DANGEROUS GAMES

Recent Titles by Sally Spencer from Severn House

THE BUTCHER BEYOND
THE DARK LADY
DEAD ON CUE
DEATH OF A CAVE DWELLER
DEATH OF AN INNOCENT
A DEATH LEFT HANGING
DYING IN THE DARK
THE ENEMY WITHIN
GOLDEN MILE TO MURDER
A LONG TIME DEAD
MURDER AT SWANN'S LAKE
THE PARADISE JOB
THE RED HERRING
THE SALTON KILLINGS
SINS OF THE FATHERS
STONE KILLER
THE WITCH MAKER

DANGEROUS GAMES

Sally Spencer

This first world edition published in Great Britain 2007 by
SEVERN HOUSE PUBLISHERS LTD of
9–15 High Street, Sutton, Surrey SM1 1DF.
This first world edition published in the USA 2007 by
SEVERN HOUSE PUBLISHERS INC of
595 Madison Avenue, New York, N.Y. 10022.

British Library Cataloguing in Publication Data

Spencer, Sally
    Dangerous games
    1. Woodend, Charlie (Fictitious character) - Fiction
    2. Police - England - Fiction
    3. Detective and mystery stories
    I. Title
    823.9'14 [F]

    ISBN-13: 978-0-7278-6468-0 (cased)
    ISBN-13: 978-1-84751-005-1 (trade paper)

All Severn House titles are printed on acid-free paper.

Printed and bound in Great Britain by
MPG Books Ltd., Bodmin, Cornwall.

This is my twenty-fifth book for Severn House, and I dedicate it unreservedly both to those loyal readers who have been with me from the start and to those who've joined us along the way. It couldn't have happened without you!

One

The canal cut right through what had once been Whitebridge's throbbing industrial heart, but now stood as little more than a grim reminder of the long and painful decline of the cotton industry. The barges and the narrow boats which had once jostled for position on it were long gone, for what was the point of such craft now that there were no bales of cotton to be unloaded nor bolts of cloth to be taken on board? And as the canal flowed sluggishly through a canyon of abandoned mills and converted warehouses, those same grim buildings stared down at it rebukingly – as if it were the waterway's fault that their golden days had disappeared forever.

There were two men ambling gently along the old canal towpath that morning in the early summer of 1965. Each carried a wicker basket in his left hand and held his fishing rod in place over his shoulder with his right. The older man was smoking a cheap briar pipe, while the younger had a Woodbine cigarette projecting from the corner of his mouth. They looked as if they might well be father and son, and – in fact – that was just what they were.

It was the older man who first noticed the yellow cord.

'Bloody rubbish!' he snorted in disgust.

'What's bloody rubbish?' his son asked.

'That is!' his father replied, using a finger of the hand holding the fishing rod to point vaguely ahead of them.

The son looked up. The length of cord was hanging limply from the railing at the centre of the bridge they were just approaching.

'What's your problem?' he asked. 'It's only a bit of rope,'

'If that's what you want to call it, you're more than welcome to!' the older man said. 'But in my day, rope *was* rope. Indian hemp! That's nothin' but a bit of nylon – the same stuff your mam's stockings are made out of.'

'It's very strong, is nylon,' said the son, almost as if, as a member of the younger generation, he felt it was incumbent on him to defend all things modern against the crotchety attacks of his dad, who held the opinion that anything produced after 1938 was a complete waste of time.

They had reached the bridge now, and though they could not touch the rope – since it was suspended over the middle of the canal – they could at least get a better look at it.

'It's got a bit of a loop on the end,' the son said, puzzled.

'So what?' asked his father who, having already made his point, was becoming bored with the subject.

'Well, I don't see why anybody would have hung a bit of rope . . .'

'A bit of *nylon*.'

'. . . with a loop at the end of it, over the bridge.'

His father shrugged. 'It's probably just some big daft bugger's idea of a joke.'

'But it's not very funny, is it? An' what's that floatin' in the canal up ahead? It looks to me like an old sack or somethin'.'

'Folk chuck all kinds of bloody rubbish in the cut these days,' his father grumbled. 'No respect for anythin', you see, lad. It was all very different when I was growin' up.'

They walked on, and soon the bridge was a hundred yards behind them, and the 'object' in the canal not more than ten yards ahead.

The son suddenly came to a shaky halt, and began to turn quite pale.

'I . . . I don't think it's a sack at all, Dad,' he stuttered. 'I . . . I think it's a body.'

'It can't be a body, you silly sod,' scoffed his father, who had slowed his pace, but was still walking on.

'I think it . . . I think it is.'

'If it's a body, then where's the bloody head?'

The older man was no more than a dozen feet from the 'object' when *he* stopped walking. For a second, he was frozen, then his left hand opened and his wicker fishing basket clattered down onto the canal path.

'Dad?' the younger man said, now more worried about his father than he was about the thing in the canal. 'Are you all right, Dad?'

'Oh God!' the older man moaned. 'Where *is* the bloody head?'

Half a dozen uniformed policemen had been stationed at various points along the canal bank. They looked bored. And so they were, since – apart from keeping nosy parkers away from the scene – they had very little to do.

The only person in the vicinity who appeared to have any real purpose at all was a delicately-boned, golden-skinned woman. She was dressed in a colourful sari, which, when seen in contrast to the dark blue uniforms of the policemen around her, made her seem almost like a flaming bird of paradise. She had been the official police surgeon ever since her predecessor had done one favour too many for his corrupt friends, and had gone to gaol as a result. Her surname was Shastri, and though she undoubtedly had a first name, too, no one in the Central Lancs Force had ever quite plucked up the nerve to ask her what it was. DCI Woodend – who simply called her 'Doc' – thought she was the best police surgeon he had ever worked with, and most of his colleagues agreed.

A second woman was approaching along the canal path. The new arrival had long blonde hair which was naturally wavy, and a rather large – though not unattractive – nose, which identified her immediately as being of central European extraction. She was wearing a business-like black-and white check suit, though the skirt was short enough to attest to the fact that she had pretty sensational legs. As she strode briskly along the canal towpath, the Beatles latest number one, *Ticket to Ride*, was playing in her head.

There were times when she wished *she* had a ticket to ride and just didn't care, she thought.

The blonde woman nodded to the constables who had been posted along the path, but did not slacken her pace until she was no more than three or four feet away from the police doctor, Then she came to an abrupt halt, and her serious expression melted into a warm smile.

'Good morning, Dr Shastri,' she said.

The doctor returned the smile. 'And good morning to you, Sergeant Paniatowski!'

Monika Paniatowski looked down at the headless cadaver, which was lying on a tarpaulin sheet on the ground. From his

hands, she would have guessed that he was in his late twenties
or early thirties – though it was no *more* than a guess. He was
wearing a boiler suit, which had once been dark blue, but now
was stained a dirty rust-coloured brown.

'It is something of a surprise – though rather a pleasant
one – to see you here,' the doctor said. 'I would have thought
that an accident of this nature would have merited only the
presence of a *uniformed* sergeant. I certainly did not expect
one of Detective Chief Inspector Woodend's brightest stars to
put in an appearance.'

'An accident?' Paniatowski repeated, looking down at the
corpse again – just to make sure she had seen it correctly the
first time – and confirming that it was indeed lacking a head.

The doctor laughed. 'Oh, I understand the source of your
confusion,' she said. 'You are wondering how he could have
accidentally lost his head.'

'Exactly.'

'The poor man undoubtedly intended to kill himself –
hanging still *is* the most popular form of suicide in this country,
you know – but I imagine he was planning only to break his
neck. I do not think he *ever* intended to decapitate himself.
In fact, it would have come as quite a shock to him – if, that
is, he had been aware of it.' Dr Shastri laughed. 'But how
could he be aware that he had lost his head, when he had lost
his head?'

Paniatowski shook her own head slowly from side to side.
'I sometimes worry about your sense of humour, Doc,' she
said.

'Don't,' Shastri told her. 'Show me a pathologist who cannot
laugh at his own work, and I will show you a pathologist who
is ripe for an extended stay at the Funny Farm.'

'So if he didn't intend to lose his head, why *did* he lose
it?' Paniatowski asked.

'Because both the laws of physics and the laws of anatomy
dictated absolutely that he should.'

'Go on.'

'I would estimate that he weighed something like a hundred
and fifty-five pounds – though that *is* only an estimate, since
the head is still missing. The ideal distance for him to
have dropped, if he wished to break his neck, was six feet
five inches. The rope he used allowed a drop of something

closer to twelve feet. It was almost inevitable that he and his head would part company.'

'So where's the head now?'

'When the police diver arrives, I confidently expect him to find it at the bottom of the canal, right next to the bridge. The body, you see, is naturally buoyant, and has floated away from the point at which the separation took place, but the head is both heavy and awkwardly shaped, and left to its own devices would have sunk like a stone.'

Paniatowski reached into her jacket pocket, took out a packet of cigarettes, and lit one up.

'So the injuries are entirely self-inflicted?' she asked.

'That would be my guess, though naturally I cannot tell you anything officially until I have conducted a complete autopsy.'

'Naturally,' Paniatowski agreed.

'And how is your lovely Chief Inspector Woodend?' Dr Shastri asked, slipping from the official to the social with the same grace with which she managed most aspects of her life.

'Cloggin'-it Charlie?' Paniatowski replied. 'To tell you the truth, with things being so quiet around here recently, I think he's rather bored.'

Dr Shastri smiled again.

'He would be,' she acknowledged. 'Mr Woodend is not a man for sitting on his hands. His mission in life is to bring murderers to justice – and the more the merrier.' She paused for a second. 'And what about your handsome Inspector Rutter? How is he?'

Why did even a mention of her ex-lover still bring a stabbing pain to her heart, Paniatowski wondered.

'Bob's fine – but rather preoccupied – at the moment,' she said aloud, and managed to sound almost normal.

'Preoccupied?'

'His daughter's going to live with him again, and that takes a lot of arranging.'

'Ah yes, his little daughter,' Dr Shastri said, with a hint of sadness in her voice. 'Am I right that she has been staying with her grandparents down in London since . . . since . . . ?'

'Since his wife was murdered,' Paniatowski supplied. 'Yes, she has. But he's decided it's time for her to come home, and I think he's probably right.'

'Though it will not be easy,' Dr Shastri said sagely.

'Life never *is* easy,' Paniatowski replied. Then, detecting the obvious edge of bitterness in her own voice, she continued hurriedly, 'Well, as I'm obviously not required here, I'll be off in search of real criminals I can bother. I'll see you around, Doc.'

Dr Shastri nodded her head. 'Since murder never seems to go in the least out of fashion, that is undoubtedly true,' she agreed.

The uniformed sergeant leaning against the MGA was in his late thirties, and was called Jack Conner. Monika Paniatowski guessed that he'd been put in charge of the headless man case, and also had a fair suspicion as to why he was so obviously waiting for her now.

'Thought that there was a good chance this vehicle might be yours, Monika,' Conner said, smiling.

'Since we both know this is the only bright red MGA in the whole of central Lancashire, you did more than just *think*,' Paniatowski countered. 'What can I do for you, Jack?'

'Do?' the uniformed sergeant asked innocently.

'Do,' Paniatowski repeated.

'We've made a provisional identification of the stiff in the canal,' the sergeant said.

'Is that right?' Paniatowski asked, disinterestedly.

'Oh, it wasn't that difficult,' Connor said, as if he feared that she'd think he was attempting to take credit where none was due. 'He had his driving licence in his overall pocket, you see. When we took it out, it was sopping wet, but still legible enough.'

He paused, as if giving Paniatowski the opportunity to say something.

'Sopping wet, eh?' she obliged.

'But legible enough,' Conner said, in the tone of a man who had just realized he was going to have to work rather harder if he was ever to get the result he wanted. 'Turns out the stiff was called Terrence Roger Pugh. He was twenty-nine years old, and he didn't live far from here.'

'And you told me all that without consulting your notebook once,' Paniatowski said, with mock admiration.

'The thing is, what with having to find Pugh's head and

everything, I've got rather a lot on my plate at the moment,' Connor said awkwardly.

'Why don't you just tell me what it is you want me to do?' Paniatowski suggested.

'It probably wouldn't take you more than a few minutes,' Conner told her. 'And it *is* on the way back to the station.'

'*What's* on the way back to the station?' Paniatowski wondered.

'Terrence Pugh's home, of course.'

'Of course.'

'The thing is, somebody needs to call on his wife, tell her we've found a body that's probably his, and drive her down to the morgue.'

'And couldn't one of your team do that?'

'Like I said, they're all busy,' Conner said, looking over Paniatowski's shoulder as a way of avoiding her eyes.

'Am I right in assuming that when you've got a shitty job like this on your hands, you normally send WPC Murray to do it for you?' Paniatowski asked innocently.

'Well, it's certainly true that Brenda Murray's done her share of talking to grieving widows,' Conner admitted.

'So why can't Brenda do it today?'

'Well . . .'

'It couldn't perhaps be because she's on sick leave, could it?'

Conner shrugged, acknowledging that she had hit the nail squarely on the head. 'Women are so much better at dealing with emotional situations than men are, aren't they?' he said hopefully.

Paniatowski laughed. 'A few years ago, when I was on the beat myself, I saw you face down a gang of hooligans who were armed with cut-throat razors and were just thirsting to spill your blood,' she said. 'You weren't scared that day – or, if you were, you didn't show it. So are you seriously trying to tell me now that you don't have the bottle to tell a woman that her husband's probably killed himself?'

Connor looked down at the ground. 'Different thing altogether,' he muttered. 'I've never been very good with women – and if you don't believe me, just ask my wife.' He looked up again. 'I really would appreciate your help, Monika. I'd owe you big time.'

Paniatowski sighed. 'I suppose you'd better give me the address, Jack,' she said, resignedly.

Conner took a piece of paper out of his pocket with some speed, and handed it over to her before she could change her mind.

Paniatowski climbed into the MGA, and slipped her key into the ignition. The engine fired first time, but then any engine which had had the amount of love and attention lavished on it that this one had *should* have shown its gratitude by starting immediately.

'Funny thing, him killing himself like that,' Sergeant Connor said from the pavement.

'Bloody hilarious,' Paniatowski replied.

'I mean, I didn't know the man myself, but he was quite a bit younger than me, and his body looked healthy enough.'

'Except it didn't have a head,' Paniatowski pointed out.

'What I'm saying is, everybody has their difficulties in this life, but however deep my own problems have been, I've never considered topping myself for a minute, and I don't suppose you have, either.'

'Oh, I've *considered* it, right enough,' Paniatowski said, but she had already shifted into gear by then, and it was doubtful if Conner heard her over the roar of the engine.

Two

Chief Constable Henry Marlowe mounted the podium, and looked down with a serious expression on his face at the handful of local reporters who were looking back up at him.

It wasn't really a very good turn-out, he thought, but he supposed he must make the best of it.

Marlowe had always liked calling press conferences. They seemed to him to be a way of appearing immensely authoritative, without necessarily knowing very much at all. And, if they were skilfully manipulated, they could be used to convey the impression of being in charge without the necessity of doing any of the tedious work that being in charge usually involved.

But as much as he'd enjoyed them previously, press conferences had never been more important to him than they were now. His disastrous attempt to become the local member of parliament – and the ignominy of his forced withdrawal from the race – had cost him a great deal of the prestige he'd been carefully building up over the years, and if he was ever to climb back to the lofty heights he had once inhabited, he needed the press on his side.

Marlowe cleared his throat.

'There are two main reasons I have asked you to attend this briefing at such short notice,' he said. 'The first is that I wanted to take the earliest opportunity to scotch all the wild rumours which have been circulating around the town since early this morning.' He paused. 'The second is that while those wild rumours are completely untrue, the case may just be bizarre enough to be of interest to the national newspapers, and if anybody is going to file this story with them, I thought it should be the hard-working members of the local press, rather than some flash bastard from London.'

You shouldn't have said *flash bastard*, Henry, he told himself. It doesn't go with the dignity of your office.

But then that was how the local reporters thought of London-based journalists, and there was no doubt that they were looking quite pleased at the prospect of earning stringers' fees from the nationals.

'A headless corpse was removed from the canal early this morning,' Marlowe continued. 'The head has since been re-covered from the bottom of the canal. The dead man's name is Terrence Roger Pugh. His decapitation was not, as some of the rumours have suggested, the result of some strange – and no doubt foreign – ritual sacrifice. In fact, it is no more than an unintended consequence of the man's suicide.'

'So you've ruled out all possibility of foul play?' one of the reporters, whose name was Arthur Williams, asked, some-what disappointedly.

Marlowe nodded, seriously. 'Yes, Arthur, I have.'

'Even before you've seen the results of the post mortem?'

'How do you know I've not seen the results of the post mortem?' Marlowe countered.

'Well, have you?'

Williams was becoming a real nuisance, Marlowe thought, and made a mental note to find some thoroughly justifiable reason to exclude him from future press conferences.

'As a matter of fact, I haven't yet seen the report,' he admitted. 'But I've had twenty-five years' experience in this force, Arthur, and – believe me – even in my sleep, I could tell the difference between a suicide and a murder.'

The rush hour was well under way by the time Paniatowski and her passenger set out on their journey to the police morgue. Ahead of them, commercial vans jostled each other for posi-tion, and office workers glanced down at their watches and wondered if the boss would notice if they happened to be a few minutes late.

Paniatowski, behind the wheel of her MGA, treated all other vehicles on her side of the road with the same disdain that a top charioteer probably displayed to his opponents in the Circus Maximus, and left behind her a trail of drivers with pale faces and hands tightly gripping their steering wheels.

Her passenger, in contrast to the other drivers, did not even appear to notice this series of near-misses and hair's-breadth escapes. Mrs Pugh, hunched down in her seat, was totally absorbed in a new and very dark world that Paniatowski had recently introduced her to.

'Why would he kill himself?' the new widow moaned, for perhaps the tenth time. 'Why?'

'We still don't know for sure that it *is* him,' Paniatowski said, changing lanes with a speed which wrong-footed the post office van driver, who had already marked out that space for himself.

'But it's *likely* to be him, isn't it?' Mrs Pugh wailed.

'Yes, it's likely,' Paniatowski agreed and hoped that by the time they reached the morgue Sergeant Conner's team would have found the bloody head at the bottom of the canal, and that Dr Shastri would have temporarily re-united it with the body for the viewing.

'Then why?' Mrs Pugh asked. '*Why* would my Terry ever go and take his own life?'

'We'll probably never know for sure,' Paniatowski said, feeling totally inadequate to deal with the situation.

'Things were going so well for him, you see,' Mrs Pugh told her. 'They'd just told him at the factory that he was going to be promoted. The general manager said he really liked Terry's positive attitude to his work. And we were planning our first holiday abroad. We were going to Spain. To the Costa del Something-or-other. Terry was looking forward to it.'

Or *appeared* to be looking forward to it, Paniatowski thought. Or was *pretending* to be looking forward to it, until he found it too much of a strain to pretend any longer. We've all played that game at one time or another.

'Whose idea was this holiday in Spain?' she asked, mainly as a distraction.

'Oh, it was Terry's,' Mrs Pugh said.

Yes, you can convince yourself of anything, if you really want to, Paniatowski thought. But holidays require planning, and the only planning Terry Pugh seemed to be involved in was planning a way to kill himself.

'I wasn't keen on it at first,' Mrs Pugh continued. 'I've never been abroad, you see. I've never been further than Blackpool, to be honest. But Terry said all that sunshine would do us good. He said it would give us the strength to deal with the baby when it arrived.'

Paniatowski, in the midst of another complex manoeuvre,

faltered for a split-second and nearly clipped the side of a milk cart with her wing.

'The baby!' she repeated.

'That's right,' Mrs Pugh agreed.

'You're pregnant?'

'Four months. We've been trying for years, and had almost given up hope. Terry was very excited when it finally happened. That's why I can't understand why he'd ever think of killing himself.'

And when you put it like that, neither can I, Paniatowski thought.

The man pacing up and down outside the phone box on Whitebridge High Street had been christened *Reginald* Lewis, but had never been quite able to live up to his full name and was always known as Reg. He was wearing the jacket from one suit (brown) and the trousers from another (blue). Both parts of his ensemble had been well past their best when he acquired them, and had suffered from a lack of care and attention since. The rest of his appearance did not exactly inspire confidence either. His hair was long and greasy, his skin had an unwashed look, and there was a five-day growth of beard on his chin. He looked like a tramp – and *smelled* like a tramp – but tramps were not known for their nervous energy, and as Lewis continued to pace, it was plain that he had plenty of it and to spare.

The old woman in the phone box – at whom he glared every time his perambulations took him past her – was wearing a thick coat despite the heat, and had a knitted woollen hat on her head which looked as if it might have felt more at home keeping a teapot warm. She had been talking non-stop for over ten minutes, showing no sign of reaching the end of her monologue.

Lewis felt an almost overwhelming urge to open the phone box door, grab her by her lapels, and fling her out onto the street.

But that would never do, he told himself – because there would doubtless be some do-gooder around who would feel the need to intervene, and then he would never get his phone call made.

The old woman was still in full flow. Lewis tapped on the phone box window and then pointed with the index finger of his left hand to his right wrist, where his watch would have been – if he'd owned a watch.

The woman smiled uncertainly, and mouthed something which could have been, 'Won't be a minute.'

Lewis glared at her, and walked on.

Up until that morning, he had been handling the situation well, he told himself.

True, the letter had unnerved him when he'd first read it, he freely admitted that, but he had worked hard at convincing himself that it had been no more than a joke in bad taste – a random stab in the dark by some malicious nutter which had just happened to hit a nerve.

He couldn't argue that any longer, could he? However much he might want to, he couldn't argue that now.

The old woman finally replaced the receiver back on its cradle and stepped out of the box.

'You want to learn to have some patience, young man,' she said, looking up at him.

'Piss off!' Lewis growled.

The woman looked shocked. 'I know a policeman,' she said.

'And *I* know where you live,' Lewis lied.

The old woman scuttled away.

Lewis grinned. Frightening her did not feel as good as placing his fist right in the centre of her stupid wrinkled old-bag face might have done, but at least it was something.

The panic hit him again the second he was inside the phone box. He found locating the right loose change in his pocket an almost impossible task. Half-crowns and pennies brushed easily against his fingertips, but though he knew there was a shilling in there somewhere, it kept on eluding him.

He should have done it earlier, he told himself, as he sweated and fumbled. When he was outside, pacing up and down, he'd had plenty of time to find the right money.

He almost gasped with relief when he located the shilling. He picked up the phone, dialled the number, and heard a ringing at the other end.

'Brown Brothers' Furnishings,' said a woman's voice.

'I want to speak to Mr Bygraves,' Lewis told her, pushing his shilling into the slot just as the pips started.

'Are you a customer?' the bloody woman asked.

'No, I'm a friend,' Lewis said, managing to keep to keep

his voice level only by a tremendous effort of will. 'It's a personal matter, and I need to speak to him urgently.'

'Hold the line,' the woman said.

It could not have been more than a couple of minutes before Lewis heard a male voice say, 'Tom Bygraves here,' but even that short wait had seemed like an eternity.

'Have you heard?' Lewis demanded.

'Who is this?' Bygraves asked.

'For God's sake, it's me!' Lewis said.

'Reg? Reg Lewis?'

'Yes! Have you heard about Terry Pugh?'

'Yes, I have, as a matter of fact. It said on the wireless news this morning that he was dead.'

'And doesn't that bother you?'

Bygraves hesitated for a second, then said, 'Not really. I haven't seen him for years. And people die all the time.'

'But he didn't just *die*, did he?' Lewis asked, and now he was almost screaming. 'He was bloody killed!'

'They said on the wireless that he'd committed suicide.'

'I don't believe that. And neither do you, Tom. Terry just wasn't the suicidal type.'

'Not when we knew him, no. But that was quite a while ago, when you think about it, and people do change.'

'Not Terry Pugh.'

'He *must* have done.'

There was something in those last four words that made Lewis realise that, of the two of them, Bygraves was probably the more frightened – so frightened, in fact, that he was doing all he could to deny the glaringly obvious reality of the situation.

And that knowledge, strangely, made Lewis suddenly feel much calmer and much more in control.

'It could be you or me next,' he said darkly.

'What you're suggesting is absurd!' Bygraves said, and now there was clear evidence of hysteria in his tone. 'This is England, for God's sake! We don't have revenge killings here!'

'Did I mention revenge killings?' Lewis asked cunningly. 'Did I *once* use the word "revenge"?'

'No, but if you're calling me like this . . .'

'I'm not the only one who got a letter, am I?' Lewis asked. 'You've had one, too.'

'I don't know what you're talking about!' Bygraves protested.

But he did! He definitely did!

'When did it arrive?' Lewis asked. 'Mine was about two weeks ago. Did yours come at the same time?'

There was a longer pause this time, then Bygraves said, 'I . . . I did receive an anonymous letter.'

'Well, then?'

'But I just thought it was the work of some crank.'

'That's what I thought, as well. Or, at least, that's what I *wanted* to think. But we have to face facts, don't we?'

'Sweet Jesus, what are going to do?' Bygraves asked, and Lewis was almost certain that he was crying now.

'We have to work as a team, like we used to,' Lewis said. 'We have to figure out who's behind this.'

'You don't think we'll *know* the man, do you?' Bygraves asked, incredulously.

'We might,' Lewis said weakly.

He heard the other man take a deep breath, as if he were trying to pull himself together.

'His connection isn't to us, you bloody fool – it's to what happened *back then*,' Bygraves said. 'He'd probably never even *met* Terry Pugh before he killed him. And if he gets us, too . . . if . . . if he does to us what he did to Terry, we'll be dying at the hands of a stranger.'

Lewis looked around him, wildly. The High Street was busy at that time of day, and any number of people were walking past the booth – shoppers, and office workers on their break; delivery men and sales representatives; school kids nicking off class, and nuns going about their holy business. And though he couldn't see him, it was possible that the killer was out there too – watching him, looking for just the right opportunity to make his move.

'So what *are* we going to do?' he asked. 'Just sit around and wait for him to get us?'

'They used to say that if a bullet had your name on it, there was nothing you could do,' Bygraves said fatalistically.

'And what does that mean, for Christ's sake?'

'It means that all any of us can do is pray we're not the next one on his list. It means that the only hope we have is that he'll be caught before he works his way round to us.'

Three

The sign outside the police morgue said that there was no waiting in the area at any time, but for the moment it was partially hidden by the old Wolseley which had parked right in front of it.

As the driver of the Wolseley climbed out of his vehicle, it would have been instantly obvious to anyone watching that he was what people in Lancashire would call 'a big bugger'. In fact, he was tall enough to scrape his head on the inside of the car roof if he wasn't careful, an occasional occurrence which he blamed – if only half-heartedly – for the thinning of his hair around the crown.

The rest of the package which made up DCI Charlie Woodend was consistent with his frame. He had a broad face which was more than amply filled by a big nose and a large mouth. It was the sort of face which looked as if it had been carved with tools that were not quite sharp enough to do really delicate work, and were wielded by an artisan who had long ago lost of his enthusiasm for his craft. But, as if to balance this, Woodend had intelligent eyes which were capable of showing great kindness and understanding, as well as great anger and steely determination. He was wearing a hairy sports jacket and cavalry twill trousers, and very few people could ever remember him ever wearing anything else. And between his nicotine-stained fingers burned the Capstan Full Strength cigarette that he would have felt almost naked without.

Woodend slammed the door of the Wolseley, but did not lock it. Nor did he bother to leave a sign on the dashboard announcing that he was a policeman on official business. That was the advantage of owning a car most drivers wouldn't be seen dead in, he thought – people soon learned that it was yours, and understood that they moved it at their peril.

He paused for a second to light a new cigarette from the

butt of his old one, then stepped through the main door of the morgue. The smell of chemicals hit him even in the vestibule, and reminded him how much he disliked visiting this place. On the other hand, he thought, there was always the consolation that his visit gave him the opportunity to talk to the lovely and charming Dr Shastri, and – like the chemicals – that was not to be sniffed at.

Shastri was waiting for him in the post mortem room. Her colourful sari was covered by a practical white coat, but she managed to wear even this mundane article as if it were fresh off the catwalks of Paris.

A wide smile filled her face when she saw him. 'Ah, my favourite policeman,' she said. 'It was good of you to get here so quickly.'

'You said it was urgent,' Woodend pointed out.

'And so it is,' Dr Shastri agreed. She gestured with her delicate hand towards the marble slab. 'Have you met the late Mr Pugh?'

The body was covered with a sheet right up to the chin, and anyone who didn't know any better would probably have assumed that the head was connected to it.

Woodend examined Pugh's face. He had expected there to be an expression of pure horror on it – for surely even a spilt second's realization that he was about to decapitate himself would have been enough to produce such a look – but Terry Pugh looked surprisingly peaceful.

'You are wondering why he does not look overly concerned at the thought of losing his head,' Dr Shastri said, reading his thoughts.

'That's exactly what I'm wonderin',' Woodend agreed.

'In my experience, dead men *rarely* mind what is happening to them,' the doctor said.

'What's that? Are you saying that this feller was dead *before* he lost his head?'

'Indeed.'

'How *long* before he lost it?'

'That is rather a tricky question to answer precisely, since we do not know when he entered the canal. I would say, from the extent of the rigor mortis and livor mortis, that he has been dead for somewhere between eight and twelve hours, but even that is a very rough approximation.'

'What killed him?' Woodend asked.

'A massive blow to the back of the head. Not a very original way of committing a murder, I will admit, but one that is so effective that it continues to be very popular with your average, unimaginative killer.'

'Was he killed on the bridge?'

'From my preliminary investigations, I would very much doubt that was where he met his end.'

Woodend lit up a cigarette, and inhaled a mixture of nicotine and formaldehyde.

'So, let me see if I've got this straight,' he said. 'He's killed somewhere else, then his body's taken to the bridge. Once the killer has him there, he puts a noose around his neck and throws him over the parapet. Is that about it?'

'That is, indeed, about it.'

'Is there any chance at all that, when the killer hanged him, he didn't know he was already dead?'

'There is always a chance of that. But in this case I would have thought it unlikely. As I said, it is a massive wound.'

'What was the blow inflicted with?'

'The proverbial blunt instrument. And, in all probability, that blunt instrument was made of metal. I hope to tell you more when I have conducted a more detailed examination.'

'So if the killer knew he was dead, why run the risk of being caught hanging him?' Woodend wondered, frowning. 'What the bloody hell was he playing at?'

Dr Shastri smiled. 'It is when I see that expression of perplexed frustration on your face that I am glad I'm no more than a simple doctor,' she said.

The Chief Constable sat at his desk. Behind him, on the wall, were framed photographs of him shaking hands with important people, and framed letters of commendation which assured him that he was a very good policeman indeed. In front of him stood the large man in the hairy sports jacket and the blonde sergeant with the big nose.

Marlowe glared at both of them in turn. 'Murder?' he demanded. 'Are you sure?'

Woodend considered the option of telling the Chief Constable that he wasn't sure at all – that there was a distinct possibility that Terry Pugh had managed to deliver the fatal blow to the back of his head himself, driven himself to the bridge, made his car disappear, and then somehow contrived to lift his own dead body over the bridge. It was a tempting and amusing idea – but, given the circumstances, it was also a very unwise one.

'I'm afraid there's no doubt about it at all, sir,' he said. 'I've seen the wound myself.'

'But I told the reporters, only a few hours ago, that it was quite definitely suicide,' Marlowe said angrily.

'It might have been prudent to wait for Dr Shastri's report before you held the press conference,' Woodend said, using what was – for him – a considerable amount of tact and diplomacy.

'The reason I delivered that particular briefing was because your Sergeant Paniatowski assured me . . .'

'Sir, I never . . .' Paniatowski began.

'Shut up, Sergeant,' Marlowe barked. 'To repeat: the reason I delivered that particular briefing to the press was because I'd been assured that the man had taken his own life.'

'What Sergeant Paniatowski told you, sir, was that all the indications *pointed* towards suicide.'

'And how would *you* know that?' Marlowe asked. 'Were you listening in on our telephone conversation, Chief Inspector? Or were you perhaps in this very office, hiding under my desk?'

Sarcasm was one of the stronger weapons in the Chief Constable's personal armoury, Woodend thought – but even there, given his preference for the crude broad slash over the delicate cut, he was an amateur at it by Lancashire standards.

'Well?' Marlowe demanded.

'I don't make a habit of listening to other people's calls, sir,' Woodend said. 'An' as for my hiding under your desk, if you'll look for yourself, you'll see that there's no room there for a feller my size. So no, I didn't hear actually hear your conversation with Sergeant Paniatowski, but she has given me an outline of what she told you and . . .'

'So if it's a choice between my word and hers, you'll take hers any day of the week?'

Woodend said nothing.

Marlowe wiped his brow with his linen handkerchief. 'There may yet be a way out of this for us,' he said.

'For *us*?' Woodend repeated.

'We might say that we deliberately released the wrong information in order to lull the killer into a false sense of security,' Marlowe continued, ignoring the comment. 'I'll apologize to the press for the deception . . .' He paused for a second. 'Or better yet, I might even say that I'll allow them to hint in their articles that they were in on the ruse – that they, too, had played a role in bringing the killer to justice. They'd like that.'

'Or you could simply admit that you'd made a mistake,' Woodend pointed out.

'Admitting that mistakes *have been made* would certainly be one way to deal with the situation,' Marlowe agreed. 'But, on reflection, I think my alternative plan is better.' He paused again. 'Of course,' he continued, 'since we can't possibly hope to keep the truth secret for long, I am going to need an arrest in the fairly near future.'

Woodend sighed heavily. 'As I've explained to you often enough in the past, sir . . .'

'You can't hurry an investigation,' Marlowe interrupted. 'It's a bit like gardening – you have to nurture your leads before you can harvest them. Is that what you were going to say, Chief Inspector?'

'More or less,' Woodend agreed.

'Then let me make my own position crystal clear to you,' Marlowe said harshly. 'If it weren't for certain pieces of information you uncovered while you were investigating the Bradley Pine murder case, I'd probably be sitting in the House of Commons right now – as Henry Marlowe, MP, a man with a brilliant parliamentary career to look forward to.'

'The information I uncovered was there to be found, sir,' Woodend said, trying to sound apologetic and not even coming close. 'And once I had uncovered it, I couldn't ignore it – because it was that information which led me directly to the murderer.'

'Perhaps that's true,' Marlowe agreed, 'but the fact remains that you owe me a great deal for costing me my opportunity to make a name for myself, Chief Inspector Woodend. You owe it to me – and you'll do whatever you have to in order to make it right.'

'Listen, sir . . .'

Marlowe slapped the palm of his hand down angrily on the edge of his desk. His in-tray and out-tray rattled, and his lamp flickered for a second.

'This is not a matter for debate, Mr Woodend,' he said angrily. 'I want Terry Pugh's killer caught – and I want him caught quickly.'

'Sir . . .'

'You can go now,' the Chief Constable said, looking down at the paperwork lying on his desk.

Four

A t this stage in most murder inquiries, a team of officers would already be hard at work, turning the basement of Police Headquarters into what Henry Marlowe liked to call 'the nerve centre of our investigation'. But since there was, as yet, no official inquiry – since Terry Pugh's death was still 'officially' a suicide – no such transformation had begun, and instead Woodend had convened what he always thought of as his 'inner' team, at their usual table in the public bar of the Drum and Monkey.

The team consisted of four people – Woodend himself, Monika Paniatowski, Inspector Bob Rutter, and Colin Beresford who had recently been promoted to detective constable. It was a team Woodend trusted – one he wouldn't have changed even if he'd been given the choice. But, like any team, its effectiveness was sometimes challenged by both internal conflicts and individual problems.

The relationship between Monika and Bob was probably the most straining of its difficulties. They had been lovers, and though they had broken off their affair before Rutter's blind wife was murdered – and though the murder itself had absolutely nothing to do with their relationship – they still both sometimes acted as if they felt responsible for Maria's death.

And that was not the half of it, Woodend thought, taking a slug of his first pint of the day. Bob Rutter had started 'seeing' Elizabeth Driver . . .

'She's a friend!' Rutter had told Woodend, when he'd asked. 'No more than that.'

. . . and Driver was the chief crime reporter for a daily tabloid newspaper which specialized in lurid headlines, and was rarely inclined to let the truth stand in the way of a good story.

Woodend had had a number of encounters with Driver over

the years – all of which had left a bad taste in his mouth – and didn't like the idea of the friendship developing at all.

But his reaction to Rutter's relationship with Driver was nothing when compared to Monika Paniatowski's. She *resented the hell* out of it, for while she didn't want Bob Rutter back herself – or *said* she didn't want him back – she certainly didn't want a scheming, unscrupulous bitch like Driver to have him.

The problems that the fourth member of the team, DC Colin Beresford, found himself facing were of quite a different nature. His mother was only just sixty-one – 'And I'm not so far from that myself,' Woodend thought unhappily – but she had been struck down by Alzheimer's disease, and though Beresford was – for the moment – managing to balance looking after her with handling his job, there was no doubt that at some point in the none-too-distant future, *something* was going to have to give.

Woodend put his pint down on the table with a slight thud, which served to call the meeting to order.

'This investigation is going to be a tricky one,' he announced, 'especially since our esteemed Chief Constable has made it quite clear that he wants us to pretend that it's a suicide we're investigating.'

'When he said that, why didn't you just tell him to stuff it, sir?' Beresford asked.

Woodend sighed, and then smiled with a sort of paternal indulgence at the newest member of the team.

A couple of months earlier, Beresford would never have spoken out like that, he thought. Back then, he would have sat at the table as quiet as a mouse, over-awed at even being in the presence of these three local CID legends. Now, he was starting to chance his arm – which was a good thing, because 'yes' men were of no bloody use to Woodend – but he still had a lot to learn about the *realpolitik* of being at the sharp end of dealings with the Chief Constable.

'If I was to tell Mr Marlowe to stuff it every time I disagreed with him, I'd end up sayin' virtually nothin' else to the bugger,' he explained to Beresford.

'I'm sure that's true, sir, but . . .'

'You have to choose your battles, lad,' Woodend interrupted. 'You have to save your energy for when the fight really matters – an', at the moment, this one doesn't.'

'I see,' Beresford said.

He didn't, of course, Woodend thought. But the longer he worked with the team, the more he would understand that what sounded like a surrender was in fact no more than common sense.

'What impressions do you have of the killer, so far?' he asked the team in general.

'He's a careful thinker,' said Bob Rutter. 'He plans things out well in advance.'

'What makes you say that?'

'The fact that he picked that particular bridge.'

'Somethin' special about it, is there?'

'Yes, I think there is. Or if not 'special', something that makes it *different* to all the others.'

'An' what might that be?'

'It'd be easier to *show* you what I mean than to tell you,' Rutter said. He produced a map of Whitebridge from his pocket, and spread it on that section of the table which was free of drinks. 'The canal enters the town here, and leaves it here,' he said, tracing out the blue line with his finger. 'Between those two points, it's crossed by six road bridges, which means that if the killer wanted to hang his victim from a canal bridge, he had half a dozen choices.'

'That makes sense,' Woodend agreed.

'Locke Bridge is close to the Locke housing estate, and takes a lot of foot traffic as well as vehicles,' Rutter continued. 'Taylor Bridge has Taylor *Street* on both sides of it, and the same could be said of that. But what's Hulme Bridge surrounded by?'

'Factories and warehouses,' Woodend said.

'Exactly. If the killer had chosen Locke Bridge, there'd always have been the chance of him being spotted by a late-night dog walker. If he'd chosen Taylor Bridge, he could have been seen by someone who couldn't sleep, and just happened to be looking out of their bedroom window. But by choosing Hulme Bridge, he could be pretty sure that between midnight – when the last customers of the local pubs had all finally gone home – and six o'clock in the morning – when the first workers started to turn up – he'd have the area to himself.'

'You might well be right about that being the reason he chose Hulme Bridge, rather than one of the others,' Monika

Paniatowski said. 'But what I don't see is why he needed to choose *any* bridge at all?'

'Meanin' what, exactly?' Woodend asked.

'His aim was to kill Terry Pugh, wasn't it?'

'That's a fair assumption, given the damage he did to the back of Pugh's skull.'

'In which case, the moment he'd struck the blow, he'd achieved all he'd set out to do, hadn't he? So why do any more than that? Why not leave Pugh where he met his death?'

'Perhaps because that particular location might have given us some clue as to who the murderer is.'

'All right then, why not drive out to the moors and dump the body there? Or simply weigh it down with bricks and throw it *into* the canal? What I'm really saying is, why would he even consider the risk involved in hanging Terry Pugh from the bridge?'

'A fair point,' Woodend agreed. 'Maybe this killer regards his victim in much the same way as Bradley Pine's killer regarded him. You remember what happened to Pine, don't you?'

The team all nodded.

Pine had been found on a lay-by, with his mouth smashed to a pulp, and his stomach slit open. Beresford had been sick, and even Monika Paniatowski had looked slightly queasy. So the sight of that particular corpse was not something that any of them were likely to forget in a hurry.

'So you think the killer hanged Pugh as a way of humiliating him, do you?' Paniatowski asked.

'It's a possibility,' Woodend told her.

'Does that also mean that you think the decapitation was intentional?'

'No, I wouldn't say that. If the killer had wanted to cut Pugh's head off, he could have done it with an axe, somewhere there was no chance of his being spotted. Going on the bridge was a risk – we're all agreed on that – however much he minimized that risk by choosing the *right* bridge. The actual process of hanging was what he was interested in, though not knowing anything about the mechanics of a successful hanging, the decapitation probably came as a surprise to him.'

'Then I still don't understand why he did it,' Paniatowski persisted. 'Bradley Pine's mutilation could have been regarded as humiliating. Leaving the victim's body naked in the main square – like in that case in Yorkshire – is humiliating. But hanging's no more of a humiliation than having your head bashed in. In fact, there's something almost clinical – almost *judicial* – about hanging.'

She was right, of course, Woodend thought.

'We're chasin' our own tails here,' he said. 'Let's set aside the question of the unnecessary hanging for a while, and concentrate on how we go about catchin' the bastard who did it. Any suggestions?'

'Post a team on the bridge,' Rutter said crisply. 'Have them display a large placard which asks anyone who crossed the bridge between the hours of midnight and five a.m. to pull over and give their details to the officers.'

'You'd use the uniformed branch for that particular job, I take it,' Woodend said.

Rutter nodded. 'I doubt they'll come up with anything useful, since, as I've already pointed out, it's unlikely anybody *did* cross the bridge within those hours – but I'd rather be safe than sorry.'

'Right, so that's covered,' Woodend said. 'But what should us smart-as-paint detectives be doin' while the uniforms are handlin' our donkey work for us?' He looked straight at Colin Beresford. 'What do *you* think we should be doing, Constable?'

Beresford felt his temperature shoot up – as it always did when he suddenly became the centre of attention at one of these meetings – but at least now he had his blushing under control. Or *hoped* he had.

'We need to establish when the victim was last seen alive, sir,' the constable said.

'Quite right,' Woodend agreed. 'We *do* need to know exactly where an' when he was last seen alive. So me an' Sergeant Paniatowski will go an' talk to the widow, because it's more than likely she'll have some idea of where he was supposed to be last night. Meanwhile, you an' Inspector Rutter can pay a visit to the place where Pugh worked. You know where that is, do you, Bob?'

'Yes,' Rutter agreed. 'I know where that is.'

'Young Beresford can talk to the workers, since, based on the evidence of the results he got at Bradley Pine's mattress factory, he's rapidly developin' the common touch,' Woodend said.

'Thank you, sir,' said Beresford, not entirely sure whether it had been intended as a compliment or not.

'An' Inspector Rutter will talk to the management, because he looks as if he's one of them himself.'

Beresford and Paniatowski grinned, since it was undoubtedly true that the Inspector had always looked more like a rising young executive than a street-level policeman.

Rutter himself continued to look serious – almost preoccupied.

'Is that all right, Bob?' Woodend asked.

'Fine,' Rutter told him. 'But I'm going to have to slip away for a couple of hours in the afternoon.'

'Why's that?' Paniatowski asked, before she could stop herself. 'Have you got a date?'

Rutter looked at her with uncharacteristic coldness.

'As a matter of fact, I have, in a manner of speaking,' he said. 'I'm interviewing nannies for Louisa.' He turned towards Woodend. 'You remember, I cleared it with you yesterday, sir.'

'Aye, now I think about it, so you did,' Woodend agreed.

Paniatowski looked mortified. 'I was speaking well out of turn,' she said. 'I'm so sorry, Bob.'

'Forget it,' Rutter said, but the tone in which he spoke the words wasn't even halfway to being forgiving.

'What else should we be lookin' for, Constable Beresford?' Woodend asked, cutting through the suddenly chill atmosphere with a reminder that they were all still police officers.

'I . . . er . . .' Beresford began. 'I suppose we should be looking for a motive for the murder, sir.'

'Aye, we most certainly should,' Woodend agreed. 'An' let's hope an' pray that Terry Pugh was a popular feller – because the last thing we need is a victim whose death makes most of the people who knew him want to throw a party.' He drained the rest of his pint. 'Right, does anyone have questions before we get stuck into the investigation?'

Beresford raised his hand, then realized what he was doing, and dropped it again, embarrassedly.

Woodend pretended not to have seen the gesture. 'Any questions at all?' he said.

'I've got a question, sir,' Beresford told him, and this time he managed to keep his hand below table level.

'Let's hear it, then,' Woodend suggested.

'How are we going to investigate a murder without the people who we're questioning in the course of that investigation knowing that's what we're doing?' Beresford wondered.

'That's a fair point, Colin,' Woodend conceded. 'You'll just have to tell them that what you're doin' is tryin' to find a motive for Terry Pugh decidin' to kill himself.'

'Aren't they going to find it rather strange that the CID would concern themselves with a matter like that, sir?' Beresford wondered.

'They'll most probably find it completely barmy.'

'Well, then . . .'

'But they'll answer your questions anyway, because most people still think it's in their best interest to co-operate with bobbies – even if the bobbies do seem a bit doolally.'

'How long do you think we'll have to keep this deception going?' Bob Rutter asked.

'There you've got me,' Woodend admitted. 'It's entirely in Henry Marlowe's hands. Until he either decides that the decent thing to do is to come clean, or is *forced by circumstances* to come clean – which is far the more likely of the two – we'll just have to play the game he wants us to play.' The chief inspector checked his watch. 'Let's get crackin' then. I'll see you all back here at six o'clock.'

Five

The house where the dead man had lived was a modest semi-detached, the kind of place that a skilled working man could take out a mortgage on and confidently expect to eventually own outright – as long, that was, as he was prepared to accept as much overtime as his employer offered him, and could resist the temptation of falling into one of those vices that were the curse of the working class.

It looked more-than-decently cared for, Woodend decided, examining it from the street. The front door and the rest of the woodwork had all been recently painted, the pebble-dashed walls were well-maintained, and there was no sign of vegetation sprouting out of the guttering. There was a small garden in front of the house, bisected by a weed-free crazy paving path and inhabited by several ugly-but-cute garden gnomes.

'If you want to light up a coffin nail, you'd better do it now – because we'll not be smoking once we're inside,' Woodend said to his sergeant.

Paniatowski nodded. 'I was aware of that, sir.'

And so she was. She knew from experience that Woodend would never smoke in a house that was in mourning, nor allow any of his subordinates to smoke either. She didn't understand why this should be so – especially since everybody else – friends and relatives alike – would probably be puffing away like chimneys themselves. Even so, she never objected. Woodend was a boss who imposed very few restrictions on her actions, and when he did put one in place, it would have seemed unreasonable to question it.

Woodend himself was not entirely sure why he should see not smoking as a mark of respect. Possibly it was something his old dad had once told him, and though he had now forgotten the occasion – if occasion there had been – the lesson had sunk in. Now, it was like an instinct to him – and his whole career had been built on having a healthy respect for his instincts.

They lit up their cigarettes. 'Nice house,' Woodend said. 'Cared for. Do you think that's due to him or her?'

'Him,' Paniatowski said definitely.

'Is that just a gut feelin'?' Woodend asked.

Paniatowski shook her head. 'All the way down to the morgue, Mrs Pugh was coming up with all the reasons why her husband wouldn't have killed himself – and at least three or four of them related to the house. Apparently, he was looking forward to turning the little back bedroom into a nursery for the baby. Couldn't wait to get started on the job, according to Mrs Pugh. "So why would he kill himself, when he had so many plans?" she kept asking me.'

'And now we know he didn't – but we're not allowed to tell her that,' Woodend said grimly.

The woman who answered their knock at the front door wore her hair in a tight perm, and was dressed in a plain, hard-wearing twin set. She looked perhaps a few years older than Mrs Pugh, but bore a strong resemblance to her.

'I'm Mrs Rogers, Mrs Pugh's sister,' she explained, after Woodend had shown her his warrant card, and she'd spent nearly a minute examining it. 'What do you want?'

'We'd like to speak to Mrs Pugh.' Woodend told her 'Is she here?'

'Our Mary's in the lounge,' Mrs Rogers.

'Then if you don't mind . . .' Woodend said, taking a step forward.

Mrs Rogers shifted position so she was blocking the doorway completely. 'Our Mary's in the lounge,' she repeated, 'but she's still very upset, and I don't think it's a good idea for her to see *anybody* at the moment.'

'We only want to ask her a few simple questions,' Paniatowski said, wheedlingly.

'Why should you want to ask her any questions at all – simple or otherwise?' Mrs Rogers countered.

'I rather think that's a matter we should be discussin' with her rather than you,' Woodend said firmly though not unpleasantly.

'My sister's husband went out last night and topped himself, leaving her alone to cope with her unborn child,' Mrs Rogers replied. 'You know it, and I know it. In fact, the whole bloody world knows it – because it's been on the bloody wireless for everybody *to* hear – so don't you think that should be an end of it?'

'Who's there?' called a cracked voice from beyond the hallway.

'It's nobody,' Mrs Rogers replied, over her shoulder.

'It's the police, isn't it?'

'Don't you go worryin' your head about who it is, our Mary. Get some rest. You need to *compose* yourself.'

'*Is* it the police?'

Mrs Rogers sighed. 'Yes, if you must know, it *is* the police,' she admitted reluctantly.

'Then I want to see them.'

Mrs Rogers shot Woodend and Paniatowski a look of pure venom, then said, 'Well, now you've gone and disturbed the poor woman, I suppose the damage is already done and you'd better follow me.'

Mrs Pugh was sitting on a deep blue velveteen sofa, around which the rest of the room seemed to have been designed. Woodend's eyes quickly swept the lounge. The pictures on the walls were mainly of seascapes and horses, and in one corner of the room there was a veneered wood display cabinet which contained ornaments mainly bought as holiday souvenirs. He liked the whole feel of the room himself – it was *cosy* – though he was sure that Paniatowski was already finding it too low-brow and much too conventional for her taste.

The widow looked up at them. Her eyes were red, and her face was puffy from crying, but she did her best to give them a welcoming smile.

'This is Chief Inspector Woodend, Mrs Pugh,' Paniatowski said. 'He's my boss.'

'I'm afraid you'll have to excuse the state of the place, Mr Woodend,' Mrs Pugh said.

'I would, gladly enough – if I needed to,' Woodend told her. 'But there *is* no need, is there? You've got a lovely home.'

Mrs Pugh looked grateful for the comment. 'What was it you were wanting to ask me?' she said.

'I was wonderin' if you knew anythin' about your husband's movements last night,' Woodend said.

'Why should that matter?' Mrs Rogers demanded angrily. 'Wherever he was, and whatever he was doing, he's still dead, isn't he?'

'In case you've forgotten, this is my house, our Elaine,' Mrs Pugh said, in a surprisingly firm voice, 'and when I'm having a conversation with a visitor, I'll thank you not to interfere in it.'

Mrs Rogers folded her arms across her chest. 'Pardon me for breathing,' she said.

'But since you seem to be so interested in knowing why it matters, I'll tell you,' Mrs Pugh continued, still talking to her sister. 'It matters because whatever they're saying on the wireless about my Terry killing himself, it's not true. He was murdered.'

'That's ridiculous,' Elaine Rogers said.

'He was murdered,' Mary Pugh repeated firmly. 'Isn't that right, Mr Woodend?'

Woodend hesitated. On the one hand, he had his clear and direct orders from a chief constable who already felt himself backed into the corner, and – like a rat which found itself in a similar position – could turn very nasty if he didn't get his own way. On the other hand, he was dealing here with a woman who desperately needed to know that the life she'd been living had been more than a lie – that she really had *known* the father of her unborn child.

'The official view at the moment is still that your husband *did* commit suicide,' he said.

'Isn't that just what I've been telling you all along!' Elaine Rogers said.

'But I can see that you don't accept that view yourself, Mrs Pugh,' Woodend continued. 'Well, I can't stop you thinkin' whatever you choose to think . . .' he paused, '. . . an', as a matter of fact, I'm not sure that I'd really want to.'

Mrs Pugh turned to his sister again, with an expression on her face which was half-despair, half-triumph.

'I'm right,' she said. 'They know I'm right.'

'*Do* you know where your husband was last night?' Paniatowski asked Mrs Pugh.

'He told me he was going to the Tanners' Arms.'

Which was not more than a quarter of the mile from the bridge where he was found hanged, Woodend thought.

'Is that his usual waterin' hole?' he wondered.

'No, he usually goes – he usually *went* – to the Bull and Bush, which is just around the corner from here.'

'An' was there any particular reason for him goin' to the Tanners' Arms instead?'

'Yes, as a matter of fact, there was. He was meeting an old school-mate of his, who he hadn't seen for years.'

'Does he have a name, this old school-mate of his?'

'Mark Hough.'

'If he hadn't seen him for years, why had he suddenly arranged to see him last night?'

'He didn't say.'

'And didn't you ask?'

'Yes, I did ask, but he was very cagey about the whole thing.'

'Then perhaps he had . . .'

'But he wasn't cagey like he would have been if he'd had something he wanted to hide from me.'

'No?'

'No! It was more like he was holding back on a nice surprise, until the time was right.'

'Was he big on surprises?' Woodend wondered.

'He . . . he *always* liked to surprise me.' Mary Pugh started to cry again. 'He . . . he was such a lovely man.'

'I think you'd better go now!' Elaine Rogers said fiercely.

'Aye, I think you're probably right,' Woodend agreed.

The sister, her footfalls beating out an angry tattoo on the floor, led the two police officers down the hallway. At first, Woodend thought it was only to make sure they really left the premises, but by the time they reached the front door it was clear that she had more to say – and that she didn't want Mary Pugh to hear it.

They stepped out into the garden, and Elaine Rogers closed the front door behind them.

'How dare you even *suggest* to her that Terry didn't kill himself?' she demanded angrily.

'What makes you so sure that he *did* kill himself, Mrs Rogers?' Woodend countered.

'If nothing else, there was the look I saw on his face when he got that letter,' Elaine Rogers said.

'What letter?'

Elaine Rogers glanced over her shoulder, as if to check that her sister had not followed them into the hallway and was now crouched down and listening through the letterbox.

'This pregnancy's been very rough on our Mary,' she said. 'She's had morning sickness as bad as I've seen it. So last week, when Terry was working shift, I said I'd stay with her overnight, in case she needed anything. That's how I happened to be here when Terry came home from work in the morning.'

'An' that's when he got the letter?' Woodend guessed.

'And that's when he got the letter,' Elaine agreed. 'I had to let him into the house, because I'd got his keys. He saw the letter lying on the mat, and picked it up. It didn't worry him – not at first. I remember him saying something like, "Well, here's a rum thing – a letter with a typewritten address." But when he opened it, and read what it said, he went very pale. And the next minute, he's rushing up the stairs to the bathroom. He closed the door behind him, but even from the hallway I could hear the sound of him being sick.'

'You didn't see this letter yourself?' Woodend asked.

'No, I don't read other people's correspondence. Besides, before he ran upstairs, he screwed it up, and jammed it into his pocket.'

'Was it a long letter?'

'No, it was a single sheet of paper. And I think it was typewritten, like the envelope.'

'What was in the letter?' Woodend asked.

'How would I know?'

'He might have said.'

'He didn't! Not then – and not later.'

'Well, then, you can't know anythin' at all about it for certain, can you?'

'No, I most certainly can't.'

'But I've got you marked down as a woman who could make a pretty good guess, whether or not, so I'd still like to hear what you think.'

For a moment, it looked as if Elaine Rogers was about to continue proclaiming her complete ignorance on the subject of the letter, then she shrugged and said, 'Who can you think of who might send a typewritten letter to a working man like Terry?'

There was only one answer to that.

'It's likely to be either council officials and debt collectors,' Woodend admitted.

'But the things that council officials write to you don't make you want to puke, do they?'

'You think he was in debt?'

'I could almost swear to it.'

'And who do you think he was in debt *to*?'

'Who do *you* think? How do fellers like our Mary's Terry ever accumulate debts they can't afford to pay off?'

'Through gamblin'.'

'Exactly. He'll have been betting more than he could afford on the horses. Or on the dogs – because they can do just as much damage. And suddenly, with the baby on the way, he realized what a mess he'd got himself into. But it was too late for second thoughts then, wasn't it? There was no going back. So he hung himself off that bridge, because he knew that no bookie will ever go after the widows and orphans for the money he's owed. Once you're dead, as far as bookies are concerned, the debt dies with you.'

'Are you still married yourself – or are you divorced, Mrs Rogers?' Woodend wondered.

'Why are you asking me that?'

'Just curious.'

'I'm divorced. And if what you're *really* asking is why I kicked the bastard out, I did it because he was a gambler as well. But that doesn't mean I've got an obsession about men and gambling.'

'Doesn't it?' Woodend asked mildly.

'No, it bloody doesn't. All it *does* mean is that when the signs are there, I know how to recognize them.'

Six

Woodend had been something of a regular in the Tanners' Arms in the days when his old dad had worked as a tackler in one of the nearby mills.

Back then, it had been a strictly 'spit and sawdust' pub – a place to which women did not choose to go, and where they would not have been welcome if they had. It had done most of its business in the hour or so after the end of a shift, and on high days and holidays had been virtually deserted.

There had been no food on offer in those days before the Second World War, and no music to listen to. The men had stood there talking loudly – since after a few years of working in the roar of the mills' machinery, they were all at least partially deaf – and knocking back as much ale as they could afford, in a fruitless attempt to rid their throats of the taste of the cotton dust.

Now, everything had changed. Cotton was no longer king in Lancashire, and though much of the new light industry had established itself in the industrial estate on the edge of town, a number of firms had chosen instead to colonize the skeletons of the old cotton mills close to the Tanner's Arms.

The pub had moved with the times, too, as was immediately evidenced by the fact that in place of the old front door – which had been latched – there were a pair of swing doors, which could be pushed open.

'Swing doors!' Woodend said, bad-temperedly. 'What do them buggers at the brewery think this is? A saloon in the Old West?'

'You tell me, Gary Cooper,' Paniatowski said, almost – but not *quite* – under her breath.

Once inside, the changes were even more apparent. The brass spittoons had gone. The heavy wallpaper – stained dark brown by generations of nicotine-laden smoke – had been stripped away, and the walls painted in a soothing pastel shade. The old wooden benches had been replaced by padded red chairs and the long wooden tables by small round ones with beaten copper tops. The pub offered 'executive lunches', and most of the customers were in suits.

The young man standing behind the bar was wearing a fancy red and white striped waistcoat which had a gold badge on it announcing that he was the assistant manager.

'I'll be with you in a minute,' he told Woodend and Paniatowski off-handedly, before rushing to the other end of the bar, where two men smoking large cigars had just indicated – by the very vaguest of gestures – that they'd like some service immediately.

'Assistant manager!' Woodend said with disgust, when the young man had gone.

'What's wrong with that?' Paniatowski wondered.

'Managers are for dull, soulless factories,' Woodend explained. 'A pub's a livin', breathin' thing. It doesn't need a *manager*.'

'Then what does it need?'

'If it's to be cherished as it deserves to be, it needs a *landlord*, who's invested both his money an' his heart in the place.'

Paniatowski laughed. 'Will you ever acknowledge that the modern world exists, sir?' she asked.

'I doubt it,' Woodend replied.

The barman working under the alias of assistant manager returned to their end of the bar. He gave Woodend a slightly supercilious look, as if to say that in this haven of made-to-measure suits, his hairy sports coat was acceptable – but only just.

'What can I do for you, sir?' he asked.

'A pint of best bitter, an' a neat vodka,' Woodend told him.

'Neat?' the barman repeated.

'Neat,' Woodend confirmed.

'Most of our customers consider that the proper way to drink vodka is with a mixer,' the young man said snottily.

'Aye, well, most of your customers are probably big girl's blouses, then,' Woodend told him. 'My friend here likes to *taste* what it is she's drinkin'.'

The barman shrugged, like a missionary who was not the least surprised to see that his words of wisdom had fallen on

stony ground. Then, he reached for a glass and started to pull
Woodend's pint.

'Were you on duty last night?' Woodend asked.

The barman looked up. 'Might I ask why you require that
particular piece of information, sir?'

Jesus! Woodend thought. Whatever had happened to the
old-style barman – the kind of man who would either have
given him a straight answer to a straight question, or else
accused him of being a nosy parker and then told him to mind
his own business?

The chief inspector slapped his warrant card on the counter.
'I *require* it, Sunshine, because askin' questions is what I do
for a livin',' he said.

'Oh, I see,' the assistant manager said.

'I rather thought you would,' Woodend told him. 'So, were
you workin' last night or not?'

'Yes, I was.'

Woodend produced a photograph of Terry Pugh, which had
been taken in the morgue after Dr Shastri had done all within
her power to disguise the fact that the body – like a Chinese
puzzle – came in two parts.

'Do you know this man?' he asked.

'He's lying down,' the barman pointed out.

'Boy, but nothin' gets past you, does it?' Woodend said.

'Is he ill or something?'

'You could say that.'

'Oh?'

Woodend sighed. 'He's been decapitated, so chances are
that he'll never ride a bike again. But I asked you a question,
Sunny Jim. Was this feller in here last night?'

The barman looked at the picture again. 'You'd never guess
he'd lost his head,' he said.

'You'll lose yours, if you don't start answerin' my question soon,' Woodend threatened.

'Yes, he was in here,' the barman said hastily.

'Now you're not just tellin' me that to keep me happy, are
you?' Woodend demanded.

'No. I promise you that he was here. Came in about half
past seven, bought a pint, and took it over to the table in the
corner. And fifteen minutes later, he was gone.'

'You're very precise,' Woodend said suspiciously.

'Well, he stood out, didn't he?'

'In what way?'

The barman shrugged awkwardly. 'You know.'

'No, I don't.'

'Most of our clientele are management. They come in here either to discuss business with each other or to entertain their lady friends. They give the place a certain tone.'

'I imagine they must.'

'This chap – the one in the picture – was wearing overalls when he came in. Of course, there's no law against that . . .'

'Though you probably think there should be!'

'. . . but it did make him rather conspicuous.'

'You probably wondered what he was doing in here at all,' Woodend suggested.

'I did at the time, but now I know that he was supposed to be meeting Mr Hough.'

'How do you know that?'

'Because after he'd left, Mr Hough himself came in, and asked me if I'd seen the man.'

'So if he'd got a meetin' with this Hough feller, why did he leave?' Woodend wondered.

'Probably because the other chap asked him to,' the barman said.

'What other chap?'

'He came into the bar about five minutes after his friend. At least, I'm assuming the man in the boiler suit was a friend of his.'

'Get to the point,' Woodend growled.

'He didn't order a drink. He went straight over to the table where his friend was sitting. I sent a waiter across – that's part of my responsibility as assistant manager – but the new arrival just waved the waiter away.'

'That could almost have been construed as a challenge to your considerable authority,' Woodend said. 'You can't have liked that.'

'I didn't,' the barman told him, oblivious to the sarcasm. 'I was just about to go across to the table myself, and tell him quite firmly that, in case he hadn't noticed, this wasn't a bus shelter . . .'

'By God, you're right!' Woodend said, looking around him. 'It isn't a bus shelter at all!'

'. . . and that if he wanted to remain in this rather pleasant environment, he'd have to order something to drink.'

'But you didn't, in fact, do that?'

'No, because the two of them stood up and left before I had the chance. The man in the boiler suit hadn't even finished his drink. There was more than half a pint left.'

'What did this *friend* look like?' Woodend asked.

'He was a big man, around forty-five years old. He had black oily hair, and he was wearing a rather crumpled suit in a garish pattern.'

'Anythin' else?'

'He was very dark – "foreign" dark, if you know what I mean.'

'Are you saying he was coloured?'

'Are you asking me if he was a nigger?'

'No,' Woodend said, with a sudden sharp edge to his voice. 'I'm asking you if he was *coloured.*'

'No, he wasn't. But his skin was a lot darker than yours or mine. I used to know a chap in Manchester who ran a Greek restaurant. He was from Athens, and this man rather reminded me of him.'

'So let me see if I've got this straight,' Woodend said. 'This Greek-looking feller comes into the bar an' talks to Terry Pugh, and five minutes later, they leave together.'

'Yes.'

'Did Pugh look as if he wanted to go with the other man? Or did he seem to be leavin' unwillingly?'

'I can't say. I was in the middle of serving a customer, and by the time I'd filled his order, the two of them were already leaving. So all I actually saw was their backs.'

Behind them, there was the sound of the double doors, which led in from the street, swinging open.

The assistant manager looked over Woodend's shoulder, and suddenly an obsequious smile filled his face.

'Who's arrived?' Woodend asked grumpily. 'Calamity Jane an' Billy the Kid?'

The assistant manager ignored him completely, and the smile on his face grew even wider as he shifted to the left, so that the new customer could get a proper look at him.

'Good afternoon, Mr Hough!' he called out brightly. 'What a pleasure it is to see you again so soon.'

'Hough?' Woodend repeated. 'Would that be *Mark* Hough?'

'Yes, that's right.'

Woodend turned around to make eye contact with the man who Terry Pugh had supposedly been intending to meet the previous evening – and found he had a clear view right to the door.

'I'm down here,' said a voice, and, from its tone, the speaker was clearly finding Woodend's obvious surprise quite amusing.

The Chief Inspector lowered his eyes a couple of feet, and saw that he had been right, and the man *was* greatly amused by his confusion.

'Mr Hough, I presume,' he said.

'Well, I'm certainly not Dr Livingstone,' the man in the wheelchair told him. '*He* had working legs.'

When Bob Rutter had wanted to sell the house in which his wife had been murdered, all the local estate agents he'd approached had been less than enthusiastic about the prospect of having it on their books.

'What's wrong with it?' he'd asked one agent. 'It's less than two years old. Any other house on that street has been snapped up almost as soon as the For Sale sign's been erected.'

'Yes, but it isn't *any other* house on the street,' the estate agent had said, awkwardly.

'No, it isn't,' Rutter had agreed, irritated. 'This one has had an entire re-fit since the fire. It's only the shell that's two years old – the inside's brand spanking new.'

'That may be true,' the agent had agreed reluctantly.

'It *is* true!'

'But the thing is, Mr Rutter, most people have seen too many ghost films to be comfortable about moving into a house where there's been a violent death, and I think I'd have real trouble shifting it.'

'It's not haunted,' Rutter had said firmly.

'Then why don't you live in it yourself?'

A good question, Rutter thought.

Because, he supposed, for him – and him alone – it *was* haunted.

He couldn't walk into the kitchen without seeing Maria preparing food, her hands feeling what her eyes could not see.

He couldn't be in the living room without remembering

how they had sat on the sofa in front of the television, with him providing a running commentary for actions on the screen which his wife could not have worked out from the dialogue alone.

He couldn't stand in the garden without recalling that everything he had planted there had been chosen for its smell alone, because though the colour and delicacy of certain plants had once given Maria great pleasure, it was a pleasure which her blindness had robbed her of.

In the end, he had sold the house – though for considerably less than would have been paid for the houses on either side of it – and bought a large Victorian semi-detached at the other end of town.

At the time of the sale, he felt as if a great weight had been lifted from his shoulders.

Now, as he parked his car outside the house in which he hoped to make a new home for himself and his daughter, he was no longer sure that he had done the right thing.

Now, it seemed to him that selling the old house had been a cowardly act – that a real man would have stayed in it, and battled the demons of rebuke and regret on their own territory.

He saw the blue E Type Jaguar parked just up the street, and thought – somewhat guiltily – of the heated exchange between himself and Monika Paniatowski, which had followed him telling Woodend that he needed to take a couple of hours off that afternoon.

'*Why's that?*' Paniatowski had asked. '*Have you got a date?*'

'*As a matter of fact, I have, in a way,*' he'd replied coldly. '*I'm interviewing nannies for Louisa.*'

Which had been perfectly true – as far as it went. But what he'd neglected to mention was that he'd asked Elizabeth Driver – the owner of the blue E Type Jag – to sit in on those interviews.

Seven

Mark Hough had all-but perfected the art of being in a wheel-chair, Woodend thought, as he watched the man skilfully manoeuvre his machine around the maze of pub tables, before bringing it to a sharp and very precise halt when he reached the table in the corner.

He was about the same age as Terry Pugh, but because of his bushy beard, which was flecked with grey, he might possibly have been taken for a few years older. He had a powerful torso, but the very breadth of it seemed only to draw attention to the withered legs beneath it.

Woodend had known several cripples who had self-consciously hidden their legs – covering them with a thin blanket even in the heat of summer – but Hough's legs were there for all to see, and even the expensive well-cut trousers could not hide just how wasted they were.

Woodend and Paniatowski followed Hough to the table, and sat down opposite him.

Mark Hough looked with something akin to real envy at Woodend's frothing pint.

'I used to enjoy best bitter myself,' he said, 'but it goes through the system far too quickly, and since going for a pee is no longer the joy it used to be, I stick to malt whisky now.'

He picked up the whisky Woodend had bought for him, took a small sip of it, and placed it on the copper-topped table.

'I rang your headquarters as soon as I heard the news about Terry,' he continued. 'I thought it was the right thing to do, in the circumstances. But, by the same token, I don't honestly see how I can be of much use to you.'

'You'd arranged to meet Terry Pugh last night?' Woodend said.

'I had.'

'Why in this particular pub?'

'Because it's close enough to my factory for me to be able to wheel myself down, and thus not have to bother anybody else.'

'Your factory?' Woodend repeated thoughtfully. 'Wait a minute, you're not *the* Hough of Hough Engineering, are you?'

'Guilty as charged,' Hough admitted.

'I read in the paper that you've just gone public,' Woodend said.

'Well remembered,' Hough said.

'What made you do it? Were you feelin' the pinch?'

'Far from it. There's a worldwide demand for precision engineering valves, and mine are some of the best on the market. The order book's full to overflowing, and it didn't take me long to realize that I either had to turn away business or expand my capacity. But expansion always takes capital, Chief Inspector, and rather than go cap in hand to the bank, I thought I'd issue shares.'

'But you refused to sell to large investors, didn't you?' Woodend asked, remembering why it was that the article in the newspaper had managed to stick in his mind. 'You told all the merchant banks an' insurance companies that were sniffin' around the company to go an' take a runnin' jump.'

'That's exactly what I told them,' Hough confirmed. 'I have great confidence in my company's future, and I saw no reason why a bunch of bloated capitalists based in London should profit from it, when I could just as easily ensure that the ordinary man in the street up here made a few bob instead.'

'You say "your company", but now you've sold the shares, it isn't actually your company any more, is it?' Woodend asked.

Hough laughed. 'Don't you believe it. I still own fifty-four percent of it – and that's more than enough to continue taking it in the direction in which I think it *should* go.'

'An' you have a very clear idea of what that direction should be, don't you?' Woodend asked.

'Oh yes, indeed,' Hough said.

Yes, you certainly look like a man who knows his own mind, Woodend thought.

'Let's get back to this meetin' you were supposed to have with Terry Pugh last night,' he suggested.

'Ah yes. I went to school with Terry, you know.'

'His wife said somethin' about that.'

'We were the closest of pals, all the way through Sudbury Street Elementary School.'

Woodend grinned. 'I went to Sudbury Street myself, though it must have been some considerable time before you did.'

'Probably so. But I don't suppose it had changed much over the years. Anyway, Terry and I fell out of touch. I expect that was mostly my fault. After I lost the use of my legs . . .' he paused for a moment, '. . . and in case you'd wondering, it was as the result of a motor accident.'

'I wasn't wondering,' Woodend told him.

'Neither was I,' Paniatowski chipped in.

Hough grinned again. 'You're a pair of liars!' he said, without rancour. 'But to get back to the point – after I was crippled, I didn't want to see anybody very much. For about two years, I just sat around the house feeling very sorry for myself. I'd been a fair-to-middling athlete in my youth, you see, and losing the use my legs seemed to take all meaning out of life.'

'That was understandable,' Woodend said.

'No, it wasn't,' Hough disagreed. 'There's never any excuse for giving in. And one morning I woke up and discovered – almost to my own surprise – that I was determined to make a new start. I can't tell you why it should have been that particular morning – or even why it should have happened at all. It simply did. I had a little capital just sitting in the bank – a legacy from an uncle of mine – and I decided to draw it all out and buy myself an engineering company which was teetering on the verge of bankruptcy.'

'Are you an engineer by training?'

'No, which makes the whole idea seem crazy, doesn't it? But though I knew I couldn't make things myself, I thought I could ensure that they were made properly. And once they *were* made, I was convinced I could sell them.' He took another sip of his whisky. 'I'm rabbiting on a bit, aren't I? You don't want to hear my life story. You're here to find out about Terry Pugh.'

'True,' Woodend agreed. 'Not that I haven't enjoyed listenin'' to your story, anyway.'

'Yes, I'm something of an inspiration, aren't I?' Mark Hough said, though the self-deprecation in his tone neutralized any element of arrogance the statement might have contained. 'At any rate, I ran into Terry in the centre of town, a few weeks ago. I must admit that my first feeling was one of guilt, for having ignored him so long, but he seemed to bear me no ill will, so I soon got over that. We had a chat about old times – as you do – then we filled each other in on what we'd been doing since we last met.'

'More him filling you in than you filling him in,' Woodend guessed. 'He'll have read all about you in the papers.'

'Possibly you're right,' Hough agreed. 'But at any rate, he was polite enough to listen, and while we were talking, it suddenly struck me that we could do each other a bit of good.'

'In what way?'

'One of the biggest headaches in any expansion programme is the manpower problem. You can get men, easily enough – but you can't always get the *right* men, especially at the shop floor management level. When I realized that Terry was working in a somewhat similar company to my own, it started to seem like a lucky chance that we'd met.'

'So you were about to offer him a job last night?'

'Not exactly. It was more a case of firming up the offer I'd already made in principle.'

'An' your job offer was based solely on the grounds that you knew him, an' he was already in the right kind of work?'

Hough laughed. 'Just because I'm in a wheelchair, you mustn't think I'm a simpleton, you know,' he said.

'I assure you, I don't,' Woodend protested.

'Knowing Terry was part of it,' Mark Hough said, 'but it was *what* I knew about him that was important. Terry was never a great brain, but he was conscientious and hard working and reliable, even in our Sudbury Street days. So if, on top of that, he was an even half-way decent engineer, then he was a real prize.'

'An' *was* he a half-way decent engineer?'

'He was better than that. They were so pleased with him at his present firm that they were about to promote him. So I told him I'd more than match whatever they were offering him, and he seemed delighted. That's why it came as such a shock to hear that he'd committed suicide. It just didn't seem like him.'

'Had you put this offer of yours in writing?' Woodend asked.

'No, it was all done over the phone.'

'So you never sent him a typewritten letter?'

'No.'

Then who the bloody hell had sent him the one that his sister-in-law claimed had worried him so much, Woodend wondered.

'What more can you tell me about Terry?' he asked aloud.

'Very little at all about his recent life,' Mark Hough admitted. 'As I said, we'd only met once in recent days, and all our telephone calls were of a strictly business nature. Perhaps that's why I don't feel the loss as much as I'd have thought I would. Even now, when I picture him, it's the young Terry I see. I never really knew the Terry who hanged himself.'

He paused again, and looked thoughtful – as if an idea had suddenly struck him.

'Or perhaps Terry Pugh didn't hang himself after all,' he continued, speaking slowly and deliberately.

'What makes you think that?' Woodend wondered.

'You do,' Hough told him. 'Why would a Chief Inspector be wasting his valuable time investigating a suicide?'

'My time's not as valuable as you seem to think,' Woodend said, trying to make light of it.

'He was murdered, wasn't he?' Hough asked. 'He was murdered, and for reasons of your own, you're keeping quiet about it.'

'No comment,' Woodend said.

'And *that* is a comment in itself,' Hough told him.

'Do you know why it's so great workin' here, Constable Beresford?' Bob Smothers asked.

From the man's tone, Beresford sensed that a joke – and probably a very weak and tired one – was on the way.

'No, why is it so great working here, Mr Smothers?' he asked, playing the comedian's dupe.

'Because this company's always on a roll!'

Beresford did his best to sound amused, but the other men sitting around the table in the staff canteen of Whitebridge Ball Bearings Ltd had heard the line so many times before that they couldn't even be bothered to raise a groan.

'Ball bearings! On a roll! Get it!' Smothers asked.

'Yes, I thought it was very funny,' Beresford told him. He turned to the rest of the men. 'So you all worked with Terry Pugh, did you?'

The men nodded.

'What was he like?' Beresford ploughed on. 'Would you say he was a popular feller?'

'He wasn't exactly popular, but he wasn't exactly unpopular, either,' one of the men said.

'He pretty much kept himself to himself,' another supplied. 'Pleasant enough with everybody, but not exactly talkative.'

'He never came on company outings to Blackpool,' a third said, almost as if he considered such a refusal little less than a grievous sin. 'Wouldn't join the darts team, either, even when we were a man short.'

'Didn't seem very interested in women, either,' contributed a fourth. 'Which was odd, because he wasn't a bad-looking lad, an' several of the girls in the typin' pool were definitely interested in him.'

'Well, he wouldn't have been interested, would he?' Beresford asked. 'After all, he *was* married.'

The men sitting around the table thought this was a far funnier joke than the one Smothers had made about ball bearings, and a couple of them were almost doubled up with laughter.

'Are you a virgin or somethin'?' Bob Smothers asked, when the laugher had subsided.

'No, of course not!' said Beresford – who was.

'Then you shouldn't be surprised that when a man gets an opportunity to dip his wick, he doesn't normally think twice about it. Most of the lads in this factory will bang anythin' that moves. An' there's a few sittin' round this table,' Smothers grinned and looked at each of the men in turn, 'that will bang it even if it *doesn't* move. It's a hotbed of sin, this place. Must come from workin' with balls all day – if you see what I mean.'

'I used to think old Terry was a bit of a homo,' another man said, 'but then I heard that he put his missus up the duff, so I must have been wrong about that, mustn't I?'

The man at the far end of the table, who looked to be round about Terry Pugh's age, had kept silent so far, but now he said, 'It was his National Service that changed him.'

'What's your name, sir?' Beresford asked.

There were several cries of, 'Oooh, *sir!*' from the other workers, and Bob Smothers said, 'You never told me you been knighted, Albert!'

'The name's Albert Knox,' the man told Beresford.

'In what way did his National Service seem to change Terry Pugh?' Beresford asked.

'I knew Terry before he got his call-up papers, which is more than any of the other buggers around this table can say,' Albert Knox told him. 'He was a bit of a lad, in them days. You know what I mean, don't you?'

'A heavy drinker?' Beresford guessed.

'Oh, he was some boozer, all right – a ten-pint-a-night man, when he could afford it. But there was more to it than that. He was never exactly on the lookout for trouble, but if it came his way, he'd get stuck in without a second's thought. An' if a shift worker was puttin' in a bit of overtime at the factory, he was always more than willing to put in a bit of overtime with the shift worker's wife.'

'But the army changed all that?'

'Like you'd never have thought possible. When he came out, he'd quietened down *a lot*.'

'That's what two years in the army does for you,' Bob Smothers said. 'Teaches you a bit of self-discipline. Makes a man of you. The worst thing the government ever did was to abolish National Service.'

His words clearly annoyed Albert Knox. 'You weren't in the army yourself, were you, Bob?' he asked.

'Well, no,' Smothers admitted, suddenly looking rather uncomfortable.

'Then you've no idea what you're talkin' about, have you?' Albert Knox asked.

'I was perfectly willin' to go,' Smothers said defensively, 'but I had flat feet, you see, so they wouldn't take me.'

'You're lucky you're young enough to have just missed it,' Knox said, ignoring Smothers and talking directly to Beresford. 'It was a waste of two years of my life. They say it'll make a man of you, but what it really tries to do is to turn you into an unthinkin', unfeelin' machine.'

'Hey, that's a bit strong,' Bob Smothers protested.

'Still, I shouldn't complain,' Knox said, continuing to ignore him. 'It's true that they made me paint stones white, an' then, when I'd finished that to their satisfaction. paint 'em black. But I was never under fire, like some poor buggers were, forced to defend an empire we should have got shut of years ago.'

'The Empire was the envy of the world,' Smothers said.

'You're talkin' through your arse, as usual, you big stupid bastard,' Knox told him.

'Did Terry Pugh seem especially unhappy in the last couple of weeks?' Beresford interjected, eager to get the conversation back on course before a fight broke out.

'Now you mention it, I think I'd have to say that he did,' a man with a squint, who was sitting next to Albert Knox, chipped in. 'It was probably the letter that did it.'

'What letter?' Beresford asked.

'He had this letter in his boiler suit pocket. He'd take it out two or three times a day, an' read it, though he must have known it by heart. An' he always looked worried after he'd done that.'

'Any idea what the letter was about?' Beresford asked.

'No. He didn't show it to me, an' I didn't ask him about it. But I can tell you that it was all crumpled, like he'd balled it up to throw it away, then thought better of it – an' I think it was typed, rather than written.'

'It'll have been a solicitor's letter, then,' Bob Smothers said. '"Dear Mr Pugh, I must inform you that Miss Big Tits from the typin' pool has a bun in the oven, an' is claimin' that you are the father".'

He checked around the table to see if his latest sally into humour was receiving the appreciation it deserved, but the other men seemed almost as fed up with him as Albert Knox was.

'If it had been a solicitor's letter, it would have been on a big sheet of paper,' the man with the squint said. 'But this was just an ordinary size – the size you might use if you were writin' a letter yourself.'

'So maybe it was from Miss Big Tits herself,' Bob Smothers said, still trying to squeeze an acceptable joke out of his less-than-adequate material.

'Did anybody else here happen to see Terry Pugh reading this letter?' Beresford asked.

Several of the men admitted that they had – so it seemed likely that Pugh had read the letter more than the two or three times a day that the man with the squint had observed – but none of them could throw any light on what the letter might actually have said.

Still, Beresford assured himself, he had made progress of a sort, and even if the letter didn't mean anything to him, it just might mean something to Woodend.

Eight

From her vantage point, in the bay window of the lounge in Bob Rutter's new home, Elizabeth Driver watched Rutter walk around his car, checking that all the doors were properly locked.

She smiled to herself. It was a smile that her colleagues in London would have immediately recognized – a smile which would have made most of them break out into a sweat. Because when she smiled like that, it meant her latest scheme was right on the track, and someone – quite possibly one of them – was about to have his life – or at least his career – seriously damaged.

Rutter had finished checking the doors, and now tried the boot, to make sure that was locked too.

He was a very careful man, Elizabeth Driver thought. A meticulous man. The sort of man who knew – down to the last penny – how much money there was in his bank account; who took his suits back to the dry cleaner's *exactly* a month after he had last collected them from the same establishment; who would have checked that the water pipes in his new house were properly lagged before the ink had even had time to dry on the contract.

So it was ironic that when such a careful man *did* make mistakes, they were such monumental ones. And Rutter had made not just one, but two.

The first had been over his affair with Monika Paniatowski. It hadn't been a mistake to *have* the affair, as far as Driver was concerned. There was nothing wrong with grabbing your pleasure where you could. No, the mistake had been to feel *guilty* about it, once it was over. Because guilt slowed you down – guilt could stop you doing what you wanted to do the next time an opportunity arose. And if you couldn't do *exactly* what you wanted, then what was the point of life?

As for his second mistake, he wasn't even aware that he'd made it yet, though it was already of such proportions that it towered above the first one as an elephant does over a rabbit.

This *second* mistake was to welcome his own destruction by allowing the enemy right into the heart of his camp – and not only allowing her in, but giving her a key to the front door.

He had lowered his guard to her – this careful man – because he thought they shared a secret which bound her to him, and made her safe. He *thought* that she was writing a book about his life with Maria, an honest book which would serve as a penance for the way he had behaved to his blind wife before her murder. He was quite wrong about that, of course. Such a book would never be written.

But there would be *a* book, and he, by making it possible for her to see into the workings of Central Lancs Police, would all unknowingly be helping her to write it. It would be a blockbuster of a book, exposing the Whitebridge force as not only incompetent, but also vastly corrupt, and her own newspaper had already promised to buy the serial rights.

She had worried, for a while, that the Lancashire force might actually turn out to be not quite as corrupt and incompetent as she might have hoped, but she had long since left that concern behind her. After all, it was not the truth she was searching for, but something that had the *appearance* of being the truth – and the myriad authentic details that Rutter could feed her with would provide her with the ideal camouflage for a score of outrageous stories of her own concocting.

She heard the key turn in the front door lock, and then Rutter stepping into the hallway.

'I'm in here, Bob,' she called out.

When he entered the living room, she inclined her head a little, so that he could kiss her lightly on the cheek.

Later on in her book's development, she thought, it might be necessary to go much further with their physical intimacy. Later on, it would probably be necessary to actually sleep with him.

The prospect did not bother her. She'd gone to bed with dozens of men – some of them really quite repulsive – in the interests of her career. And Rutter was not repulsive at all. In fact, he was so dishy that she felt an urge to seduce him at that very moment.

She forced herself to hold back. The role she was playing for Rutter's benefit called for her to act more like a penitent nun than a raging nymphomaniac. Besides, a good commander never throws all his soldiers into the first battle – he saves his elite troops for the final devastating assault.

Rutter checked his watch. 'The first girl will be here in about ten minutes,' he said. 'Now the way I suggest we handle the interviews is . . .'

'I can't do it,' Elizabeth Driver interrupted him.

'Can't do what?'

'Help you to interview the nannies.'

'Why not?'

Because she had no interest at all in children or in children's nannies, Elizabeth Driver thought, and she was afraid that her lack of interest would shine through, however much she might try to disguise it. Because the only kind of interviewing she really enjoyed was aggressive interviewing – interviewing which pulled the subject apart and left him in pieces on the floor – and there was always the danger that, however much she tried to avoid it, she would get caught up in the heat of the moment and reveal her true self.

'I'm sorry, Bob, I really did want to help you,' she said, looking penitent. 'In fact, when I talked to my editor a few minutes ago, I told him I had something really important to do, so I simply couldn't follow up the lead he'd just been given on a hot story in Preston. I won't tell you exactly what he said in reply,' she smiled impishly, 'but his language would have made a docker blush.'

'But you promised,' Rutter said, rather like a disappointed child.

'I know I did,' she replied, wondered if she should brush her finger against his cheek, then deciding that, at this stage of the game, it was a step too far. 'And honestly, I'm really upset that I can't do it. But my editor was most insistent that I leave right away.'

'Then why did you bother to come at all?' Rutter asked, with just a hint of petulance evident in his tone.

'I don't know how long I'll be gone,' Elizabeth Driver lied. 'It could be weeks. And I felt I just had to see you before I left.'

'That was sweet of you,' Rutter told her.

She smiled. 'I *am* sweet. Under this tough exterior, there lurks a real big softie.'

Rutter looked at her strangely – questioningly – and she wondered if she'd been over-acting.

'You haven't asked me about the case I'm working on,' he said. 'Why is that?'

'I didn't really think I should,' Elizabeth Driver replied seriously. 'After all, I am a crime reporter, and when we talk about your work, it should be on a purely official basis.'

Rutter frowned. 'Yes, but it does seem a great pity that, on this occasion, I *can't* talk about it.'

It seemed to Elizabeth Driver that she might not be the only one to be guilty of over-acting. And suddenly, she understood exactly what game Bob Rutter was playing.

'A pity?' she repeated.

'Yes, you see, I've never come across a case quite like this one before, but it's just possible, given your paper's tendency to focus on the bizarre . . . I'm sorry, I didn't mean to offend you.'

'I'm not offended. I know what my paper does.'

'Well, then, given that your newspaper has a propensity for the bizarre and sensational side of crime, I think it's just possible that you *might* have come across a case like it.'

'I suppose it is,' Elizabeth Driver said, noncommittally.

'And if you *had* come across a similar case, then your insights might prove to be very useful to me.' Rutter paused. 'But since, as you've just pointed out, you *are* a crime reporter . . .'

'This is a ridiculous situation,' Elizabeth Driver said, with mock exasperation. 'I'm your friend, aren't I?'

'Well, I certainly like to think so.'

'And *as* your friend, I'd like to help you out in any way I can. And I don't really see why my job should get in the way of that.'

Rutter pretended to be on the horns of a dilemma. 'If you could give me your word that you won't . . .'

'Publish anything that you tell me?'

'Yes.'

'You have it.'

'In that case, there's absolutely nothing to stop me from speaking freely to you.'

Rutter told her all about the Terry Pugh case.

'So you're sure he was dead long before he went off the bridge?' she asked, when he'd finished.

'Dr Shastri's convinced of it.'

'But all the local press still think it was suicide?'

'That's right. If one of the reporters managed to work out the truth, he'd have a real scoop on his hands.' Rutter paused again. 'So what do you think?'

'Think?'

'Does this particular case remind you of any other that you might have come across?'

'Not even remotely.' Elizabeth Driver looked at her watch. 'I really *do* have to go.'

'Well, if you must, you must,' Rutter agreed.

This time, when he kissed her, she moved her head at the last moment, so that his lips lightly brushed against hers.

'I'll be back as soon as I can be,' she called from the hallway. 'After all, we really do need to get started on your book.'

'Yes, we do,' Rutter said, from the lounge.

She was conscious of his eyes following her as she made her way towards her Jaguar, so she walked slowly.

As if she were reluctant to leave.

As if it were only with a tremendous effort on her part that she was preventing herself from turning around and rushing back to him.

She did not allow herself to break into laugher until she was sure she was out of his range of vision, but once she gave way, she could not stop for well over a minute.

Did Bob Rutter really think he could trick her quite so easily, she asked herself. Did he really believe that he could put her to a test without her even noticing it?

He had offered her the bait of the suicide-that-was-really-a-murder, and the following morning he would no doubt anxiously pick up her newspaper, half-expecting to see the story under her by-line.

And when it wasn't there, what conclusion would he draw? That he could trust her!

It would never even occur to him that she might have chosen to forgo a short-term gain in favour of a much larger long-term one. Because men like Bob Rutter simply didn't think deviously enough.

She'd passed an important milestone. Conquered a major peak. From now on, it was going to be easy.

Reg Lewis stood in a back alley, sobbing like a baby. It had been the empty cigarette packet he held in his hand which had opened the floodgates to his tears. He'd been so sure there'd be at least *one* more cigarette inside it – and there hadn't been. Yet even as he wept, he knew the cigarette wasn't the real problem – that the absence of it had been no more than the final straw.

The real cause of his anguish was his fear – a fear that had been gnawing away at his insides like a hungry rat ever since he received the letter, but now threatened to swallow him whole.

Terry Pugh was dead! Hanged! Decapitated!

And that was only the start!

'*They used to say that if a bullet had your name on it, there was nothing you could do,*' Tom Bygraves had told him. '*All that any of us can do is pray we're not the next one on his list. The only hope we have is that he'll be caught before he works his way round to us.*'

He needed a smoke. Just a few puffs of blessed nicotine would make all the difference. He got down on his hands and knees, and started rummaging through the rubbish on the floor of the alley.

He found a flattened half-smoked cigarette lying close to a pile of dog shit. For a moment, he thought this was too low to go – even for him. Then, carefully avoiding the canine droppings, he picked up the discarded cigarette and rolled it around between his fingers until it was more or less cylindrical again.

With trembling hands, he stuck a match, lit up the cigarette, and took in a deep drag.

What was he to do, he wondered.

What the *bloody hell* was he to do?

He needed to get away from Whitebridge, change his name, and start a new life. But that required money. And he didn't have any. Not even enough to buy himself another packet of fags.

In a couple of days' time, he would be able to pick up his unemployment benefit at the dole office. It wouldn't be much money, but it should just about cover a train ticket to London,

and London was a big city where any man could hide if he
really wanted to.

Yes, that was what he would do, he decided. He would go
to London. And so what if, once he was there, he had to live
on the streets and could eat only what he found in rubbish bins?

At least he would be alive! At least he wouldn't end up
hanging from the end of a rope on some bridge!

He felt better for having made the decision, but the feeling
didn't last. Because two days was a long time to wait for his
money. And what was he going to do – where was he going
to *be* – while he was waiting?

He couldn't go back to his grotty little bedsit – with the
leaking tap and the only toilet in the house down the other end
of the hallway – because he would be a sitting target there.

But he couldn't stay out on the streets, either.

Perhaps he could hitch-hike to London. But who would
ever pick up a man who had long scraggly hair and was dressed
almost like a tramp?

Perhaps he could *walk* to London.

Or Birmingham.

Or Manchester.

But he knew himself well enough to understand that he was
already too beaten down by life to ever make that kind of effort.

So maybe the only real choice he was left with was to give
himself up to the police – to walk into Whitebridge Police
Headquarters, and explain to the sergeant behind the desk why
he should lock him up.

And then, like the sun emerging from behind a very dark
cloud, a bright shining new idea suddenly came into his head.

There was still one man in Whitebridge who would help
him – who would really have no choice *but* to help him.

Reg Lewis took another drag on the rescued cigarette, and
found that it tasted better than his previous ones – found that
it tasted *wonderful*.

It was all going to be all right, he told himself. He would
not only have a new life, he would have a better one.

Despite the fact there was at least one more puff left in the
cigarette, he threw it carelessly away. And when he walked
back up the alley, there was a definite spring in his step.

Nine

The assistant manager and the waiter in the Tanners' Arms had both given the police artist a description of the suspect who had left the pub with Terry Pugh, and the resulting black-and-white sketch was of a man with greased-back hair, a largish nose, and a dimple in his chin. What was missing was any expression in the eyes. They were neutral, which was the fault neither of the witnesses (who had never got close enough to him to really see them), nor of the police artist (who had consequently had nothing to work towards). Nobody's fault then, but the simple truth was that without a clear impression of the eyes, the sketch did not really come alive – without the eyes, Woodend and Paniatowski had no real idea of the kind of man they were dealing with.

Monika Paniatowski picked the sketch up from where it was lying on Woodend's desk, looked at it first from one angle and then another, and finally placed it back where she'd found it.

'It's not *just* the eyes that are the problem,' she said. 'It's the lack of a complexion as well. We've no idea of his actual colouring from this. Even so, I'd have to say that he definitely looks foreign, and he could well be Greek.'

'Or Turkish,' Woodend said gloomily, dragging on his Capstan Full Strength. 'Or Yugoslav, or Albanian or Romanian. Or perhaps he's not European at all. Maybe he's Anglo-Indian.'

Paniatowski laughed uncertainly. 'That's not a very positive attitude to take, is it, sir?' she asked.

'No, but I can't help that,' Woodend told her. 'This is a very nasty case – an' I've got a feelin' in my water that it's goin' to get even nastier.'

'How could it possibly get any nastier than *decapitation*?' Paniatowski wondered.

'When a perfectly ordinary feller like Terry Pugh dies in

the way he did, you can pretty much guarantee that he's been killed not for somethin' he's done on his own, but because he's part of somethin' bigger,' Woodend said. 'An' it's that "somethin' bigger" – whatever it is – that's goin' to get nastier.' He picked up the police artist's sketch, gave it a cursory glance, and listlessly dropped it back on his desk. 'This picture, even without the eyes, should be a big breakthrough for us – but I just don't think it's goin' to be.'

'It's early days yet, sir,' Paniatowski reminded him.

'Aye, it is,' Woodend agreed. 'But even at this stage of the investigation, a clue like that sketch should already be producin' significant leads. An' it hasn't. There's nobody filed in our records who looks even remotely like this feller. An' none of the bobbies who've seen the picture so far can recall ever seein' him in Whitebridge – despite the fact that if he was here, he should stick out like a nun in a knockin' shop.'

'So perhaps he's new to the area,' Paniatowski suggested.

'Perhaps he is,' Woodend countered sourly. 'But if that's true, it just makes things look even murkier, doesn't it?'

'Does it?'

'Let's follow that argument of yours through, shall we? A stranger comes into town, an' looks around for somethin' to amuse himself with. An' what does he come up with? He thinks, "I know what I'll do. I'll find some feller who works in a ball bearin' factory – an' then I'll pull his bloody head off"!'

There was little point in arguing with Woodend when he was in this mood, Paniatowski decided.

'Have you had the sketch sent down to the Central Records Office in Scotland Yard, sir?' she asked.

'Oh aye. They should get it first thing in the mornin'.'

'Then perhaps they'll be able to give us a result. Their records are so much more extensive than ours, you know.'

'Yes, strange as it might seem, I *did* already know that,' Woodend said. He paused. 'I'm sorry, Monika. That must have sounded really ratty.'

'No rattier than several other things you've said in the last few minutes,' Paniatowski pointed out.

Woodend shook his head. 'You're right, I'm wrong, an' again, I apologize,' he said. 'An' maybe you're right about somethin' else, as well. Maybe, whatever my misgivings,

Central Records *will* be able to put a name to the face. But if I was you, I wouldn't hold my breath while I was waiting.'

Paniatowski glanced up at the heavy old-fashioned clock which hung on the wall.

'Isn't it time that we headed out for the Drum and Monkey, sir?' she asked.

'Just about,' Woodend agreed, glancing up at the clock himself. 'An' I suppose it's just possible that when we get there, we'll find that either Constable Beresford or Inspector Rutter has come up with a brilliant lead which will crack the case wide open.'

'But we shouldn't hold our breaths while we're waiting?' Paniatowski suggested.

'But we shouldn't hold our breaths while we're waitin',' the Chief Inspector agreed.

Reg Lewis' head ached, and though he was sure he had his eyes open, he couldn't see a thing.

He'd heard somewhere that people could go blind through drinking too much. But *he* hadn't drunk that much, had he? At least, not that day.

He'd needed to calm his nerves, so he'd knocked back five pints in quick succession at lunch time. No – five and a half. He'd managed to scrape together just enough copper from the bottom of his pocket to buy that last half. But five and a half pints wasn't a lot. For him, it could almost be called 'moderate'. It certainly wasn't enough to make him go blind!

He tried to remember what he'd done since he'd drained that last half pint, and discovered that he had no idea.

He didn't even know what time it was now. And how could he, when he couldn't even tell whether it was day or night?

He closed his eyes – not that that made much difference – and tried to remember what he'd done after he'd left the pub.

He'd been standing in the alley, crying like a baby.

He'd picked up a flattened cigarette end off the ground, rolled it back into shape, and smoked it.

And then?

And then *nothing*.

He realized that he was being bounced around, and with that realization came another – that he was not standing on his feet, but lying down.

There had been a steady hum accompanying his thoughts, like background music. Now the hum changed briefly to a minor roar, before settling down to something much more regular again.

A car engine, he told himself. That was what the noise was.

No, not a *car* engine. From the sound of it, it was more likely to be a van or a small lorry.

So . . . he was in some kind of motor vehicle, he was lying down, and his head hurt.

He had not thought to move before, but now, when he did try, he found that he couldn't. His hands, which were behind his back, refused to separate. And his ankles were being equally uncooperative.

He was tied up! He was in the back of a van, and he was tied up.

But why? *Who* had tied him up, and for *what* purpose?

He tried to speak, but his lips seemed to be glued together. His whole face was beginning to prickle, and he guessed that was because it was in close contact with an itchy woollen fabric.

He had a hood over his head, he decided – probably like the ones that he'd seen army interrogators slip over their suspects' heads, before they started to question them. It had been fun watching that happen – working out from their panicked body language what their facial expressions must be under the hoods – but it wasn't fun when it happened to you.

And he wasn't in the army now.

He wasn't . . . in the army . . . now.

It was as if he had stumbled on the right key to open the door of his closed mind. Suddenly, all the events of the afternoon came flooding back to him with perfect clarity.

He knew who had put him in the van now.

And he knew *why* they had done it.

And now he understood what was in store for him, he felt his bowels open and he soiled himself.

Woodend drummed his fingers impatiently on the surface of the corner table in the Drum and Monkey, then checked his watch again.

Bob Rutter was already three-quarters of an hour late, he noted. That was not at all like the conscientious inspector who had been with him since his days at the Yard – and it was certainly *not* a good sign.

Possibly the reason that Rutter was so late was because interviewing the potential nannies for Louisa had taken him longer than he had anticipated, Woodend told himself.

But that wasn't an excuse. In a murder investigation, there *were* no excuses. You worked all the hours that God sent, and if your private life happened to fall to pieces in the middle of it, then that was just tough.

What the bloody hell was the matter with him, he suddenly found himself wondering. The thoughts which had just passed through his head didn't belong there – didn't belong to *him* – at all.

Some chief inspectors he knew *did* regard their teams as little more than robots programmed to do their will – but he certainly wasn't one of them. He valued the members of his team, despite their weaknesses. In fact, those weaknesses were often more of an advantage than a hindrance. Because if they didn't have any of their own, how would they ever understand the human weakness they came across in the course of the investigation? And if they didn't understand that weakness, how would they ever solve the case?

He'd swung from one extreme to the other in a matter of seconds, he told himself, and now it was time to try and strike a balance.

He took a deep breath. Certainly, allowances had to be made, he argued – but it was also necessary to draw the line somewhere. And it was very worrying indeed that even though baby Louisa was still in London, she had already begun to distract Rutter from the job.

'We might as well make a start, I suppose,' he said aloud.

'What about Bob?' Monika Paniatowski asked.

'What about him?'

'He's not here yet.'

'I can see that for myself, but we can't wait for him forever. If he wants to keep up to speed, he'll just have to read our reports.'

'It's not the same,' Monika said firmly.

'I know it isn't,' Woodend agreed. 'But what can we do?'

'We could give him a bit longer to get here.'

'Monika . . .'

'You know as well as I do that Bob's mind works in a

different way to yours and mine, and that he often picks up on points that would have slipped by the rest of us completely. So if he's not here when we go through our findings, there's a bloody good chance we'll overlook what could turn out to be a vital lead in this investigation.'

It was tragic to see how much she still loved Bob Rutter, Woodend thought. She might snipe at him when he was there . . .

Might? a voice said in his head. There was no *might* about it. She bloody *did*!

. . . but when he wasn't there, she seemed to feel under an obligation to defend him to her dying breath.

'We really do have to crack on, Monika,' he said heavily, and without giving her time to respond, he turned to DC Beresford. 'So, what little pearls of wisdom have you managed to glean from your visit to the ball bearing factory, young Colin?' he asked.

Beresford outlined what he had heard in the works canteen, and Woodend told him what progress he and Paniatowski had made.

'So let's review what we know so far,' Woodend said. 'Terry Pugh, from what Monika and I have learned of him, was a quiet sort of feller who did his work conscientiously, an' generally kept his head down.'

He saw that Monika Paniatowski was smiling – and thank God she still could – at his unfortunate choice of words.

'Sorry,' he said, grinning despite himself. 'What I *meant* was that Pugh seems to have pretty much kept himself out of trouble.'

'Although one of his work-mates did say that he was rather wild when he was in his late teens,' Beresford reminded him.

'Which of us wasn't?' Woodend asked.

And then he thought: You weren't, Colin. Given your mother's condition, you haven't been allowed that luxury.

'On the other hand, we know that, one bright spring mornin', Pugh received a typewritten letter which really disturbed him,' he continued, 'a letter which not only made him puke up the first time he read it, but which he kept *re-readin'* – as if he couldn't help himself – even when he was at work. Now, what could have been in that letter?'

'I think his sister-in-law could be right about the gambling debts,' Paniatowski said.

'So what are you suggestin'? That the bookies have decided that breakin' legs isn't a sufficient incentive to make their clients pay up any more, an' have moved their persuasion techniques up a notch?'

'Of course not,' Paniatowski said. 'But it can't do any harm to have the bookies checked out, can it?'

Woodend nodded. 'No, it can't do any harm at all,' he agreed. 'When it comes to secret vices, it's often the quiet ones you have to watch, because they're always the best at keeping it to themselves.'

'So we'll have the bookies checked out?'

'Why not? What have we got to lose? And while they're bein' questioned about Pugh's possible gamblin' habits, they can also have a look at the sketch of the Unknown Greek.'

'What I don't understand is why Terry Pugh left the pub with this Greek feller in the first place,' Beresford said, sounding troubled.

'Go on,' Woodend said encouragingly – because a troubled thought could often turn out to be a fruitful one.

'The meeting he'd arranged to have with Mr Hough was important to him, wasn't it?' Beresford asked.

'Very important. Hough was about to offer him a much better job than the one he had at the time – an' he could have used the extra money, what with the baby bein' on the way.'

'And from what you've said about him expanding his factory, Mr Hough must be a very busy man.'

'I imagine he is.'

'So, since his time is valuable, he won't have taken kindly to being stood up, will he? He might even have withdrawn the job offer, for all Pugh knew. Yet despite that, he decides to leave the pub with the Unknown Greek – a stranger, who he's only been talking to for a couple of minutes.'

'You're right, that doesn't make sense,' Paniatowski agreed. 'The Greek can't have been a stranger to him at all.'

'On the other hand, they're unlikely to have met in Whitebridge, because we've already established that if the Greek had been here for any length of time, one of our lads would have been bound to notice him,' Woodend said thoughtfully. He nodded at Beresford. 'Well done, lad. You've not only raised some interestin' questions, but you've landed yourself a job for the mornin'.'

'What job's that, sir?'

'I want you to find out if Terry Pugh's done much travellin', and especially if he's ever been to Greece.'

'Or Turkey. Or Yugoslavia. Or Romania,' Paniatowski said.

And then she grinned, just in case Woodend had missed the point that what she was doing was mocking him for his earlier pessimism.

'Aye, or any of them other strange weird an' wonderful foreign places as well,' Woodend agreed, grinning back at her.

He suddenly realized he was feeling much better than he had earlier. The black mood that this investigation had induced in him – and which had coloured his view of life in general, and Bob Rutter's absence in particular – had been somewhat lifted by talking through the case with Paniatowski and Beresford.

Of course, he understood that they still had a long way to go before they were in a position to make an arrest. And, of course, it didn't help that the Chief Constable was still insisting that they pretend Terry Pugh's murder was a suicide. But these were no more than occupational hazards.

He took another sip of his pint, and decided that letting the beer settle for a while had improved the flavour no end.

What he didn't realize – but very soon would – was that in so many ways, he was like a prisoner already kneeling before the execution block, yet still convinced that a last-minute reprieve would come through. And when the axe fell – as it was about to – it would come as a complete surprise.

Ten

The building site was on the corner where the road into town and the road to Preston intersected. It had been a large, old-fashioned cinema, which in its heyday had shown the biggest and best of the Hollywood epics, but in its later years had survived mainly by screening 'naturist' films for the delectation of sniggering schoolboys and dirty old men. And when even this had failed – when, some evenings, the staff outnumbered the customers – the owners had finally decided that they could no longer compete with that evil little monster, the television set, and had sold up.

The space had been bought – much to the consternation of several local small businesses – by a large retail chain. Soon, in place of the old decrepit cinema, there would be a brand spanking new supermarket, offering cut prices, trading stamps and free gifts. For the moment, however, there was little more than a steel skeleton, surrounded by a chain-link fence and guarded, at night, by Harry 'Bone Crusher' Turner, who had once been the most formidable prop forward ever to have played for Whitebridge Rugby Football Club.

If Harry – who time had turned into a somewhat cantankerous old-age pensioner – had had a dog with him as he went on his rounds, that particular site would probably never have been chosen for the events of the evening.

But he hadn't – and it was.

Turner had, in fact, asked for a dog on his first day on the job, and had gone into a second-childhood sulk when his request had been immediately – and somewhat ungraciously – turned down.

'But I *need* a dog, if I'm to do the job properly,' he'd protested to the young site manager, who went by the name of Wickshaw.

'It's not the crown jewels you're guarding here, you know,

Harry,' the site manager had replied. 'There's no gang of international building material thieves planning to swoop down on the site in the dead of night, and make off with a couple of thousand Accrington bricks.'

'I know that, but . . .'

'The Secret Cement Cartel isn't just waiting for our guard to be down before they have it away with a dozen bags of Portland Finest.'

The site manager was too much of a smart-alec for his own good, the night-watchman thought. He was little more than a lad, still wet behind the ears – but because he had his City and Guilds Certificate, he thought he knew everything there was to know.

'What about the machinery?' Turner had grumbled. 'It's very valuable, is that machinery, Mr Wickshaw.'

'So it is,' the site manager had agreed. 'But it's also virtually impossible to nick.'

'I'm not so sure about that.'

'You're not? So tell me, how's anybody going to steal a crane or a digger? Drive it away?'

'They could.'

'Talk sense, Harry! Heavy plant's not exactly built with a speedy getaway in mind, you know. A bobby on a push-bike could catch up with it, if he pedalled hard enough.'

'So if there's no risk of anythin' valuable bein' stolen, what am I goin' to be doin' here, night after night?' the watchman had wondered.

'I'll tell what you're doing here, Harry,' the site manager had said, his patience almost at an end. 'You're here so that some chap living just down the road – who happens to be in need of a couple of concrete flag-stones – won't be tempted to just walk in and help himself.'

'But suppose he does give way to the temptation,' the watchman argued. 'I could be in danger.'

'If we thought there was any danger, we wouldn't entrust the security of the place to an old feller like you,' the site manager had said, exasperatedly.

'Thanks for the vote of confidence,' Turner said.

And he was thinking: I may be old, but I reckon I could still drop you if I had to, you thin streak of piss an' wind.

'You're still looking worried,' the site manager had said, mistaking anger for fear. 'For God's sake, Harry, nobody's going to put you in hospital for a couple of pipes or a few yards of copper wiring, now are they?'

And so it was that Turner was dog-less and alone when he discovered the breech in the chain-link fence that surrounded the site.

It was perfectly obvious what had happened, Harry Turner thought, as he examined the breech in the light of his torch. Some bastard had taken a pair of wire cutters, sliced his way through the chain link, and then peeled back a flap so he could get access. And now he was somewhere on the site, in any one of the dozen or so places he could have chosen to hide.

There should be searchlights I could switch on, Harry Turner thought.

But there were no lights, just as there was no dog.

He was not afraid, he told himself, but it would probably wise to be a little *cautious*.

He turned away from the fence, to face the site.

'The police have been called!' he bawled out in that same loud voice that had sung a thousand dirty rugby songs. 'There's no gettin' away, an' if you give yourself up now, they'll probably go easy on you.'

He heard a single foot-fall from somewhere to his left, and was just about to turn again when his head suddenly seemed to explode. And then everything went black.

Rutter had finally arrived at the Drum and Monkey. He was looking somewhat flustered, but also a little triumphant.

'One of the nannies who I was supposed to be interviewing couldn't make it this afternoon,' he explained.

'Well, that *is* a promisin' start,' Woodend said dourly.

'It wasn't her fault,' Rutter said, completely missing the warning signal. 'Apparently, there was some kind of domestic crisis in the place where she's currently employed. And since – on paper at least – she looked the best of the bunch, I thought I'd better allow a little leeway.'

'Very good of you, I'm sure,' Woodend said. 'An' since we seem to be discussin' leeway, is there any reason you couldn't have phoned to tell us you were goin' to be late?'

'I did make a call to the station, but you'd already left, sir,' Rutter said defensively.

'This pub has a phone,' Woodend pointed out. 'We've all used it, often enough.'

'I didn't want to disturb you here, especially since I knew that within half an hour or so . . .' Rutter trailed off. 'You're quite right, sir,' he continued. 'I could have phoned, and I'm sorry I didn't.'

His problem was that Bob was feeling very guilty about the way he'd behaved towards his daughter, Woodend thought. For quite a while after Maria's death, he'd not believed he was able to take care of Louisa at all, and the grandparents had been forced to bear the burden. And now he finally felt he could handle it, he was trying to compensate for that earlier neglect by giving her his total commitment.

'Did you hire a nanny in the end?' Paniatowski asked.

'Yes, I did,' Rutter told her. 'I actually hired the one who I interviewed last – the one who made me late. I think she's going to be really excellent.'

'Well, that's all right then,' Woodend said – though his tone made it clear that was far from the case.

Later, when he was talking it through with the police, Harry Turner would calculate that he could not have been unconscious for more than five minutes. But at the time, as he was slowly coming round, his thoughts were not about that at all, but instead were focused on the loud noise coming from beyond the shell of the supermarket, at the other end of the site.

'The crane!' he gasped. 'He's stealin' the bloody crane!'

That should certainly teach the smart-arsed site manager a lesson in humility, he thought.

But his feeling of smugness didn't last for long, because he had been brought up in an age when you were taught to take your responsibilities very seriously, and it was *his* responsibility to protect the site.

Using the chain-link fence for support, he pulled himself to his feet. His head hurt – and when he gently probed the back of his skull with his index finger, he felt something sticky, which he assumed was drying blood.

But all-in-all, he told himself, he was not in bad shape.

Certainly he was steady enough on his feet, and his vision did not seem to be in the least bit blurred. In the old days, on the rugby pitch, he'd have shrugged off an injury like this one, and there was no reason he shouldn't do the same now.

The crane engine continued to roar at the other end of the site, but so far the thief had made no attempt to slam it into gear and drive away.

Harry shone his torch along the ground, searching for something he could use as a weapon. Its beam fell on a short iron bar, which should have been returned to the tool shed, but clearly had not.

He bent down and picked it up.

It would serve nicely, he decided – not too heavy, but capable of doing a good deal of damage if wielded properly. It would be a more-than-adequate tool to teach the bastard who had hit him that there was a great deal of difference between 'old age pensioner' and 'old and helpless'.

He walked around the edge of the construction shell, picking out his steps carefully, because there could be nothing more undignified than tripping over and twisting his ankle.

When he was no more than half way to the crane, he heard the engine judder for a few seconds, and then die away completely.

'Idiot!' he said softly to himself. 'Bloody incompetent idiot. What's the point in stealin' a crane if you don't even know how to operate it?'

He was expecting the thief to make another attempt to start the crane, but as he got closer, and it still remained silent, it became clear that he was going to do no such thing.

That was the trouble with young people today, he thought. No bloody resilience at all. Try something once, and if it doesn't work first time off, bloody give up.

He had reached the edge of the building, and an open space of perhaps five yards lay between him and the crane. He swept the area with his torch – because he was damned if he'd let the swine ambush him again – but there was no sign of a waiting enemy.

He took a few steps forward, and shone the torch into the cabin of the crane. It seemed to be empty.

That was it, then, was it? The thief had given up his attempt to steal the heavy machine, and had made his escape.

So, apart from the blow to his head – which had now almost completely stopped bothering him – no real damage had been done, Turner thought.

And then he looked up at the arm of the crane, and realized he couldn't have been wronger.

Beresford had gone home to look after his mum, so there were only three of them at the table in the Drum and Monkey when the landlord called across the bar that there was a phone call for Woodend.

The chief inspector climbed to his feet, and ambled over to the bar, as he had done a hundred times before.

Paniatowski waited until he was out of earshot, then said to Rutter, 'You want to be careful.'

'Careful about what?'

'Careful to show that you still have an interest in doing your job.'

'I do have an interest in my job,' Rutter said angrily. 'I *love* my job. But I also love my daughter, and if it's a question of either her or . . .'

'It isn't a question of either/or,' Paniatowski interrupted him. 'You can have both, but you've got to learn to balance things better.'

'Now that I've got a nanny for Louisa . . .'

'You talk as if that's the answer to all your problems. But it isn't, is it? So what if you've got a nanny? She can't be there all the time. And what will you do when she isn't?'

'Then *I'll* look after my daughter.'

'What if we're in the middle of an important case?'

'I don't know,' Rutter said weakly. 'I plan to cross that bridge if, and when, I come to it.'

'There's no "if" about,' Paniatowski said. 'It *will* happen.' She paused for a moment. 'Listen, I'll help out all I can. Once in a while, I'll baby-sit for you, so that you can at least give the *appearance* of being a full-time officer.'

'You'd do that?' Rutter asked surprised.

'I've just said I would, haven't I? Anyway, is there any reason why I wouldn't?'

Rutter shrugged, awkwardly. 'Well, you know . . .'

'Because she's Maria's baby?'

'Yes, I suppose that is what I meant.'

'Maria may have hated me – God knows, she had reason enough to – but I never hated her. And even if I had, what's that got to do with Louisa? She's just an innocent child.'

'You never cease to amaze me,' Rutter said softly. 'You never cease to *touch* me.'

'Yes, well, let's not get all sentimental and gooey about it,' Paniatowski said brusquely. 'Especially since the boss is coming back.'

Woodend was indeed returning to the table – and he looked grim.

'Has something happened, sir?' Rutter asked.

The chief inspector nodded. 'Aye, somethin' happened,' he said. 'There's been another one.'

Temporary police spotlights had been set up on the building site, and now the whole area around the crane was drenched in a bright, harsh light.

There were no shadows at all. Small stones, embedded in the ground – and until now practically invisible – shone like gems. The crane itself stood naked and exposed, all the dents and scratches in its bodywork, which were hardly noticeable in the daylight, on display for all to see.

But nobody was looking at the ground, and nobody was looking at the cabin of the crane. Instead, all eyes were focused on the *arm* of the crane, which was thirty feet in the air.

Woodend tore his gaze away from the hanging corpse, and looked at the uniformed inspector, who had been the first ranking officer on the scene and so had taken charge of the site.

'Do you have to leave the poor bugger hangin' there like that, Sid?' he asked. 'Can't you get him down?'

'Believe me, sir, I would if I could,' the inspector replied. 'But until the fire brigade gets here, we're helpless.'

'Am I to take it that the crane's liftin' mechanism's been nobbled, then?' Woodend said.

'That's what we think must have happened. When the night watchman, Harry Turner, first arrived, the feller on the end of the rope was still kicking. So Turner climbed up into the cabin of the crane, to see if he could work out how to lower the arm. But he couldn't even start the engine. And neither could any of my lads, however much they tried. So my guess would be that before the killer left, he found a way to jam it.'

There was the sound of a siren in the distance.

'That'll be the fire brigade now,' the uniformed inspector said. 'If you don't want me for anything else, sir, I suppose I'd better go and explain to them what it is they have to do.'

'Aye, you take yourself off,' Woodend said.

The inspector walked away, and Woodend turned to his team.

'Comments?' he said.

'The killer's learning from his mistakes,' Monika Paniatowski said. 'The way he chose to do it this time, there was absolutely no chance of him decapitating his victim.'

'No chance of a quick death for the poor bugger, either,' Rutter said grimly. 'The victim can't have survived for that long, but it must have been hell for him while he did.'

'So was it important to the killer that he suffered?' Woodend wondered. 'Or was the only thing that mattered to him that his victim should hang?'

'Terry Pugh was already dead when he was hanged,' Paniatowski reminded him. 'I'm starting to think that the killing and the hanging are two entirely separate things.'

'Meanin' that the actual killing is practical – an' any means will do – while the hangin' is more of a symbolic nature?' Woodend asked.

'Yes,' Paniatowski agreed. 'Although, in this case, he managed to find a way to combine the two.'

'What do you think, Bob?' Woodend asked.

'I think it's important to him that other people get to see his handiwork,' Rutter said thoughtfully. 'And in that way, too, he's learned from his previous mistakes. The only people who saw Terry Pugh's body were two fishermen and half a dozen bobbies. This time, the killer's ensured that his victim is not only seen by more policemen and an entire fire brigade crew, but by *them* as well.'

The 'them' he was referring to was the crowd which had gradually been building up on the other side of the chain link. There were at least a hundred people there now, most of them in such a hurry to take in the spectacle that they were still in dressing gowns and carpet slippers.

Woodend nodded in agreement. 'To kill his victim, all he

had to do was raise the crane's arm far enough for the man's feet to be a couple of feet off the ground,' he said. 'To prevent the night watchman from rescuing him, he only had to add eight or ten feet to that. But he wanted to make a real show out of it – and that's why he raised the arm so high before he sabotaged the motor.'

'What *is* his game?' Paniatowski asked.

'I'm buggered if I know,' Woodend told her. 'But I'd like to see Mr Marlowe explain *this* away as a suicide tomorrow mornin'.'

Eleven

That two hangings were of a great deal more interest to the press than a single one was clearly demonstrated by the fact that the next morning's press conference was so popular they could have sold tickets to it.

'Just look at them!' said the Chief Constable, looking through the glass porthole of the door leading into the room where the hacks had been assembled. 'They're like bloody vultures, squatting there. They can't wait for me to trip up so they can start tearing into my flesh.'

And whose fault was that, Woodend wondered, though he said nothing.

'I blame *you* for this,' the Chief Constable said, answering his chief inspector's unspoken question. 'And that bloody sergeant of yours, too – she must take part of the blame. I knew my predecessor was making a mistake when he promoted her.'

'Monika Paniatowski's a good bobby, sir,' Woodend said. 'A *very* good bobby.'

There was a dangerous edge to his voice which would have made most men proceed with caution, but Marlowe seemed not to notice it.

'Paniatowski's place isn't out in the field,' the Chief Constable said. 'It's in the kitchen – waiting for her man to come home, so she can cook him whatever he tells her to.'

'I think you're overlookin' all the excellent work she's done, sir,' Woodend said, and the edge to his voice was getting sharper.

'And if it's not in the kitchen, it's in the bedroom,' Marlowe ploughed on regardless. 'In the bedroom, I repeat – lying flat on her back, and with her legs spread wide open. That's where she belongs. That's where *all* women belong.'

There were a couple of ways to deal with a comment like

that, Woodend thought – and one of them was a two-part solution involving his fist and the Chief Constable's mouth.

'It seems there was this sex expert, givin' a lecture, an' the first thing he told his audience was that there were only seventy-six positions in which to make love,' he said, opting for the second course of action.

'What in God's name are you talking about now, Chief Inspector?' Marlowe demanded.

'Anyway, he hears a voice from the back of the hall call out, "Seventy-seven positions"!' Woodend continued, ignoring the interruption. 'Well, naturally, the expert's pissed off at bein' contradicted. "I have studied the subject for over twenty years," he says, "an' I can assure you there are *seventy-six* positions." "Seventy-seven positions!" the feller at the back of the hall insists. The lecturer decides it might be best just to pay him no more attention. "In the first position, the woman lies on her back," he says. "*Seventy-eight!*" the heckler shouts.'

'Have you gone mad?' Marlowe wondered.

'No, sir. I was merely pointin' out that there are other ways for a woman to have sex than lyin' flat on her back with her legs spread.'

'And what has that got to do with *anything*?'

'Well, if you must insist on confinin' all women – which must include Mrs Marlowe – to either the kitchen or the bedroom, you could at least try to ensure that the time your wife spends in the bedroom is just a *little bit* interestin' for her.'

'I'll break you, Woodend,' Marlowe said, in a low hiss that would not have disgraced the mouth of a poisonous snake. 'I swear to God that one day soon, I'll break you!'

The Chief Inspector smiled. 'Maybe so, sir – but not before the press conference,' he said.

Marlowe and Woodend sat side by side, facing the press. Marlowe had been quite correct when he'd said that the hacks couldn't wait to start tearing into his flesh, Woodend thought, but they seemed to him to be much more like ravening hyenas than vultures.

'Rather than make a formal statement, I think I'll simply take questions today,' the Chief Constable said. He looked around the room. 'Let me see, I think we'll start with you, Miss Forbes.'

Woodend grinned inwardly. This was not the random choice that Marlowe was trying his damnedest to make it appear. Annie Forbes was a spinsterish-looking woman, with greying hair pulled back in a tight bun. She normally wrote cosy pieces for readers much like herself, and was probably only there that day because the usual reporter couldn't make it.

'Well, Miss Forbes?' Marlowe said.

Annie Forbes gazed back at him over the top of her glasses, in much the same way as a wised-up school-ma'am might have looked at a particularly recalcitrant male pupil.

'Will we be allowed to ask as many questions as we may wish to, Chief Constable?' she asked.

'Within reason, yes. If you have a second question, to follow on from your first, I will certainly endeavour to answer that too.'

This response did not seem to quite satisfy Miss Forbes.

'I think I may have expressed myself badly,' she said, smiling apologetically. 'What I really meant to ask was if every reporter in the room who wants to ask a question will be allowed to ask it.'

Marlowe reddened slight. 'In an ideal world, I'd certainly be willing to stay here for as long as you all wished me to,' he said. 'But, as I'm sure you understand, I am heavily involved in an important police investigation.'

Annie Forbes smiled again, though this time the smile seemed more malicious than regretful. 'So the answer to my question is, "No, they will not," is it?' she asked sweetly.

'Yes, I'm rather afraid it is,' Marlowe conceded.

'In that case, I'd like to give the time that you've allotted to me to my colleague, Mr Williams.'

Woodend almost chuckled aloud. Arthur Williams, he knew from past experience, was to polite, deferential journalism what Jack the Ripper had been to flower arranging.

Williams stood up quickly, before Marlowe had the opportunity to come up with a reason why he shouldn't.

'You assured us yesterday that Terry Pugh's death was a suicide, Chief Constable,' he began. 'Do you still stand by that?'

Marlowe forced himself to smile benignly. 'No, I don't,' he said. 'In fact, there's nothing to stand by. At the time I

made the statement, I already knew it was not a suicide we
were investigating.'

'Then why did you . . . ?'

'I apologize for deceiving you, but I can assure you that I
did it from the best of all possible motives. I hoped that by
lulling the killer into a false sense of security, we would be
able to apprehend him before he killed again. Unfortunately,'
he turned to look briefly at Woodend, 'the officers I have
working under me have not been quite as effective as I would
have wished them to be.'

'So the two murders are *related*?' Williams asked. 'They
were both carried out by the same man?'

'Yes, that is the conclusion we have reached.' Marlowe
turned to Woodend again. 'Isn't that true, Chief Inspector?'

'They would . . . er . . . certainly appear to be connected,'
Woodend said uneasily.

'So there is also a connection between the two victims, is
there?' Williams asked him.

'Since we don't yet know who the second . . .' Woodend
began.

'We are keeping the second victim's identity a secret for
the moment,' the Chief Constable interrupted him, 'and though
we *do* have a definite connection between the two deaths, I
am still not at liberty, for operational reasons, to reveal exactly
what it is.'

'What the hell were you pullin' in there, you bloody idiot?'
Woodend demanded, once he and Marlowe were safely away
from the press, and back in the Chief Constable's office.

'Do I need to remind you who it is that you're talking to,
Chief Inspector?' Marlowe asked angrily.

Woodend looked down at the floor. 'No, sir.'

'Then please let me hear you ask your question again –
and with a little more respect this time.'

Woodend took a deep breath, and looked up. 'What the hell
were you pullin' in there, you bloody idiot, *sir*?' he said.

Marlowe had turned as red as a beetroot.

'I was doing all that was in my power to maintain the repu-
tation and credibility of this police force!' he bellowed. 'I was
attempting to create the impression that the force in general
– and *you* in particular – had a firm grip on the situation.'

'By tellin' *lies*?'

'Was I telling *lies*? Is that what they were? So tell me, Chief Inspector, isn't it highly likely that the two victims were connected in some way?'

'Yes,' Woodend admitted, grudgingly.

By Woodend's standards, the Chief Constable recognized, this was almost a climb-down, and it did something to restore his good humour.

'There you are, then,' he said. 'That's all I told the reporters.'

'But there are other possibilities as well – possibilities you didn't even bother to raise,' Woodend pointed out.

'We are not interested in any other possibilities, Chief Inspector,' Marlowe told him firmly.

'But we have to be,' Woodend protested. 'We can't just . . .'

Marlowe raised his hand to silence him, and this time the Chief Inspector obeyed his instruction.

'Find a link between the two victims, Chief Inspector,' Marlowe said in a voice that had sunk to a deadly whisper. 'Find it for both our sakes, but most especially for yours – because I can't keep on covering up your incompetence for ever, you know.'

In Woodend's office, the usual fug of smoke hung in the air like the poisonous cloud it actually was, but the chief inspector noticed immediately that there were only two people contributing to it.

'Where's Inspector Rutter?' he asked.

Paniatowski looked up. 'He's stepped outside for a few minutes, sir,' she said.

'A few minutes, eh? An' do we have any idea just how long that *few minutes* is likely . . . ?'

'We've managed to identify the second victim, sir,' Monika Paniatowski interrupted.

'That was quick work,' Woodend said approvingly. 'Not that you'll get much credit for it from upstairs, since Mr Marlowe's told the press we *already* knew who he was.' He straddled the chair opposite his sergeant. 'How did you get on to him so fast? Did he have some sort of identification on him that we managed to overlook last night?'

'Not exactly,' Paniatowski replied. 'There was no driving licence, or anything like that – but there was a pawn ticket, and I sent DC Beresford to the pawnbrokers' as soon as it opened.'

'The feller behind the counter was very co-operative,' Beresford said. 'He knew immediately who the ticket belonged to, because the man was a regular customer by the name of Reg Lewis.'

'So we've got a name,' Woodend said. 'Do we have any background on this Lewis?'

'It's only been an hour since we got his name,' Paniatowski said. 'You can't expect miracles, sir.'

'But I *do* expect miracles,' Woodend told her with a smile. 'And fortunately, you usually provide them.'

Paniatowski smiled back. 'We do have a little information on him,' she admitted. 'He was twenty-nine years old . . .'

'Which is roughly the same age as Terry Pugh was, isn't it?'

'That's right, sir. And we also know that he lived in a bedsit on Balaclava Street.'

'Or Rat Alley, as it's popularly known,' Woodend said. 'A very salubrious address.'

'Lewis was born in Whitebridge,' Paniatowski continued, consulting her notes, 'but he doesn't have any family living here any more. His mother and father are dead, and his only brother moved away years ago.'

'So what's kept *him* here?'

Paniatowski shrugged. 'Why would he move? Whitebridge is as good a place to draw his unemployment benefit as anywhere else.'

'I suppose I should have guessed he'd be on the dole the moment you told me where he lived,' Woodend said. 'What else have you got for me?'

'The longest he's ever held down a job, as far as I've been able to discover so far, is a couple of months. He also has a prison record.'

'He wasn't banged up for bein' a bookie's runner, was he?' Woodend asked, hoping to establish a connection between the two dead men.

Paniatowski shook her head. 'No. He did six months for receiving stolen property, and two years for burglary. He hasn't been in any trouble recently, but I suspect that's more of case of not getting caught than it is of keeping his nose clean.'

'You'd really make my day if you could tell me that Terry Pugh had been in the same prison at the same time, an' that they'd both shared a cell with a foreign-lookin' man,' Woodend told her.

'I imagine I would,' Paniatowski agreed. 'But unfortunately, it wouldn't be true. Terry Pugh was only arrested once – eight or nine years ago – for being drunk and disorderly. But he got away with paying a fine. And there was no one in prison with Lewis who matches the description of the man Terry Pugh was seen leaving the Tanners' Arms with.'

'Then maybe they both attended Sudbury Street Primary School,' Woodend suggested hopefully.

'I'm afraid that I'm going to have to piss on your chips yet again, sir,' Paniatowski told him regretfully. 'When he was a kid, Reg Lewis lived right on the other side of town from Terry Pugh. In Millbank, as a matter of fact.'

'So he went to Millbank Primary.'

'That's right.'

Woodend lit up a cigarette, because if he was going to breathe in smoke, it might as well be his own.

'Mr Marlowe wants us to find a link between Pugh and Lewis,' he said. 'An' I do, too. Not because I give a damn about pullin' him out of the shit – he talked his own way into that, an' he can find his own way out – but because I think there simply has to *be* one.'

'Unless the killer just has something against men in their late twenties,' Beresford said unhelpfully.

'If he does – if that's his only motivation – then we're *really* up the creek without a paddle,' Woodend told him.

The phone rang, and Woodend answered it.

'There's a man on the line who wouldn't give me his name when I asked for it, but says he has some very important information on the murders, sir,' the switchboard operator said. 'Shall I put him through?'

'I don't know, Daphne,' Woodend said. 'What's your opinion of him? Do you think he's on the up-an'-up, or is he one of the nutters who always rings when a case makes the papers?'

'I don't recognize his voice,' the operator replied cautiously. 'And he doesn't sound like one of our usual nutters. Which is not to say he isn't upset. In fact, I think he sounds rather desperate.'

'Put him through,' Woodend said.

There was a click on the line, then he heard a worried voice say, 'Chief Inspector Woodend?'

'That's me,' Woodend agreed. 'What can I do for you, Mr . . .'

'You . . . you haven't released the name of the second victim, yet,' his caller said, refusing the invitation to supply his name.

He was a local man, Woodend guessed. Not posh, but not exactly rough, either. He sounded as if he were in very early middle age, but it could just be that he was trying to disguise his voice.

'I said, you haven't released the name of the second victim,' the caller repeated insistently.

'I know that.'

'I . . . I was wondering if you might tell *me* who it was.'

'An' why should I do that?'

'Because I *need to know.*'

Woodend sighed. 'Listen, the only reason I took this call at all was because I was told you had some important information to give me – and so far you've told me absolutely nothin' at all.'

'Please give me the name!' the other man begged.

'Do you have some sort of connection to these murders?' Woodend asked. 'Or are you just one of those sick bastards who get a twisted pleasure out of this kind of thing?' he continued, his voice hardening.

'Was it . . . was it Reg Lewis, by any chance?' the caller asked, almost hysterical now.

'Before we can go any further, I'm goin' to need your name an' address,' Woodend told him firmly.

'It was Reg, wasn't it? I can tell it was from the way your voice changed once I'd said the name!'

'You can read into my voice whatever you want to, sir,' Woodend said, 'but I'm afraid I'm in no position to either confirm or deny your suspicions. An' it's my duty to warn you that if you're holdin' back any information which might be pertinent to this inquiry . . .'

But he was talking to a dead line.

Twelve

If she had been asked, two weeks earlier, how she would describe her life, Rosemary Bygraves would have said, with absolutely no hesitation, that it was perfect.

Not *all right*.

Not *quite good*.

But *perfect*.

There would have been reason enough for this assertion. She had a nice home – a substantial semi in a good street – which she always kept in the most immaculate condition. She had two wonderful children, who never earned less than the highest praise from their teachers. She was a force for good in the community, regularly contributing to charity drives and being one of the stalwarts of the Brighter Neighbourhood Committee which she had helped to found.

She could have been complacent about all this – but she wasn't. For though she knew that she had worked hard to achieve the life she wanted, she *also* knew that the foundation stone on which it was all built was her husband, Tom.

Tom would not have been every woman's choice. He was not particularly handsome or witty. In his work, he was steady, rather than innovative and inventive – but that had served him well in Brown Brothers' Furnishings, a conservative company in which steadiness was one of the cardinal virtues, and where he had already risen to the position of assistant manager in the soft furnishings department. In the bedroom, Rosemary suspected that he was not a great lover – and since she had been a virgin when he married her, all she *could* do was suspect. He seemed clumsy and awkward during their love-making, and sometimes, as he entered her, he would tense up – as though he found the very act distasteful. But his lack of flair, both in life in general and between the sheets in particular, did not really bother Rosemary, because he was a good man – a kind, gentle and thoughtful man – and she knew that he loved her and the children with all his heart.

But that was all two weeks ago. In the fortnight *since* then, Tom had begun to change. It had been little things at first – an uncharacteristic flare-up of temper, a refusal to look her in the eye – but it was getting worse all the time. When he had arrived home from the shop the previous day – arrived home *early*! – she could almost have sworn he had been crying. And that morning he had refused to get out of bed, even though he knew as well as she did that punctuality was regarded as one of Brown Brothers' most important measures of their employees' performance.

Things had gone from bad to worse as the morning wore on. When he *had* finally got up, and found her polishing the cocktail cabinet in the lounge, he'd announced that she would have to leave the room because he needed to make a private phone call.

'A *private* phone call?' she'd repeated incredulously.

'That's what I said.'

But there was no such thing as a *private* phone call in the Bygraves family. In the family, there wasn't really a private *anything*.

'Who is it you're going to call?' she'd demanded.

'That's none of your business,' he snapped back.

And then he'd practically *bundled* her into the kitchen, and told her to stay there until the call had been made.

And so, there she was now – polishing a fridge-freezer which had been gleaming clean before she'd even touched it. There she was now – unable to hear the precise words her husband was speaking, yet still catching the note of desperation in his tone.

She heard the sound of the receiver being slammed down on its cradle, and waited for her husband to come into the kitchen and apologize for his behaviour – or at least try to *explain* it.

It didn't happen that way. Instead of seeking to placate her, Tom went straight upstairs.

She followed him, and found him in the bedroom, throwing his clothes distractedly into an open suitcase on the bed.

'What's happening?' she asked, on the verge of tears.

'I have to go away,' he snapped back, giving no sign that he had even noticed her distress.

'Away?' she repeated dully. 'Where to?'

Tom continued to hurl clothes into the open case. 'I can't tell you. It's best you don't know.'

'But . . . but how long will you be away?'

'I don't know that, either.'

Tears were streaming down her face now. Surely he would soon stop what he was doing, and make some attempt to console her.

'You have responsibilities,' she sobbed. 'To me. To the children. To your work.'

He suddenly looked so angry that she was afraid that – for the first time in their entire marriage – he was about to hit her.

'For God's sake, woman, I'm fighting for my life here,' he said, as she shrank back.

'I . . . I don't understand.'

'Of course you don't understand! How the bloody hell could you *possibly* understand?'

He closed the suitcase, and barged past her onto the landing. She followed him downstairs and into the street.

It was a lovely day. The sun was shining and there was a gentle breeze in the air. Normally she could have relied on Tom to seize on the weather as a worthy subject for conversation, but she doubted if – at that moment – he'd have noticed if there'd been a blizzard going on around them.

She watched with horror as he opened the boot of the car and put the suitcase inside it.

'You . . . you can't really be going,' she said, though she now finally accepted that he was. 'You just can't.'

'The rubbish!' Tom said, exasperatedly.

'The what? I don't know what you're talking about.'

Tom turned and headed back towards their home. But he didn't enter the house itself. Instead, he went down the passageway between the side of the house and the fence, which led to the back garden.

'Tom!' Rosemary said, still hot on his heels.

But he ignored her.

The garden was looking nice – as it should have done, after all the work they'd both put into it – but Tom had no interest in admiring the flowers or the small immaculate lawn. Instead, he strode straight to the end of the garden, where the potting shed was.

He came to an abrupt halt next to the rubbish heap – a collection of grass cuttings and other garden waste which they were planning to turn into a compost heap – and squatted down beside it.

'What are you doing?' Rosemary asked. '*Please* tell me what you're doing, Tom.'

He reached into his pocket, and pulled out his lighter.

'We can't have a fire until it's time to burn the autumn leaves,' she said. 'We passed a resolution about it at the Brighter Neighbourhood Committee Annual General Meeting.'

He continued to ignore her, and held the lighter next to the grass cuttings, until they caught alight.

'It was *my* resolution. I was the one who put it forward,' Rosemary said, but even as she spoke the words, she was wondering what the hell she was saying – why she should be bothered about the Brighter Neighbour Committee and its bloody resolutions, when her life was being turned upside down.

Tom rose to his feet again, and walked quickly up the garden path to the front of the house. When he reached the car, he opened the door and climbed inside.

'What . . . what have I to tell them at the shop?' Rosemary asked, for it was plain to her now that her husband had no intention of ringing Brown Brothers' himself.

'Tell them anything you like,' Tom said dismissively. 'I don't care one way or the other.'

'And the children? What shall I tell them?'

Finally she seemed to be getting through to him, she thought. He paused, in the middle of inserting his ignition key, and looked directly at her for the first time since she'd gone upstairs.

'Tell them I'll miss them,' he said.

And she could see that he was crying, too.

He started up the car, and pulled away.

As he turned the corner, Rosemary noticed that a black van, which had been parked up the road, had begun to move in the same direction. Though she knew most of her neighbours' vehicles, she did not think she had seen this one before.

In Whitebridge Police Headquarters, the Chief Constable was mounting the podium for the second time that morning.

'Since you all seemed so eager to learn the name of the second victim earlier, I have decided to release it,' he said to the gathered journalists. 'His name was Reginald Lewis. He was an unemployed man of twenty-nine, and he lived in a bed-sitting room at an address in Balaclava Street. That is all I have for you for the moment, so if you'll excuse me . . .'

'Not two hours ago, you refused to reveal his name for what you said were operational reasons,' Arthur Williams called out.

Marlowe considered ignoring the comment, then realized that if he did so, he would only be giving Williams more ammunition for his column.

'For once, you seem to be quoting me correctly, Arthur,' he said, smiling to show that he was only joking.

Williams did not smile back.

'So what's changed in a couple of hours?' he asked.

'I'm afraid I'm not prepared to go into that.'

'Operational reasons again?'

'Just so.'

Now Williams *did* smile.

'Or could it be that you didn't *know* his name then, but now that you do you want to release it before we find it out ourselves, and make you look a complete prat?' he wondered.

Yes, that was exactly it, Marlowe thought, wishing that the bastard wasn't quite so sharp.

'It has always been my policy to keep the local press abreast of developments as far as possible, Mr Williams,' he said coldly. 'That is, of course, as long as the press in general – and specific reporters in particular – behave in a responsible manner.'

'Is that a threat, Mr Marlowe?' Williams asked, suddenly looking a little concerned.

Marlowe grinned at him. 'Of course not, Arthur. It's no more than a policy statement.'

'Why isn't Chief Inspector Woodend here with you?' one of the other reporters asked.

Now *that* was the kind of question he liked, Marlowe told himself – the kind of question he could turn to his own advantage.

'Based on information received, I have suggested some

possible lines of inquiry in the case,' he said, 'and Mr Woodend, who always looks to me for guidance, is out pursuing them.'

'I wouldn't keep a dog in a place like this,' Woodend said, looking around Reg Lewis' bedsit in Balaclava Street.

He had a point, Paniatowski thought.

The fixtures and furnishings of the room consisted of no more than a narrow single bed, a table, a chair, a chest of drawers, a sink and an old kitchen unit. The sheets on the bed were torn and grey with filth; the table was scarred with cigarette burns, and there was something nasty growing out of the plughole in the sink. There was a window over the sink, but it was so encrusted with grime that even when the sun was on it – as it was now – very little light was allowed to enter the dreary space in which Lewis could have done no more than just exist.

'I'll bet there's some germ-warfare scientists somewhere who'd pay a fortune to be left alone in here for an hour or so,' Woodend commented. 'That said, I'm afraid we're still goin' to have to search it.'

Not that there was much to search. The chest of drawers was virtually empty, and most of Lewis' discarded clothes had been flung carelessly onto the filthy floor, where they competed for space with empty whisky bottles and crumpled cigarette packets.

'Aside from the fact that they were around the same age, and lived in the same town, the two victims seemed to have had absolutely nothing in common,' Monika Paniatowski said, as she gingerly poked at a rotting grey sock with the toe of her shoe.

'You're right about that,' Woodend agreed. 'Terry Pugh was a reliable man with a steady job – the kind of man that most fathers hope an' pray their daughters will end up marryin' – while Reg Lewis was the sort of feller who gives even toe-rags a bad name.'

'So what is the link?' Paniatowski asked.

'I'm buggered if I know,' Woodend admitted.

Paniatowski's radio crackled, and then a metallic – and virtually inaudible – voice began to speak.

'I'll just slip outside, sir, where there's probably better reception,' the sergeant said.

'Good idea,' Woodend agreed.

Left alone, he looked around the thoroughly depressing room again. He supposed he'd better continue the search, he told himself, though it was almost certain to lead nowhere.

He opened the drawer next to the sink. It contained several mis-matched knives and forks, which had clearly not been used for some considerable time, and a bottle opener which undoubtedly had. But then he saw what was at the back of the drawer, and felt his pulse start to quicken.

Paniatowski re-entered the room.

'Message from the station, sir,' she said. 'Mark Hough called. He said he'd heard the name of the second victim on the local radio news . . .'

'Bloody Marlowe!' Woodend said in disgust. 'I asked him to keep quiet, but he just couldn't wait to get his name back in the papers, could he?' He paused. 'Sorry, what was that you were sayin', Monika?'

'Mr Hough said that the second he'd heard Reg Lewis' name, he realized he had something very important to tell you. He also said that he's willing to come down to head-quarters to talk to you at any time it's convenient for you.'

'When you've got a killer on the loose an' somebody thinks they have important information that might help catch him, you don't make appointments at "convenient times",' Woodend said. 'That's altogether far too cosy.'

'Meaning that we'll go and see him – and we'll do it right away?' Paniatowski asked.

'Exactly,' Woodend agreed. 'Mind you,' he cautioned, 'I wouldn't go gettin' yourself too het up thinkin' about what it might be he wants to tell us, because I've got a sneakin' suspicion that I already know.'

'Since when?' Paniatowski asked sceptically.

'Since I found this,' Woodend told her, holding out a Royal Lancashire Fusiliers cap badge for her inspection.

Tom Bygraves had not chosen to take the dual carriageway to Accrington because he wished to go in that particular direction – he had simply selected it as the quickest way to leave Whitebridge behind him. But now, once the dual carriageway had come to an end, and he was back in the much slower two-way traffic, he was starting to realize that he couldn't continue running blind forever, and that what he needed to come up with was a plan.

But what kind of plan could a man like him possibly produce, he found himself asking.

Apart from the time he was away in the army, he had lived in Whitebridge and district for his whole life, which meant, in effect, that the area beyond the Mid Lancs cotton towns was almost like a foreign country to him.

He had no friends outside Lancashire who could offer him the refuge that he needed, so if he wanted to have a roof over his head, he would have to pay for it. But he had no money, either, apart from the normal walking-around money which he always kept in his wallet.

He'd read in American true crime magazines about men who'd lived as fugitives for years, but he hadn't a clue how to go about becoming one of them himself. He was an assistant manager in the soft furnishings department of a furniture store, a man who knew how to obey instructions from his superiors and do his job reasonably well. But that was about it. That was about all it had *ever* been, even when he was in the army. And the simple truth was that he had neither the courage nor the wit for a life constantly on the run.

He was already approaching Clitheroe, and soon he would see a sign which would tell him that he was entering Yorkshire.

But he didn't *want* to go to Yorkshire!

He *wanted* to go *home*!

But if he did go home, what then?

He could carry on with his normal routine of work and leisure, as if nothing had happened. But something *had* happened, and how was it possible to act normally when you knew that sooner or later you would end up swinging from the end of a rope?

He could do as the letter had suggested – had *ordered* – and go to the police, but then the life that he had known would be just as much over as if he were already dead.

He saw a roadside pub looming up ahead. He knew – with absolute conviction – that it would be a big mistake to stop there, but with equal conviction he knew that that was exactly what he was going *to* do. He signalled, checked his rear-view mirror, then pulled onto the pub car park.

He did not open his wallet until he was walking across the

tarmac to the pub's main entrance, but when he did, he saw that all it contained was two pound notes and a ten shilling note.

Two pounds ten! He wouldn't get far on that! A few pints with whisky chasers and almost half of it would be gone.

His brain told him to conserve what few resources he had, but his legs were already taking him into the pub.

He did not look back, but if he had, he would have seen the black van pulling into the parking space next to his car.

Thirteen

Hough Engineering, like all the other old mills which surrounded it, had a grim, forbidding red-brick exterior, and, but for the fact that thick black smoke no longer belched out of its tall chimney, it would have been possible to believe – from a distance – that there had been no change in its *raison d'être* since it had first opened its doors over a century earlier.

Closer to, there was clear evidence that it had, in fact, moved with the times. The main entrance had a frontage which was both modern and aggressive, and seemed to exemplify an embracing of 'the white heat of technology', which the Prime Minister was currently setting so much store by.

Once through the doors, Woodend and Paniatowski found themselves in a high-ceilinged foyer which seemed to be constructed entirely out of smoked glass and chrome – and made the chief inspector grimace.

There was a reception desk at the end of the foyer, but before they could reach it, their path was blocked by a young woman with honey-blonde hair, deep blue eyes and white regular teeth.

She was not beautiful in any classic sense of the word, Woodend thought, but she was rather pretty. He put her age at around twenty-four, and guessed that she was unmarried.

The young woman smiled and said, 'Are you the detectives? Because, if you are, I'm Priscilla Charlton, Mr Hough's secretary.'

Woodend smiled back. 'An' if we're *not* the detectives, who are you then?' he asked.

Good God, he was almost *flirting*, he told himself – and with a woman not much older than his own daughter.

'Sorry about that,' he said, before Priscilla Charlton had had time to answer. 'Yes, we're the detectives – DCI Woodend and Sergeant Paniatowski.'

'Pleased to meet you,' Priscilla Charlton said, offering them both her hand. And as she led them across to the lift, she added, 'Mr Hough's cancelled all his other appointments. He's just *bursting* to see you.'

'Is he now?' Woodend asked. 'Bursting, you say?'

'Bursting,' Priscilla Charlton repeated. 'He'd never admit it – even to me – but I think he's really rather intrigued by the idea of helping the police in a *murder* inquiry.'

They took the lift up to the first floor. When the doors slid open, they found they were looking at a small outer office, at the end of which there was an imposing teak door.

'The inner sanctum,' Priscilla Charlton said, and giggled.

She knocked on the teak door, but did not wait for her boss to say anything before opening it, stepping inside, and gesturing to Woodend and Paniatowski that they should follow her.

Woodend took a quick but all-encompassing look around him. The office was furnished in minimalist good taste, the only furniture being a large mahogany desk in the centre of the room, and the two chairs in front of it.

The walls were painted in a soft pastel shade. A number of framed posters hung from them, all of which advertised exhibitions and cultural events, and were linked by the fact that the words 'Sponsored by Hough Engineering' appeared on all of them. The chief inspector noted that one of the events Hough had sponsored was the Dunethorpe Festival, and hoped that Monika hadn't noticed it too – because Dunethorpe would remind her of her post-Rutter affair with Chief Inspector Baxter of Dunethorpe CID, and though he himself didn't know what had gone wrong between the two of them, he suspected it had been painful.

At the far end of the room, close to the window, were two thin metal pillars, about four and half feet high, which had been fixed to the floor. They were roughly three feet apart, and were joined by a steel rod. Woodend wasn't quite sure what they for – but thought he could make a pretty good guess.

Hough himself was sitting in his wheelchair behind the desk. He seemed genuinely pleased to see the new arrivals.

'Take a seat,' he said expansively, then turned to his secretary and said, 'Thank you, Miss Charlton, that will be all.'

Priscilla Charlton did not move. 'Don't forget that you have your water therapy session booked for three o'clock, Mr Hough,' she said.

Hough looked bemused. 'Water therapy? I have no idea what you're talking about.'

Priscilla Charlton shook her head in a gesture of disbelief. 'Of course you have.'

'Ah, you mean I'm planning to have a swim at around that time,' Hough said, as if enlightenment had finally dawned.

'You can call it what you like, but I make out the cheques, and I know that what you're paying for is water therapy,' the girl said. 'And you've missed the last two sessions, because – *you say* – you have too much work on. Well, I'm not going to allow you to get away with it today.'

Hough grinned. 'You're a hard task master,' he said.

'And *you* are a fool to yourself,' Priscilla Carlton said severely. Then she smiled, to take the edge off her words, and continued, 'Will there be anything else you'll require, sir?'

'A cup of coffee might be nice,' Hough said, almost diffidently. 'Or perhaps our guests would prefer tea?'

'Coffee's fine,' Woodend told the girl.

'For me, too,' Paniatowski added.

Hough watched his secretary intently, until she had finally left the room, then turned to Woodend and said, 'I think I may have found something to connect your two dead men for you.'

'The Royal Lancashire Fusiliers?' Woodend asked.

Hough looked slightly disappointed. 'How long have you known?'

'About half an hour.'

'The three of us – Terry Pugh, Reg Lewis and I – were all called up at the same time, and we served in the same unit,' Hough said. 'We were in Aldershot at first, for our basic training. Then, when the powers-that-be had decided they'd probably turned us into real enough soldiers to face enemy bullets, they shipped us off to Cyprus.'

'Cyprus!' Woodend exclaimed.

And he was thinking: Maybe the feller who Terry Pugh left the pub with wasn't a Turk or a Yugoslav after all. Maybe he was a Cypriot.

'It's a funny thing, you know,' Hough continued, 'I hadn't thought about Reg Lewis for years, yet the moment I heard his name on the radio, I was transported back to that little island in the Mediterranean, where people always seemed to be trying to kill us.'

'It was rough, was it?' Woodend asked.

'Oh, nothing like the show I imagine you were in,' Hough said dismissively, 'but I suppose it was rough enough. The Greek Cypriots wanted their independence from Britain, our government didn't want to give it to them, and us fellers in the poor bloody infantry were caught right in the middle.'

'Like fellers in the poor bloody infantry always are everywhere,' Woodend said with feeling.

'We never knew, when we got up in the morning, if we'd still be alive to see the sunset,' Hough mused. 'Of course, that's true of everyone, isn't it? But in addition to the hazards that normal people have to face, we had to deal with snipers who could be hiding virtually anywhere, and roadside bombs which could reduce our Land Rovers to no more than scrap metal in an instant.'

'Is that how you lost the use of your legs?' Woodend asked.

Hough laughed. 'As the result of a roadside bomb?'

'Yes.'

'No, it wasn't! I wish it had been, because at least then I'd have been crippled doing what I'd been trained to do, and might possibly have got a medal out of it. But they don't hand out medals to men who get blind drunk and fall into the path of a military lorry.'

'I'm sorry,' Woodend said. 'I shouldn't have asked.'

'Think nothing of it,' Hough assured him. 'We all have to live with our mistakes, and however much we wish we could turn the clock back and do things differently, we eventually have to accept that we can't. And it could have been worse, you know. A few more inches, and the lorry would have run straight over my bloody head!'

The door opened, and Priscilla Charlton entered, carrying a tray with three coffee cups.

'I hope this is all right for you,' she said, as she handed Woodend and Paniatowski their cups. 'I have to make it rather strong, because that's the way that Mr Hough likes it.'

'We like it strong, too,' Paniatowski assured her.

'She makes the best coffee in Whitebridge,' Hough said proudly. 'Don't you, Cilla?'

'Priscilla!' the girl said. 'It's *Priscilla* – and if I've told you that once, I must have told you a hundred times.'

Hough put his hand to his mouth in mock horror. 'I keep forgetting,' he said. 'Please forgive me.'

The secretary seemed to be considering the request. 'All right,' she said finally. 'But make sure it's the last time.'

She flounced out of the room, and when she'd gone, Hough said, 'I know I really shouldn't tease her, but it's such fun to see her pretending to be annoyed with me.'

Woodend felt slightly uncomfortable. He knew that Hough had asked to see him, rather than the other way round – and that the factory owner himself had felt no embarrassment himself over the exchange he'd just had with his secretary being witnessed by others – but even so, the chief inspector still could not help feeling as if he had barged in uninvited on an intimate moment.

He cleared his throat and said, 'How well did you know Reg Lewis, Mr Hough?'

'Much better than I'd have wished to,' Hough replied frankly. 'I never liked the man personally, but in Cyprus I learned to depend on him. We all learned to depend on each other, when we were out there. We had to. You must know how that happens yourself.'

'Aye, I do,' Woodend agreed. 'There were fellers in *my* war who I entrusted my life to on a daily basis, though I doubt I'd have wanted anythin' to do with them if I'd met them *before* the war, back in Civvy Street.' He paused to light up a cigarette. 'How did Pugh an' Lewis get on?'

'Terry had much the same relationship with Lewis as I had – and for much the same reasons.'

'How many other lads were there from Whitebridge who served in Cyprus with you?'

'I couldn't say, exactly. If I had to make a guess, I'd say that it was round about a couple of dozen, though sitting here, I can only actually put a name to eleven of them.'

'If you could give us those names . . .'

'I've done better than that. I've given them to Priscilla. She'll hand you the list on your way out.'

There was one question that Woodend had really wanted to

ask since the moment he'd walked into the room. He was tempted to ask it now, but since Hough's answer could well turn out to be of significance to the development of the case, he decided to postpone it until the very end of the interview, when the other man's guard would be down.

So, instead of asking that question, he reached into his pocket, pull out the police artist's sketch, and laid it on the desk.

'Do you know this feller?' he asked.

Hough studied the sketch carefully, for perhaps a minute.

'Is he a Cyp?'

'You tell me.'

'He reminds me a little bit of a lot of men I knew in Cyprus,' Hough said finally, 'but,' he added with regret, 'there's not a close enough resemblance to any one of them for me to be able to say, for example, "That's Costas, who ran the little bar down by the harbour".'

'To go back to a couple of the points you raised earlier,' Woodend said casually. 'You say that there were around two dozen Whitebridge lads serving on Cyprus?'

'More or less.'

'And that Lewis and Pugh weren't particular pals?'

'No, they weren't.'

'So what I *don't* see is why it should be them.'

'Why *what* should be them?'

'If the killings are connected to Cyprus, I don't see why the killer should have chosen those particular two men – out of the twenty-four he had available – for execution.'

'Maybe he didn't,' Hough said, with a laugh that could have been no more than bravado. 'Maybe he intends to kill us all.'

Woodend shook his head. 'I don't think so. He'd have to be a very stupid man indeed to believe he could get away with that.'

'Why?'

'Because only a very stupid man would fail to understand that at some point we'd detect a pattern – and that once we'd detected it, we'd be bound to catch him in the act eventually.'

'Perhaps he *is* stupid,' Hough suggested.

'Not goin' by his form so far.'

'His form?'

'There were any number of bridges he could have hung

Terry Pugh from, but he chose the one where he was least likely to be interrupted. An' when it came to selectin' a buildin' site on which to execute Reg Lewis, he picked one that was guarded by one old man who didn't even have a dog with him. So you see, he's far from stupid. In fact, he's bloody clever.'

'Maybe you're right,' Hough agreed reluctantly. 'In which case, I don't envy you your task in tracking him down at all.'

'So what we always come back to is this: that a careful, logical killer like this one must have seen some connection between his victims. An' what *is* the connection?'

Hough shrugged. 'Beats me.'

'I think it has to be tied in with somethin' they both did while they were on Cyprus,' Woodend said. 'What do you think of that as a theory?'

'It's certainly an interesting one,' Hough conceded.

The moment had finally come to put *the question*. Woodend looked Hough straight in the eyes and said, 'Can you think of somethin' they might have done together that could have engendered that kind of hatred, Mr Hough?'

'No, I can't' Hough said.

Both Woodend and Paniatowski had been going over the interview in their minds on the drive back to police headquarters, but it was not until they were crossing the car park that Woodend said, 'What do you think?'

'I think he was being reasonably honest and straightforward for most of the interview,' Paniatowski replied, 'but I also think that he was lying when he said he couldn't think of anything Pugh and Lewis might have done which could have caused their deaths.'

Woodend nodded. 'Good, then we're in agreement.'

'What I don't see is *why* he would lie,' Paniatowski said.

'There could be a hundred reasons,' Woodend told her. 'Maybe he's so ashamed of not having said somethin' earlier that he simply can't bring himself to say it now. Maybe he doesn't want the truth to come out, because he thinks that now the two of them are dead, all it will do is cause unnecessary sufferin' to Terry Pugh's widow. Maybe he's worried that people will think he was involved in whatever it was that went on. Maybe he *was* involved, if only on the periphery.

We're never goin' to know for sure, until we find out exactly what it was that Pugh an' Lewis did.'

'And how do you propose that we do that?' Paniatowski wondered.

'For a start, there's the lads on Hough's list to interview. After them, there's the other lads from Whitebridge, whose names Hough can't remember, but who will still be listed by the War Office. An' if we've still come up with nothin', I suppose we could always widen our search.'

'Widen it how?'

Woodend stopped to light a cigarette. He didn't want to talk about how he planned to widen the search yet – partly because he hadn't yet thought through all the implications, and partly because if he did decide to go ahead, he still hadn't worked out how the bloody hell he *could* do it.

'Widen it how?' Paniatowski repeated, sounding intrigued.

'I think we're gettin' ahead of ourselves,' Woodend said. 'Before we go on to pastures new, we should make sure we've sifted through all the cow pats in the field we're about to leave behind.'

'That's almost poetry,' Paniatowski said.

Woodend grinned. 'Thank you.'

'Almost – but somehow not quite. It's the ball that bounces off the crossbar, instead of going straight into the net; the arrow that gets caught in a crosswind and just fails to miss the target; the . . .'

'I think I get the picture,' Woodend interrupted, still grinning.

'So what particular cow pat would you like to talk about?' Paniatowski asked.

'The interview with Mark Hough. Is there anythin' else you'd like to say about it?'

Paniatowski opened her handbag and took out her own cigarettes. 'Not really,' she admitted. 'Except to say that I came away from it feeling very sorry for Mr Hough.'

'Because he's in a wheelchair?'

'No. He seems to have come to terms with that.'

'Then why?'

'Because of his secretary.'

'Because of his secretary? What's she got to do with it? I think she's a very nice lass.'

Paniatowski grinned. 'You made that more than apparent,'

she said, then, deepening her voice so it sounded a little like Woodend's, she added, '"An' if we're *not* the detectives, who are you then?"'

Woodend looked suddenly sheepish. 'Did I really say that?' he asked.

'You know you did.'

'Aye, well, there's no fool like an old fool,' Woodend conceded. 'But you have to admit, the girl's got *something*.'

'Oh, I will admit,' Paniatowski said. 'And it's probably because of the something that Hough's so deeply in love with her.'

'Deeply in love with her?'

'Don't tell me that you didn't notice any of the banter that passed between them.'

'I *did* notice it – an' to tell you the truth, it made me feel slightly uncomfortable – but I thought that was no more than affection.'

Paniatowski shook her head in wonderment, 'Most of the time, I'm almost in awe of the way that you can read people, Charlie, but there a few occasions – and this is one of them – when you can be really thick.'

'So he's in love with her,' Woodend said, accepting his sergeant's assessment. 'How does *she* feel about *him*?'

'That's harder to say. She's certainly very fond of him. But as for actually *loving* him, I certainly *hope* she doesn't.'

'Why's that?'

Paniatowski sucked greedily on her cigarette, as if she were drawing in new – and necessary – energy from it.

'Because if she loves him, that will only make matters worse all round,' she said.

'Will it?'

'Yes. You don't know what it's like to love somebody – and believe that they love you – but at the same time have to accept that you can never have the kind of relationship that any couple in love are entitled to expect.'

'No, you're quite right, I don't,' Woodend said.

But you do, don't you? he added silently, as they started walking towards the back entrance of police headquarters.

Fourteen

The lifts to the upper floors of police headquarters were halfway between the duty desk and the back door, and so it was perfectly possible to go from car park to office without once crossing the path of either a member of the public or a junior officer. The Chief Constable, Woodend was sure, found this arrangement totally admirable, but it did not suit him. His own habit, before taking the lift, was to walk the extra few yards to the duty desk, and have a quick word with whichever of the half a dozen veteran sergeants was manning it. That late afternoon, however, he decided to abandon his usual practice for once, because the sergeant on duty seemed to have his hands more than full.

What was occupying all the sergeant's attention was a woman. At first glance, she looked to be in her late twenties. She was smartly – though not expensively – dressed, and she appeared to be in what, in Lancashire, was known as 'a right old state.'

'You have to do *something*!' she was screaming at the duty sergeant.

The sergeant, a man who had seen pretty much everything during his long service on the force – and as a consequence was rarely surprised, and almost *never* disconcerted – shook his head regretfully.

'There's nothing I *can* do, madam,' he said. 'Your husband's only been missing for a few hours, and, by your own admission, he left your home of his own free will.'

'But it's not like him,' the woman bawled. 'He has two little children, who he adores. It's . . . it's just not like him at all.'

That's what most deserted women said after they discovered their husbands had done a bunk, Woodend thought as he walked over to the lift. Even when all the signs had been there for months – and sometimes even for years - they never actually saw them until the fellers had gone.

'If you'll just fill in this form, we'll act on it as soon as an appropriate time has elapsed,' the desk sergeant said soothingly.

Woodend pressed the button, and heard the sound of the lift coming to life overhead.

'You don't understand!' he heard the woman say. 'This can't wait. Something terrible may *already* have happened.'

'Don't be so pessimistic, Mrs Bygraves,' the desk sergeant said, shifting smoothly from a measured approached to one which attempted to jolly the woman along. 'For all you know, your Tom may be waiting for you at home even now.'

The lift doors slid open, but instead of stepping inside, Woodend reached into his inside pocket and pulled out the list of names that Priscilla Charlton had given him as he left Hough Engineering.

The one that he was looking for was halfway down it – Pte Thomas Bygraves.

The Chief Inspector turned, and walked back to the duty desk.

'Excuse me, Mrs Bygraves, but when your husband did his National Service, did he happen to be posted to Cyprus?'

The woman sniffed. 'Yes, he did serve in Cyprus, but what's that got to do with . . . ?'

But Woodend already had his hand on her shoulder, and was guiding her gently towards the lift.

'I think what we both need to do is to go up to my office an' have a little talk,' he said reassuringly.

His first impression – that Mrs Bygraves was in her late twenties – had been spot on, Woodend thought, looking at her across his desk. He'd been right about the 'respectable' side of things, too. Before she'd come to the police station, she'd taken the trouble to put on her make-up, though, in her obvious distress, she'd made a really botched job of it.

'It's so unlike my Tom to do anything like this,' Mrs Bygraves said, making an effort to fight back the tears.

'Have a sip of your police canteen tea, love,' the chief inspector said gently. 'There's not much to recommend it in the flavour stakes, but at least it's hot an' sweet.'

Mrs Bygraves did as she'd been instructed, but it didn't seem to be helping much.

'He's normally so steady,' she said, with a sniffle. 'So reliable. They said at work that they could set their clocks by him.'

'When did you start to notice a change in your husband's behaviour?' Woodend asked.

'It must have been over two weeks ago now. I thought at first it might be something to do with his job. He can get in a real tizzy during the half-yearly stock-taking. But that was all over and done with by last Friday, and instead of just looking exhausted – as he usually does when it's finished – he seemed to have more nervous energy than ever.'

'An' did he suddenly get worse yesterday – say around early afternoon?' Woodend suggested.

'How could you have known that?' Mrs Bygraves asked, amazed.

Because that's about the time he would have learned that Terry Pugh was dead, Woodend thought.

'It was just a guess,' he said aloud.

'He came home from work at about one o'clock. He said he wasn't feeling well, and had decided to take the rest of the day off. But he *never* does that kind of thing.'

'Did you meet your husband after he'd left the army, or did you know him before that?'

'Before. We got engaged just before he was called up.'

'So he'll have told you all about it?'

'Well, yes. I mean, no. I mean, I don't know *what* I mean! He did tell me about it at the beginning. And he did talk about it when he came home on that unexpected leave from Cyprus, because of his mother's condition. But after that, well, it was almost as if he wasn't the same man at all, so I don't really know how to answer your question honestly.'

'Maybe it would be better if we took each leave in turn,' Woodend suggested. 'Do you think that might make it easier?'

'Maybe.'

'So let's start with the first one.'

'That was after basic training. He hadn't enjoyed the training at all. He said that it seemed to him as if they were trying to turn him into some kind of unthinking, unfeeling machine.'

Woodend grimaced, remembering his own early days in the army.

'When you see an enemy soldier, don't think about whether he's got a wife and kids at home,' young Charlie Woodend's Sergeant Major had bawled at the men as he'd strode up and down the line along which they were standing stiffly to attention. 'Don't think about him at all. You kill the bastard – before he kills you!'

'What did your husband have to say about his time in Cyprus?' Woodend asked.

'I don't see what this has to do with Tom's disappearance,' Mrs Bygraves told him.

'I don't expect you do,' Woodend agreed. 'But humour me, an' it will all become clear later.'

Mrs Bygraves nodded. 'He came home on compassionate leave shortly after he'd been posted there. His mum was having a very serious operation,' She paused. 'Did I say that before?'

'More or less. But it doesn't really matter why he was there. Just tell me what he said.'

'He said he really liked the place, and that if that was "abroad", then he was all for it. He even went as far as to suggest that, if we could afford it, we might spend our honeymoon there. But soon after he went back, things turned very nasty, what with the terrorists and everything.'

'Was he scared when things turned nasty?'

'I think he must have been.'

'You *think* he must have been?'

'Yes, but I can't know for certain, because the next time he came home he'd already been demobbed, and he wouldn't talk about the place at all. In fact, he's *never* talked about it to this day.'

'Not even when he's been out for a few drinks with some of his old comrades?'

'He doesn't.'

'Doesn't what? Doesn't drink?'

'No, not that. He likes the odd tipple – though always within reason. But he's never been out with the men he served with. I don't even know who they are.'

Now that really was amazing, Woodend thought.

His own wife, Joan, knew almost as much about his old comrades as he did himself, because after what he'd been through with those lads, he couldn't *help* talking about them. And as for never going out for a drink with them, he couldn't understand that either, because there were times when every man *needed* to talk about his war – and the people he needed to talk about it *to* were those men who'd been through the same experience themselves.

'Tell me about what happened this mornin',' he suggested.

'Tom wouldn't get out of bed at first. I asked him if he was still feeling poorly, but he wouldn't even answer me. Honestly, it was just like talking to a brick wall.'

Or a man almost paralysed with fear, Woodend thought.

'Anyway, I went downstairs and started doing a bit of cleaning up in the lounge,' Mrs Bygraves continued. 'I find dusting and polishing has a very soothing effect on me.'

'I'm sure it does,' Woodend agreed.

'I heard him turn on the little radio we keep by the side of the bed, just in time to catch the local news, and I thought: *Well, at least he's taking an interest in something.* And the next thing I knew, he was rushing down the stairs like the house was on fire. He said he had to make a phone call – a *private* phone call – and he bundled me into the kitchen as if I was no more than a pile of rags.'

And as soon as he'd done that, he rang me and pleaded with me to tell him the name of the second victim, Woodend thought.

'Then he packed his suitcase, got into the car and drove away,' Mrs Bygraves continued. 'He wouldn't tell me where he was going. To be honest, I don't think he knew himself.' She paused. 'He is going to be all right, isn't he?'

She had no idea why her husband had run away, Woodend thought. She had made no connection in her mind between him and the two hanged men. But from the tone of those last few words of hers, it was plain that she already had the smell of death in her nostrils.

'It's early days yet,' he told her, hoping he was sounding reassuring, yet almost certain that he was not. 'There's absolutely no point in worryin' yourself about him unnecessarily. Is there anything else you can remember which might help us to find him quicker?'

Mrs Bygraves thought about it for a moment. 'There is one strange thing he did just before he left,' she said finally. 'But I don't see how it could possibly have anything to do with where he is now.'

'Tell me about it anyway,' Woodend encouraged.

'He seemed in such a rush to get away – he'd just *thrown* his clothes into the suitcase, and that wasn't like him at all, because he's normally such a careful packer and . . .'

'He seemed in such a rush to get away,' Woodend said, steering her back on course.

'That's right. But then he suddenly decided to go into the back garden and set fire to the garden rubbish we were planning to turn into a compost heap. Don't *you* find that strange?'

'Very strange,' Woodend said levelly.

'I didn't understand why he was doing it at the time, and I *still* don't understand. Do you have any idea why he might have done it?'

'Not a clue,' Woodend said.

But he was lying. He thought he knew *exactly* why Tom Bygraves had set fire to the nascent compost heap. He'd done it to destroy evidence.

Fifteen

The sun was just beginning to set as Woodend drove towards RAF Blackhill. The road he was travelling along was there solely for military purposes, coming to a dead halt when it reached the base, and that showed in the road surface, which presented no challenges at all to an RAF lorry or sturdy Land Rover, but was drawing considerable complaints from the suspension of the chief inspector's ageing Wolseley.

Woodend remembered the last time he had visited the base. It had been three years earlier, during the Cuban Missile Crisis.

Reading about the crisis in their history books, he thought as his suspension emitted another whine of agony, future generations would probably wonder what all the fuss had been about. Russia had wanted to establish a missile base on the island of Cuba, they would learn, and the United States of America had said it couldn't. The two powers had argued hotly about it for a few days, then America had made some token concessions, and Russia had backed down as gracefully as they could. A simple problem, then, those students of the future might well decide. A simple problem, simply resolved.

But it hadn't felt like that at time, Woodend told himself, as he saw the barbed-wire fence of RAF Blackhill up ahead of him. It hadn't felt like that *at all*.

Back then, it had seemed with each successive, and ever-worsening, news bulletin that nuclear war was inevitable – as if the end of the world was not only likely, but imminent. People in Whitebridge had walked round in a daze, almost like sleep walkers, their stomachs gripped by fear, their minds attempting to fight off an all-engulfing panic. And then, in the middle of this count-down to destruction, a young girl had gone missing.

Her name was Helen, and she had been the daughter of Squadron Leader Dunn. From the very start of the investigation, Woodend had been almost certain that she'd been kidnapped by a dangerous psychopath, and was already as good as dead – but that had not stopped him from driving his team of officers harder than he'd ever driven a team before.

As he approached the gate of the base, Woodend slowed down, coming to a halt just in front of the barrier. Two sentries had been watching him for some time, and now one of them walked over to him.

'This is a military installation, sir,' he said, politely but firmly.

'I know that,' Woodend replied, looking up the towers at the corners of the perimeter fence, and thinking it would be difficult to miss the fact. 'I'm Chief Inspector Woodend of the Central Lancs Police, an' I've got an appointment with Group Captain Featherington-Byres.'

The sentry first ran his eyes over Woodend's hairy sports coat and then over the Wolseley. He did not seem unduly impressed with either.

'I'll have to ring through and get confirmation,' he said.

'Of course you will,' Woodend agreed.

The sentry returned to his box and picked up the phone.

Watching him only vaguely, Woodend found his mind returning to the Helen Dunn case.

He'd been totally wrong about the nature of that investigation, he thought. But that hadn't been his fault, because what he'd believed had been what he'd been *intended* to believe – what he'd been *manipulated* into believing. Helen's abductor, as he discovered when he personally rescued her, was no sexual deviant – and her kidnapping was less to do with the girl herself than with the Cold War between the West and the USSR.

The barrier was lifted, and the sentry waved him on.

Woodend slipped the car into gear, and eased it forward. He would never have imagined, three years earlier, that he would ever be raising the Helen Dunn case again, he thought. But there he was, doing just that – and once again, though Helen might be the centre of the discussion, it was not really *about* her at all.

The bar in the officers' mess couldn't quite decide whether it was just a basic watering hole in which brave fighting men met to tell each other stories of breathtaking escapes, or a pleasant social club in which an officer and a gentleman could comfortably entertain his lady wife – and, as result, it was not really satisfactory as either of those things.

Woodend entered it under escort, and was taken over to the table where Group Captain Featherington-Byres was waiting for him.

Featherington-Byres was in his middle forties, and had one of those handlebar moustaches which most flyers had stopped sporting at the end of the War. He stood up when Woodend drew level with him, gave the chief inspector a broad smile and a firm handshake, and indicated that he should sit down.

'But he's edgy,' Woodend thought. 'An' I can't say that I blame him for that.'

'I'm assuming that since this is an informal meeting . . .' Featherington-Byres began. He paused for a moment. 'It *is* informal, isn't it?'

'More or less,' Woodend replied.

He had been wondering about how to go about handling this meeting since the idea of it had first come into his head. For a while, he had toyed with simply asking for what he wanted right from the start. But that would never work. Group captains were probably as much political animals as chief constables were – and if they saw no need to make concessions or grant favours, then no concessions would be made, and no favours granted.

So he had decided to employ an entirely different strategy. He would keep Featherington-Byres guessing about what he wanted. He would allow him the freedom to speculate on what his demands could possibly be. Then, at the point where he judged the group captain's imagination had all but settled on something completely outrageous, he would present his comparatively modest request. And, with any luck, Featherington-Byres would feel so relieved that he would agree to it without too much argument.

'So the meeting's informal, but as yet undefined,' Featherington-Byres said, when it became plain that Woodend had said all he was going to for the moment. 'At least, it's undefined to *me* – because while you clearly must know the purpose of it, I'm still very much in the dark.'

'That's right, you are,' Woodend agreed.

Featherington-Byres gave him another opportunity to say more, but Woodend didn't take it.

The group captain cleared his throat. 'So, given its informality, I thought it might be better to hold it here rather than in my office,' he said.

'Especially since that means we can take full advantage of facilities while we chat,' Woodend replied.

It was clearly not the comment Featherington-Byres had been expecting, and it seemed to throw him even more off-balance than he was already. 'I'm sorry,' he said. 'I'm afraid I don't quite follow you.'

'We could have a drink,' Woodend explained helpfully. 'At least, I'm *assumin'* we could. Unless, of course, all the alcohol I can see around me is just here for show.'

Featherington-Byres laughed unconvincingly. 'Very good!' he said. 'You can be quite amusing when you want to be, can't you? And naturally we must have a drink, Chief Inspector. What's your poison? Pink gin?'

Woodend shook his head. 'Unlike you fellers in the RAF, I like to keep both of my feet firmly on the ground,' he said, 'so, if you don't mind, I'll stick to best bitter.'

They said nothing more until the drinks had arrived, and even then Featherington-Byres did not speak until Woodend had taken a deep slurp of his pint. Then he asked, 'Is the beer to your satisfaction?'

'Not a bad pint at all,' Woodend told him.

Featherington-Byres took a sip of his pink gin, then said, 'It's been a long time since we last met, hasn't it, Mr Woodend?'

'Three years,' Woodend agreed.

'During the Cuban Missile Crisis, wasn't it?'

Oh no, I'm not lettin' you get away with that, Sunshine, Woodend thought.

'I suppose it *was* durin' the Cuban Missile Crisis,' he said aloud, 'but I tend to think of it more as bein' durin' the Helen Dunn Kidnappin' Crisis.'

'Ah yes, the Helen Dunn kidnapping,' Featherington-Byres agreed uncomfortably. 'But happily, that crisis – much like the other one with the missiles – was brought to a successful conclusion.' He paused. 'Wouldn't you agree, Chief Inspector?'

'I suppose it all depends how you measure success,'

Woodend said. 'It's certainly true I managed to rescue the girl, but let's not pretend that she wasn't psychologically damaged by the experience. An' let's not forget that there was a suicide involved, as well – the details of which could have been very embarrassin' for the RAF, if they'd got out.'

Silence descended over them again, until Featherington-Byres eventually broke it by saying, 'Though I'm perfectly willing to repeat it now, I think I *did* thank you at the time for all you'd done, didn't I?'

'Aye, you did,' Woodend agreed. 'But, do you know, I could never quite work out what it was exactly you were thankin' me *for*. Was it for findin' Helen? Or was it for keepin' the lid on things – for makin' sure that the details of what actually happened never became public knowledge?'

'For rescuing Helen.'

'Really?'

'Of course. I saw no need to thank you for the other thing – since you only did what any other decent patriot would have done in your place.'

I didn't do it to be patriotic, Woodend thought. I did it because the poor girl had suffered enough, without havin' her name dragged through the gutter press.

'From what you've just said, it sounds to me as if you think that the interests of the RAF an' the interests of the country are identical?' he said to Featherington-Byres.

'Yes, that is what I think, as a matter of fact.'

'An' does the same hold true of the Army?'

Featherington-Byres scowled. 'I imagine that *every* branch of the armed forces assumes it has the right to expect the co-operation of the citizens it is prepared to lay down its life to protect,' he said.

'In other words, yes?'

'As I said, I imagine it to be the case, but I really can't speak for the Army.'

'But do you speak *to* the Army?'

'I beg your pardon?'

'I was wonderin' how much back-scratchin' goes on between the services?' Woodend said.

'And what exactly do you mean by that?'

'I was wonderin' if an RAF group captain, for example,

has pals in the army who might, in turn, have influence in the War Office?'

'Are we talking here about RAF group captains in general terms? Or are we talking about me in particular?'

'We're talkin' about you in particular.'

'Do you know, I rather thought we might be,' Featherington-Byres said. 'And in answer to your question, I've always thought it was a pity there was so much inter-service rivalry, and so I have done my best to cultivate contacts in both the army and the navy.'

'I'll take that as another "yes" then.'

Group Captain Featherington-Byres sighed softly. 'I knew this would happen one day,' he said.

'Knew *what* would happen one day?' Woodend asked innocently.

'Knew that since you'd done us some small service by managing to keep the details of the Helen Dunn situation out of the papers . . .'

'I thought you told me that was no more than my patriotic duty.'

Featherington-Byres grinned, a little shamefacedly. 'I didn't think that kind of moral pressure would work on a man like you, but I had to give it a try, anyway,' he admitted. 'Where was I?'

'Since I'd done you some small service by keeping Helen Dunn out of the papers . . .'

'. . . I knew you'd eventually be back here, demanding your quid pro quo.'

'That'd be Latin, would it?' Woodend asked.

Featherington-Byres laughed. 'Don't think you can pull that country bumpkin act on me, Chief Inspector. I've seen the way you work, so it simply won't wash.'

'So you're right, an' I'm here because I want my pound of flesh,' Woodend admitted.

'And that will involve . . .?'

'I'd like you to grease a few wheels for me – to make sure they're runnin' smoothly when I have to give them a little push.'

'What wheels?'

'I want a member of my team to have access to the service records of all conscripts who were on active duty in Cyprus seven years ago.'

'And may I ask why?'

'Because I'm lookin' for a really bad apple – or maybe even a few really bad apples.'

'But you're not interested in going after the whole barrel?'

'Definitely not.'

Featherington-Byres considered the matter. 'It might be difficult,' he said finally.

'It wasn't *easy* keepin' all the details of the Helen Dunn case out of the papers,' Woodend pointed out.

Featherington-Byres nodded. 'So let me see if I've got this completely clear,' he said. 'You would like me to use my contacts to influence their friends to order their subordinates to allow you to look at military records. Is that it?'

'That's it.'

'And if I do that, then any debt you feel I may owe you will have been paid in full?'

'Not quite.'

Featherington-Byres frowned. 'No?'

'No. There is just one more little thing I'd like you to do for me,' Woodend said.

Sixteen

Sitting across the pub table from her boss, Monika Paniatowski found herself studying Woodend closely. He had been late for the meeting in the Drum and Monkey – which was unusual for him. And he had offered no explanation for his tardiness, which was quite out of character. So just what was his game?

The chief inspector drained his pint, looked around to make sure that the rest of the team had almost finished their own drinks, and signalled to the waiter to bring a fresh round.

He had a surprise up his sleeve, Paniatowski decided, and he was holding it back until just the right moment, when he would produce it with great flourish, in much the same way as music hall magicians used to produce rabbits from their hats. It wasn't a game Woodend played very often – he normally liked to keep his team completely up to date with developments – but on the few occasions when he *was* tempted, he played it for the maximum effect, and Paniatowski couldn't help wondering just what this particular rabbit would be.

The drinks arrived, and Woodend took a healthy slurp of his pint of bitter. 'The uniformed branch have been able to establish no link between Pugh an' the bookies, but given what we've learned since we started playin' around with that theory, it doesn't come as much of a shock,' he began.

Rutter nodded. 'Pugh might possibly have been a secret gambler, but Lewis didn't have the money for betting, and Bygraves didn't have the inclination,' he agreed.

'Exactly,' Woodend said. 'So now that we've got that particular red herrin' out of the way, let's review what we actually *do* know so far,' he suggested. 'We know that our killer's got a list of names, an' though we don't know how long that list is, we can be pretty sure that he's workin' his way through it. Terry Pugh was the first on the list, Reg Lewis was the second, and Tom Bygraves at least *believes* he's the third, which is why he's done a runner.'

'Do you think that by running away he's managed to escape the killer, sir?' Bob Rutter asked.

'He may have,' Woodend replied. 'On the other hand, it's equally possible that that's just what the killer *wanted* him to do.'

'I don't quite follow that,' Beresford admitted.

'Then I'll explain it to you. Our killer's more than clever enough to have worked out that we're probably onto him by now, an' that we may have identified Tom Bygraves as his possible third victim. Now that could make killin' Bygraves in Whitebridge very difficult. An' why is that, DC Beresford?'

'Because we might have assigned men to watch Bygraves, in the hope that the killer *would* make an attempt?' Beresford guessed.

'Just so. Once Bygraves has left Whitebridge, however, he's exposed, like a frightened deer caught in the crosshairs of a rifle sight. Not that the killer *is* likely to shoot him. If Bygraves dies, it'll be by hangin'. Anyway, we've taken all the precautions we *can* take, haven't we, Monika?'

'That's right, sir,' Paniatowski agreed. 'Every motor patrol in Central Lancs has been given the model and license number of Bygraves' car, and has been told that finding him is a top priority. In addition, every foot patrol officer in Whitebridge has been issued with pictures of Bygraves himself, and of the man Pugh was seen leaving the Tanner's Arms with.'

'The main problem is, we don't know who else is on that list,' Woodend continued, 'an' we can't depend on the people concerned comin' forward an' volunteerin' that information themselves, can we, Beresford?'

'No, sir.'

'An' why is that?'

'Because Bygraves didn't.'

'Exactly! Even though he felt his life was in danger – even though he was nearly shittin' himself – he still didn't come to us. An' there can be only one reason for that – because he just couldn't bring himself to tell us what this was all about. So in order to afford these fellers the protection they're so obviously in need of, we're goin' to have to find out their names ourselves.'

'And how will we do that?' Rutter asked.

'We got the names of the fellers that Mark Hough remember bers servin' with, an' by tomorrow mornin' the Ministry of Defence will have sent us the names of *all* the Whitebridge men who served in Cyprus. An' so we'll need to talk to each an' every one of the buggers, in the hope that we can find at least one who's sensible enough – or perhaps *frightened* enough – to tell us what we need to know.'

'Isn't that pretty much putting all our eggs in one basket?' Bob Rutter wondered.

'It would be, if that was all we were goin' to do,' Woodend agreed. 'But we've got a second basket – our Monika.'

Ah, the flourish! Paniatowski thought.

'Me, sir?' she said aloud.

'You,' Woodend agreed. 'You're off to Cyprus.'

'Cyprus! The *island* of Cyprus?'

'Well, I'm certainly not talking about Cyprus Street, Accrington.'

'*When* am I going?'

Woodend checked his watch. 'In about five hours from now.'

'Five hours!'

'You'll just have time to go home an' pack. Only, if I was you, I wouldn't worry too much about includin' your bikini in the packin', because, while I've no doubt you'd look pretty sensational in it, you'll be far too busy doin' other things to even *think* of lyin' about in the sun.'

Paniatowski grinned. 'I imagine I will,' she said.

'You'll have two main jobs while you're over there,' Woodend continued. 'The first is to try an' put a name to the face of our prime suspect. An' what's the second?'

'To do my best to find out just what *did* happen over there, seven years ago?' Paniatowski guessed.

'That's right,' Woodend agreed. 'Because if you *can* find that out, we'll at least have some chance of protectin' any other poor buggers who happen to be on this nutter's list.'

'I assume I'll be flying from Manchester,' Paniatowski said.

'Then you assume wrong,' Woodend told her.

'But there's no way I can get down to London in only five hours.'

'That's true,' agreed Woodend, 'but you'll not be flyin' from there, either. You'll be goin' from RAF Blackhill.'

This was not just a rabbit, Paniatowski thought. This was a positive flock of white doves.

'However did you manage to talk the RAF into that, sir?' she asked.

'I used my charm,' Woodend said, smiling.

'Your *charm*?' Paniatowski repeated, incredulously.

'That's right, Monika. You know me – I can charm the birds down from the trees, if I really put my mind to it.'

Tom Bygraves had no idea of how long he had been in this derelict cottage in the middle of the moors. He didn't even know how he'd got there in the first place, or even who had taken him there. All he *did* know was that his hands had been tied together and then attached to an old ceiling beam, and that the only way his feet could touch the floor was if he stood on tiptoe.

It had been a mild early evening when he'd regained consciousness, but now darkness was beginning to fall, the temperature was dropping, and he was starting to shiver.

There were other discomforts to deal with, too. His head hurt from the blow it had received earlier, his wrists and feet ached from being trussed in such an unnatural position.

He had wanted to urinate from the moment he came round. At first he had resisted the temptation, then he had simply given way, and allowed the hot piss to trickle down his trouser leg.

But none of these things were what was really worrying him. He would have immersed himself in ice cold water if he had to, endured being strung up for days on end, urinated until his thighs were as degradingly sticky as fly-paper – as long as the fear would go away.

But the fear *wouldn't* leave him. It was in his eyes and in his ears, in his brain and in his heart, in every tiny nook and cranny of his entire body. Because he knew that he was in the power of a madman – and there was absolutely nothing he could do about it!

He heard the sound of a engine, growing louder with each second, and by twisting round he saw – in what little light of the day was left – that a dark van was approaching the ruined shell in which he was being held.

He prayed that the new arrival would be the police, in an

unmarked vehicle. Or, if not them, a neighbouring farmer who would not expect to find him there, but would release him the moment he did.

He prayed – but even as he was doing it, he did not *believe*.

A man, carrying a torch in his hand, climbed out of the van, and walked towards the ruined building. As he stepped through the doorway, he shone the beam of the torch directly into his prisoner's face.

Tom Bygraves closed his eyes, but the light was still blinding. He turned away from it as far as he could – pirouetting on his toes like a ballet dancer – and that made it a little better.

'So you are not asleep any more, my friend,' said a voice with a heavy foreign accent.

'Who . . . who are you?' Bygraves gasped.

'Why don't you see for yourself?' the other man suggested, removing the light beam from his face.

Bygraves swivelled back to his previous position, but he could still see only the bright lights before his eyes. Then, slowly, his vision returned to something like normal, and as it did he saw that the other man was shining the torch on his own face.

'Well?' his captor asked.

'I'm . . . I'm not sure I know you.'

'Think back. Imagine me seven years younger. Imagine me *happier*.'

'I'm afraid I still don't . . .'

'Of course you don't,' his capture said in disgust. 'All Cypriots look alike to you, don't they? They are only Mediterranean monkeys.'

'I never thought of you like that.'

'Is that true?'

'Yes, it is. I promise.'

'Liar! I remember you – all of you – even if you do not remember me. I know how you treated us – how even innocence was no protection from you.'

'It wasn't me! I swear that whatever you're thinking of, it wasn't me!'

'It *was* you!' the Cypriot said firmly. 'You and your little band of friends. Tell me, how many of you were there?'

'I don't know. I'm not even sure what you're . . .'

'How many?' the other man demanded. 'Tell me, or I'll kill you.'

'Six!' Bygraves screamed. 'There were six of us.'

'Yes, six,' the other man agreed. 'And now there are only three.' He paused. 'Tell me about the game.'

'I don't know which game you mean.'

'Yes, you do. And if you do not speak now, I will cut out your tongue, and you will never speak again.'

'It was called '"What if?"'

The Cypriot nodded. 'And how did it work?'

'You must know already, or you'd never have . . .'

'*How did it work?*'

'We'd sit around and wonder what we'd do if something bad happened to one of us.'

'Like what?'

'Well, for example, we'd say, "What if one of us had his arm blown clean off by a roadside bomb?"'

'And what did you decide?'

'We decided that when we got back to England, the rest of us would each give him a tenth of whatever we earned for the rest of our working lives.'

The Cypriot laughed. 'How . . . how *cosy*. Is that the right word, Mr Bygraves? Cosy?'

'Yes, that's the right word.'

'Or do I mean *sentimental*?'

'It could be that, too,' Bygraves told him.

'You'd agree with me whatever I said, wouldn't you?' the Cypriot asked him, in disgust. '"*Testicles*! Is that the right word?" "Yes, it is." "Shit! Is that right?" "It's perfect." You want me to like you – but I never will. You want me to pity you – but that is impossible.'

'What's going to happen to me?'

'What do you think is going to happen to you?'

'I . . . I don't know.'

'Don't know?' the Cypriot repeated. 'How can that be, when you *do* know what has happened to the others?' He paused for a moment, as if turning the question over in his mind. 'Oh, now I see,' he continued. 'You are thinking that if I was going to hang you, I would have done it already. Is that right?'

'Please . . .'

'I hung – or is it "hanged"? I am never sure – Terry Pugh

from a bridge, and it created quite a sensation. Is *that* the
right word – *sensation?*'

'I don't know,' Tom Bygraves sobbed. 'I d–don't know.'

'But if I had hanged – or is it hung? – Reg Lewis in the
same way, people would not have been as much shocked. So
I used a crane instead. Each time more impressive, you see.'

'You can't mean . . . ?'

'Your death will be even more impressive still. But the
machinery for your hanging will not be ready until tomorrow
night. If you had not run away from home like a frightened
rabbit, I would have allowed you one more day of freedom.
But you *did* run, and forced me to act much earlier than I had
planned.'

'You . . . you can't hang me,' Tom Bygraves blubbered.

'Instead of complaining about your fate, you should be
counting your blessings,' the Cypriot told him harshly. 'You
will die tomorrow, it is true, but if justice had truly been
served, you would have died long ago.'

There was no physical barrier which prevented the 'ordinary'
civil servants from walking down that particular corridor on
the third floor of the Foreign and Commonwealth Office. There
wasn't even a sign in evidence to prohibit such an action. Yet
the drones and minor bureaucrats who worked in the building
steered well clear of the area, because although they only had
the vaguest idea of what was going on there, they had long
ago decided that a *vague* idea was more than enough.

The man bent over his desk in the room at the far end of
the corridor was still hard at work, even as Big Ben rang out
the chimes of midnight in the near distance. He was in his
middle fifties. He had short grey hair which always looked
as if it had recently been trimmed, and his long slim fingers
showed evidence of a regular manicure. He was wearing, as
he habitually did, an expensive herring-bone suit, grey woollen
socks, and black Oxford shoes. He went under a number of
names, depending on the situation, but in this building he was
usually known as Mr Forsyth.

The gentle tap on his door served as a switching mechanism for his keen mind, temporarily closing it off from the
problem he had just been dealing with, and preparing it for
the one which was undoubtedly soon to present itself.

The bearer of the new problem entered the room. His name was Barrington, and while he was younger than Forsyth, he was just as ambitious and probably nearly as brilliant.

'Sorry to disturb you, but a name's just been flagged up which I believe may be familiar to you,' he said in a voice which was deferential, but in which that deference rested on a solid foundation of self-confidence.

'And what name might that be?' Forsyth asked.

'Woodend. *Chief Inspector* Woodend.'

Forsyth smiled slightly. 'Cloggin'-it Charlie! Yes, I do know him. I came across him during that rather unpleasant business at Haverton Camp.'

'What's he like?'

Forsyth thought about it for a moment. 'Tenacious,' he said. 'Dogged. Bloody minded.' He paused. 'What's Charlie done now to make us take an interest in him?'

'He's investigating the murders – or perhaps *executions* might be the more appropriate word – of some ex-servicemen living in the North.'

'So?'

'All these servicemen did a tour of duty in Cyprus. In '58.'

'I still fail to see why that should concern us.'

Barrington extracted a single sheet of paper from his jacket pocket, and laid it on the desk. 'You will when you've read this.'

Forsyth quickly scanned it. 'Ah, now it's starting to make sense,' he admitted. 'But Whitebridge is a long way from the Med, you know, and I doubt if even a sharp chap like Charlie could reach a conclusion which we might regard as unfortunate without him actually going to . . .'

'One of his team's on the way to Cyprus, even as we speak,' Barrington interrupted.

'And do we have a name for this team member?'

'She's a Sergeant Paniatowski.'

Forsyth smiled again, quite fondly this time. 'Monika!' he said. 'Quite a formidable lady, in her own way. Down at Haverton Camp, she facilitated the death of . . .' He pulled himself up short, suddenly aware that Barrington might not have been briefed on that particular incident. 'The details don't matter,' he continued. 'Suffice it to say that quite an important personage died as a result of Monika's deliberate actions.'

'And she was allowed to get away with it?' Barrington asked, surprised.

'Indeed,' Forsyth agreed. 'As it happened, her quasi-homicidal tendencies turned out to be quite convenient for us.' He frowned. 'But it *is* a problem that she'll be in Cyprus.'

'So what are we going to do about it?' Barrington asked.

'For the moment, I suspect that, since the secrets she's attempting to dig up are buried very deep, we need do no more than monitor her progress.' He paused again. 'They *are* deeply buried, aren't they?'

'Yes, I believe they are,' Barrington said.

'Very well, then, the chances of her uncovering anything are minimal. But if she does look as if she's getting close, we'll have start applying a little pressure, because though we all like to see justice done whenever possible, we don't necessarily want to see it done in this particular instance.'

Seventeen

The Blackburn Beverly C.1. transport plane was ninety-nine feet long and had a wing-span of a hundred and sixty-two feet. Its maximum weight for take-off was nearly a hundred and fifty thousand pounds. It could reach a top speed of two hundred and seven knots, fly at sixteen thousand feet and had an operating range of one thousand, one hundred and twenty-nine miles. It had seen service in military operations in the Middle East and Far East, and was generally agreed to be one of the most successful planes of its kind ever built.

Monika Paniatowski had known none of this when she had entered the tail boom through the parachute doors, but a young flight lieutenant, who was the only other passenger, had been more than willing to fill her in on all the details.

He had a great deal to say about Cyprus, too.

'We'd occupied it since the latter half of the nineteenth century, as a result of the Treaty of Berlin,' he said, 'but it wasn't until the end of the First World War that it became an actual colony, and even then, it was almost by default.' He paused, and grinned sheepishly. 'I'm a bit of a history buff,' he admitted.

Paniatowski smiled. 'I think I was beginning to gather that,' she said.

'I kept it to myself at first, but then my mother found out about it, and she's had me lecturing to half the Women's Institutes in the Home Counties, when I'm home on leave. But there isn't any reason you should have to endure it.'

'It's no hardship at all,' Paniatowski protested. 'I really am interested. And I've got a question I'd like to ask, if I may.'

'By all means, go ahead.'

'If we got Cyprus mainly by default, why did we make such a fuss about giving it its independence?'

'Ah, that was because conditions had changed in the

meantime,' the lieutenant said. 'In 1954 we pulled our forces out of Egypt, and, for want of any real alternative, it was decided to make Cyprus the military headquarters of our Mediterranean zone of operations – and that was as good as saying that we intended to keep it as a colony for ever.'

'But the Cypriots didn't like that?'

'You can't really talk about the Cypriots as such, you know,' the lieutenant said.

'You can't?'

'Absolutely not. There's the *Greek* Cypriots, who make up about eighty percent of the population, and the Turkish Cypriots who make up the other twenty percent. The Greek Cyps wanted the island to be united with mainland Greece, which is all of five hundred miles across the Med. The Turkish Cyps looked on Turkey as their homeland, which is not really surprising, considering that it's a mere forty-three miles away.'

'But it was the Greek Cypriots, rather than the Turks, who were actually fighting us, wasn't it?' Paniatowski asked, feeling slightly ashamed that she was so vague about something which was still very recent history.

'That's right, it was the Greek Cyps, though they did occasionally take time off from fighting us, so they'd have the opportunity to have a go at the Turkish Cyps as well. The organization that actually led the terrorist campaign was called EOKA. The name comes from the Greek words . . .' the lieutenant closed his eyes, as if he really needed to concentrate, '. . . *Ethniki Organosis Kyprion Aguniston.*'

'And that means?' Paniatowski asked.

'The National Organization of Cypriot Fighters. They were led by a chap called Grivas, who'd been a colonel in the Greek Army during the war, and had led a pretty heroic resistance campaign against the Germans. And all the skills he'd learned in that war, he turned on us. There couldn't have been more than a few hundred guerrillas at most, but it needed more than 40,000 British troops to even *contain* the insurgency, never mind defeat it.'

'So in the end, we just gave up?' Paniatowski suggested.

The lieutenant looked quite shocked. 'Great Britain *never* gives up,' he said, then seeing the sceptical look in Paniatowski's eyes, he continued, 'But in 1960 we did . . . er . . . decide to compromise a little, by granting the island its independence, as long as the new government was prepared to guaranteed us two British bases in perpetuity.'

'What's the island itself like?' Paniatowski asked.

'Small by the standards of some islands in other parts of the world, but quite big for an island in the Med.'

Paniatowski smiled. 'And what does that mean exactly?'

'It's a hundred and forty miles long, and – if I remember correctly – it's fifty-nine miles in breadth, at its widest point.'

'Is it mainly flat?'

'Not at all. It's a very mountainous place, with the Kyrenia range in the north, and the Troodos massif to the centre and west. It was in the mountains that the guerrillas hid out in the early stages of the conflict, though later they moved into the towns.'

'So, no beaches?' Paniatowski said disappointedly – though she had no idea why she *should* feel disappointed, since, as Woodend had pointed out, there'd be no time for sunbathing.

'There are some very fine beaches,' the lieutenant said. 'Look out of the window, and you'll see for yourself.'

Paniatowski *did* look out of the window – and realized immediately it was a mistake. This was her first ever flight, and up until that moment she'd pretty much been able to ignore the fact that she was in a big metal tube, high in the sky and with no visible means of support. The sight of the island below made such self-denial no longer possible, and with slightly trembling fingers she opened her handbag and took out her cigarettes.

The flight lieutenant shook his finger at her in a slightly chiding way. 'There's no smoking on RAF flights,' he said. 'Didn't they tell you that when you were on the ground?'

Of course they had, Paniatowski thought – but she'd managed to very conveniently forget. And the last thing she needed right at that moment, she told herself, was a bloody flight officer – who seemed to have no fear of the situation at all – reminding her of the regulation. Still, she supposed that rules were rules, even if it was the last rule she ever lived to obey.

'Sorry,' she said, slipping the cigarettes back into the handbag.

The plane's smooth downward progress was suddenly interrupted by a series of rapid bounces.

'Nothing to be alarmed about!' the flight lieutenant said. 'We just hit an air pocket.'

It should have reassured Paniatowski – but it didn't.

An air pocket, she thought. What the hell was an *air pocket*? The words didn't make any sense, because what else would anyone expect – up in the bloody air – if not *air*?

In an effort to stem her rising panic, she forced herself to focus her mind on the case.

Something had happened on that island below her – an island on which she might eventually land safely! – which had cost the lives of two men seven years later, and could yet be the cause of more deaths.

So what had Terry Pugh *done* that had merited decapitation?

What crime had Reg Lewis *committed* which meant that he ended up hanging from a crane?

'We should be landing in another two or three minutes,' the flight lieutenant told her, looking out of the window.

I'll believe it when I see it, Paniatowski thought, looking in quite the other direction.

Before his wife Maria had been murdered, Bob Rutter had always eaten a hearty breakfast each morning – though he had never been able to match the championship artery clogging efforts of his boss, Charlie Woodend – but since her death he had found it difficult to manage even a slice of toast. Now he usually contented himself with a cup of strong coffee, and two or three cigarettes, and that morning – as he scanned the morning newspapers – was no exception.

The papers were full of the murders, which was hardly surprising, given both the sensational nature of the crimes and the chief constable's eagerness to re-establish his own position by talking almost constantly to the press. But though Elizabeth Driver's own paper had gone to town on it more than most, there was no article which bore Elizabeth's by-line.

There hadn't been an article by Elizabeth in the previous morning's paper, either, despite the fact that – after she'd promised to keep it to herself – he had fed her information which would have put her well ahead her rivals.

So, it seemed to him, his gut feeling had been right. Despite both Monika's and Woodend's scepticism, Elizabeth was no longer the woman she'd been when they first met. She was trying to become a better, more honest, person. And if she could make that change, then perhaps he could too.

He tried not to think about her in a sexual way, though that was becoming increasingly difficult as time went by. He knew that he didn't love her, he told himself. Not as he had once loved his wife, and not as he still loved Mo . . .

An iron grille came down in Rutter's head, slicing through that particular line of thought before it could wriggle even further into his brain.

He took a deep breath, and started again.

He knew that he didn't love Elizabeth as he had once loved Maria, but he did yearn to hold her – to feel her firm and exciting body pressed against his.

But he must resist that temptation. The book they were to write together was all that mattered. He must not do anything that might get in the way of that.

Monika Paniatowski stood on the hot tarmac at Akrotiri Base, looking up at the Blackburn Beverly which had brought her there, still not quite able to understand how the heavy metal bird had managed the trick.

She was still looking at it wonderingly when she heard a Land Rover pull up close to her, and voice call out, 'Sergeant Paniatowski?'

She turned. Sitting behind the driving wheel of the vehicle was a boy. He was wearing a lightweight military uniform which consisted of a grey socks, shorts, and a short-sleeved shirt which sported a single chevron on one of the sleeves.

'A boy!' Paniatowski thought with horror. 'I just called him a *boy!*'

The word had automatically come to her mind, because he was clearly several years her junior. And that had to make him a boy!

Didn't it?

Except that he wasn't. Looking at him objectively, it was difficult to see him as anything but a young *man*.

Paniatowski realized she was suddenly starting to feel very, very old.

The boy – the young man – was still sitting behind the wheel of the Land Rover, waiting for an answer.

'Yes, I'm Paniatowski,' she heard herself say aloud.

The lance corporal grinned. Was she allowed to call it a *boyish* grin, she wondered.

'I'm Bill Blaine, Sarge,' he said. 'Why don't you hop into the vehicle, and I'll take you to meet the boss?'

DC Colin Beresford knew that many of his colleagues stayed in bed until the last possible moment. Then, in a flurry of activity, they shaved while they smoked their first cigarette of the day, ate a bowl of cereal while they dressed, and were out of the house in fifteen minutes flat.

He couldn't do that.

He had responsibilities.

The first thing he had to do, this morning as every morning, was to cook his mother's breakfast. The second was to sit there and make sure she ate it. That accomplished – and sometimes accomplishing it wasn't easy – he always set aside five minutes for talk, because the doctor had told him that it was important to make sure that his mother talked – that though it would not stop the slide into dementia, it might possibly slow it down a little.

These tasks having been completed, he walked around the house, making sure it was a safe place in which to leave his mother.

The main fuse in the kitchen had to be removed and hidden, because once she had turned on the cooker, forgotten she'd done it, and burned her hand badly.

The stopcock in the bathroom had to be turned off, to prevent a recurrence of the time the bath had overflowed and the flood had almost brought down the living room ceiling.

And finally all the locks had to be checked, to make sure that his mother couldn't leave the house even if she wanted to, since she had an inclination to wander, even if she were only wearing her night-gown.

When all that was done, he'd kissed her on the cheek.

Some mornings, she would look at him strangely, as if wondering why a complete stranger would ever do such a thing.

But this morning was one of her good ones. This morning, she smiled at him, and said, 'Take care, Colin.'

'I will,' he promised.

As he stepped through the front door – and then carefully locked it behind him – he felt as exhausted as if he had already done a full day's work. But that day's work still lay ahead of him.

In his pocket, he had a list of several men who had served in Cyprus at the same time as Terry Pugh and Reg Lewis – and he was rather hoping that they could explain to him why the two of them were now dead.

When Mrs Bygraves appeared at her front door, it was clear to Bob Rutter, from the haggard expression on her face, that she'd had little sleep the night before. Then she saw who'd been ringing the bell, and her face flooded with hope.

'You've found him, haven't you!' she gasped with relief. 'You've found my Tom. I knew it was stupid of me to worry.'

'I'm afraid we haven't found him yet,' Rutter said gently, 'but it is still early days.'

'If you haven't found him, then why are you here?' Mrs Bygraves demanded, as hope immediately gave way to anger and aggression. 'Why aren't you out *there*?' she gestured expansively towards the wider world beyond her home. 'Why aren't you still looking for him?'

'We *are* still looking for him,' Rutter assured her. 'We've got scores of men out there involved in the operation. But that's not what I've been asked to do. My job is to search the house.'

'Search the house? Go through all our personal things – through the life we've had together? What good could that possibly do?'

'We might find some clue as to where he's gone,' Rutter explained.

'Have you got a search warrant?' Mrs Bygraves demanded.

'No, I haven't,' Rutter admitted. 'I didn't think I'd need one. I thought you'd want to help.'

'Of course I *want* to help,' Mrs Bygraves said, close to tears. 'But don't you think that if there was something here, I'd already have found it?'

'With the greatest respect, madam, you don't have a policeman's trained eye,' Rutter said.

'No, but I *do* know my husband. And I know there's nothing in the house that will tell you where he went – because when he left, he didn't know where he was going himself.'

'Well, I can't force you to let me in, if you don't want to,' Rutter told her. 'We'll let you know if your husband turns up. Good morning, madam.'

He turned towards the garden gate.

'Wait!' Mrs Bygraves said.

'Yes?'

'Do you really think you might find a clue of some sort?'

'I can't promise *anything*, madam.'

Mrs Bygraves brushed a tear from her cheek.

'You'd better come inside,' she said. 'I'm sorry for the way I spoke to you just now. I really don't know what's come over me.'

'It's perfectly understandable, madam,' Rutter said.

And it was.

First there'd been desperate hope, but that had been rapidly followed by despair, anger, defiance and eventually misery. These were the string of ever-changing emotions that people felt when they believed – and yet at the same time *refused* to believe – that they had lost their partner.

And he should know, because he had run the whole gamut himself – at least a dozen times – after Maria had been murdered.

Captain Howerd was in his mid-thirties, but already greying at the temples. He looked at Paniatowski as if she were something that the cat had dragged in.

'We're not accustomed to the civilian police force carrying out investigations into army personnel,' he said.

'The men I'll be investigating haven't been in the army for a number of years,' Paniatowski replied.

'But they'll still be able to recite their whole army pay book number without a second's hesitation,' Howerd said.

'I'm afraid I don't quite get the point,' Paniatowski admitted.

'You wouldn't,' the captain said dismissively.

'Though perhaps I just might, if you were to take the time to explain it to me.'

The captain sighed. 'In a way, we are a little like the Jesuits,' he said.

'We?' Paniatowski repeated. 'Who's *we*?'

The captain sighed again, even more heavily this time, as if it were a real strain to have to explain *anything* to this stupid civilian.

'*We* are the army,' he said. 'The *professional* soldiers. The fighting force that has kept Britain safe for the last five hundred years, and will continue to keep it safe for the next five hundred.'

'I see,' Paniatowski told him. 'Do please carry on.'

'We take our raw material at a young age, as the Jesuits do, and we mould it into exactly what we want it to be. And once that's done, it's ours for ever. It *belongs* to us. So from our perspective, Sergeant Paniatowski, there's no such thing as an *ex*-soldier. There are only soldiers who are no longer on active duty.'

'You resent me being here, don't you?' Paniatowski said.

'While you're on the Sovereign Base Areas, you'll be granted the same status as a sergeant in the military police,' the captain said, ignoring her question. 'A billet has been made available for you in the sergeants' quarters, and Lance Corporal Blaine will be your driver. You will be issued with a military pass, which will allow you to go wherever you wish to on the island. You have my permission to speak to whoever you feel the need to, provided that, in doing so, you do not compromise the position of the army vis-à-vis the local authorities. Any questions?'

'What kind of support can I expect?'

'As I've already said, Lance Corporal Blaine will be your driver.'

'No one else?'

Howerd smiled bleakly. 'You surely wouldn't expect us to do your job *for* you, would you, Sergeant?'

'What about access to your records?'

'We cannot allow you to trawl through them wholesale. If there is a specific record you wish to see, you must request it *specifically*. We will then consider your application.'

'And how long will that take?' Paniatowski wondered.

Howerd shrugged. 'Could take days. Perhaps even longer.'

'I imagine it could,' Paniatowski said. 'I imagine it could take until I'd already left the island.'

'That's a possibility,' Howerd admitted. 'I should also mention that you do not need to report your activities to anyone in the military chain of command. In fact, we'd much rather *not* know what you're doing. Any more questions?'

'No, that just about covers it,' Paniatowski said.

'In that case, I will detain you no longer,' the captain told her.

It was as Paniatowski was walking to the door that Howerd added, 'There is *one* more thing, Sergeant Paniatowski.'

'Yes?'

'We've been ordered to pull out all the stops for you, and I think you'll agree that we have.'

'In some respects, yes.'

'I can't ever remember having to do that before, not for a mere *civilian*. You must have friends in very high places.'

'It's not so much that I've got friends in high places myself as that I know a man who knows a man who has,' Paniatowski said.

Captain Howerd nodded, as if, understanding the way the world worked, that was just the answer he'd expected her to give.

Eighteen

When Paniatowski emerged from Captain Howerd's office, it was to find that Lance Corporal Blaine was just where she had left him, sitting behind the wheel of his Land Rover and basking in the sunshine.

When he saw Paniatowski approaching, he smiled.

'Did Captain Howerd give you a right proper bollocking, Sarge?' he asked.

'Now why should you ever think that?' Paniatowski wondered.

'He never bothers to see anybody personally unless a bollocking's on the cards,' Blaine said, with a total lack of guile that Paniatowski found remarkably refreshing.

'I think he did *try* to bollock me, but it just didn't take,' Paniatowski told him.

Blaine's smile transformed itself into a very wide grin. 'Good for you!' he said. 'So where are we off to now, Sarge?'

A good question, Paniatowski thought.

'Do you have any idea of how many of the soldiers on this base would have been here seven years ago?' she asked.

'Are we talkin' about the infantry, or the technical staff?'

'The infantry.'

Blaine grinned again. 'Then that's an easy question to answer, Sarge. None of them.'

'None at all?'

'Not a one.'

'Wonderful,' Paniatowski said, dejectedly.

'The longest anybody serves here is two years. I've only got a few months to go myself. Must say, I'll miss the place. A lot of the other lads will, as well. After living in the sunshine, by the sea, it'll be a bit of a wrench to have to return to wet old Blighty.'

'Yes, I can understand that,' Paniatowski said absently. Her mind had already moved on, searching for new lines of inquiry, and deciding that there were depressingly few open to her.

'Of course, if you want to talk to somebody who *was* here at the time, you could always pay a call on the Real McCoy.'

'The real *who*?'

'Sergeant Ted McCoy. He'd been in the army for donkey's years, but he said that of all the places he'd been, Cyprus was the absolute best. So when the time came for him to be demobbed, he married a local girl and stayed on. Bought himself a little taverna in Larnaca, he did, and called it the Real McCoy. It's a bit of a play on words, you see.'

'Yes,' Paniatowski agreed. 'I do see.'

'The place is a great favourite with the lads, when they're off duty. Some nights you can hardly get through the door.'

'When *exactly* did this Sergeant McCoy of yours leave the army?' Paniatowski asked.

'Let me see now,' Blaine said, scratching the top of his head. 'From what McCoy said to me the last time I was in his pub, I think it would have to have been around six years ago.'

Paniatowski climbed into the passenger seat of the Land Rover. 'Take me to the Real McCoy,' she said.

The inside of the Bygraves' house produced no surprises for Bob Rutter. It was, as it should have been, the aspiring middle-class home of an aspiring middle-class family. It was tidy and cared-for, and where corners had been cut, a valiant attempt had been made to disguise the fact.

There was nothing in Tom Bygraves' personal papers to suggest where he had gone – nothing to even hint that he had somewhere he *could have* gone – and after an hour, Rutter was prepared to admit defeat.

'I'm sorry,' he said to Mrs Bygraves, as if it were his fault that her husband had not left a paper trail.

'You did your best,' the woman said, as if *she* thought that it was his fault, but was trying not to blame him *too* much.

He did not want to leave with nothing, and it was the vague hope that he still might rescue a little from the visit which made him say, 'My chief inspector mentioned that one of the last things your husband did before he left was to light a small bonfire in the back garden, Mrs Bygraves.'

'Yes?'

'You don't happen to know what it was that he burned on it, do you?'

Mrs Bygraves shrugged, as if it were a stupid question – and Rutter silently agreed that it probably was.

'It was garden waste,' Rosemary Bygraves said. 'Leaves, grass cuttings, that kind of stuff.'

And suddenly, she was looking thoroughly ashamed of herself.

'Is anything the matter?' Rutter asked.

'We . . . we have this committee – the Brighter Neighbourhood Committee – and I'm one of the founder members,' Rosemary Bygraves said.

'I see,' Rutter replied – though he didn't.

'We drew up a set of rules which were designed to stop us from bothering the people who lived around us. One of them is that if we play the radio in the garden, we have to keep the volume very low. Another is that if we have a party, we must make sure there's no noise after eleven o'clock at night.'

'I'm not sure I'm following you,' Rutter admitted.

'And then there's the rule about fires,' Rosemary Bygraves said hurriedly. 'We can have fires in the garden, but only in the autumn, when there are a lot of leaves to burn. And even then only on Saturdays.'

'And this isn't autumn, and yesterday wasn't a Saturday,' Rutter said, catching on.

Rosemary Bygraves nodded. 'As soon as Tom had left, I went into the back garden and doused the fire. Isn't that terrible? My husband had gone, and all I could think about was what the neighbours would say about me breaking the rules.'

'We all do that,' Rutter said. 'We all worry over the little problems because we can't face the big ones.'

But though the sympathy in his voice was real enough, it was all he could do to restrain himself from pushing the woman aside and rushing straight into the back garden.

The first two men, who DC Colin Beresford had already ticked off on his morning list of visits, had been of absolutely no help to him at all.

'Yes, I remember Pugh and Lewis vaguely,' one of them had said. 'But they had their own mates, just as I had mine.'

'When I read in the paper that a Reg Lewis had been

murdered, the name did ring a bell,' the second had told him, 'but I never thought for a minute that it might be somebody I'd been in the army with. To tell you truth, I doubt if I could even put a face to the name, after all this time.'

The third man on Beresford's list was called Martin Murray, and he lived above his model shop on one of the quaint twisty old lanes in the centre of Whitebridge that the planners hadn't quite got around to gleefully pulling down yet.

The shop itself re-awakened the child in Beresford. Models of Second World War bomber and fighter planes, all of them beautifully painted, hung from the ceiling, as they re-fought old battles. Soldiers made of lead, and wearing uniforms from the Peninsular War, stood to attention on the numerous shelves which ran around the walls.

But it was the model railway, which took up most of the floor space between the counter and the door, that was the true marvel. There were tunnels and stations, signal boxes and level crossings. As the train made its slow graceful journey around the track, tiny figures watched it from the doorways of tiny houses, and little white sheep – no doubt frightened by the roar – seemed caught in the act of running away across painted fields.

'It's taken me six years to make,' said Martin Murray, noticing Beresford's fascination. 'Six long years, working way into the night, and all through the weekends.'

'It was worth it,' Beresford said, admiringly.

Murray smiled. 'Thank you.'

The man was probably still only in his late twenties, Beresford thought, but he looked a lot older. His face was round and pasty. His white curly hair had already started to desert his pate. His shoulders – perhaps due to spending so much time bent over his model railway – had developed a stoop. And if his eyesight had been as poor a few years ago as the thick lenses in his glasses seemed to indicate that it was now, he'd never have been accepted into the army in the first place.

'I want to ask you about Terry Pugh and Reg Lewis,' Beresford said.

'They're both dead,' Martin Murray told him, as if that were all he needed to know.

'Were you a close friend of theirs?'

'Who's to say? We think we know people, but we don't

really. We think we know ourselves, and then something happens to show us that we couldn't have been wronger about that.'

'Something happens?' Beresford repeated wonderingly. 'Like what?'

'It could be anything,' Murray told him. 'For example, you might think you love somebody – that you'd do anything in the world for them – but the moment the relationship becomes difficult for you, you find excuses for yourself and cast them aside.'

Beresford thought of the problems he was having with his mother – and shivered.

'Is that what happened to you?' he asked.

Murray shook his head. 'No, I've never really loved anybody, and nobody has ever really loved me. My personal revelation came more out of hatred than it did out of love.'

'Can I ask you what you mean by that?' Beresford asked.

'You can ask,' Murray replied. 'But I won't answer.'

'Do you have any idea why Terry Pugh and Reg Lewis should have been murdered?' Beresford wondered.

'Because it was meant to be,' Murray told him. 'Because once they had set their feet firmly on a particular road, there was only one possible destination.'

'What road are we talking about?'

'Do you know why I like spending so much time with my model railway?' Murray asked.

'No, but that's not really why . . .'

'It's because it creates a world of its own, a world which is both understandable and ordered. The train will go around this track, without mishaps, for ever. None of the cars will break down on the railway crossing, and be smashed into by the train. There'll be no bombs detonated on the station. The little people who watch the train are happy to go on doing just that. They feel no urge to go on the rampage with a Sten gun, killing everybody in their path.'

'It *is* only a model,' Beresford felt obliged to point out.

'Is it?' Murray countered. 'It seems to me to be much more than that. For me, it is an inspiration – a golden city to which we should aspire, in which evil and ugliness have no place.'

'What exactly happened in Cyprus?' Beresford demanded.

'In Cyprus? The train came off the track – and none of us who saw it happen have ever been able to put it back again.'

'You're not being very helpful,' Beresford said exasperatedly.

'Why should I be helpful?' Murray wondered. 'I don't have to answer to you.'

'Then who do you have to answer to?'

Murray smiled. 'To the model maker, of course.'

The rubbish heap was at the very end of the Bygraves' garden. It was a couple of feet high, and Mrs Bygraves had been right when she said it contained mostly leaves and grass cuttings.

If Tom Bygraves had bothered to set it alight properly, it would have burned out completely by the time his wife got back to it. But he'd been in a hurry, so he hadn't made a proper job, and though he was no expert on fires, Bob Rutter guessed that it had only been at the smouldering stage when Rosemary had poured the water on it.

Rutter squatted down, and began to carefully remove the blackened grass cuttings.

'What are you looking for?' he heard Rosemary Bygraves' voice ask behind him.

'I don't know,' he admitted.

Anything near the surface of the heap would probably have been destroyed, he thought, as he continued his painstaking work. But something that Bygraves had considered important enough to burn would also have been important enough to hide properly – deep down in the heap.

He found what he was looking for under a pile of orange peel.

A letter.

A *typed* letter.

The fire had damaged it, but parts of it were still legible.

Rutter stood up. 'I'm going to ring the police laboratory,' he told Mrs Bygraves, 'and I think you'd better come with me.'

'Why?'

Because I don't trust you not to mess with evidence while I'm away, Rutter thought.

'Because it will be better that way,' he said aloud.

'Have you . . . have you found something that will help to find my Tom?' Mrs Bygraves asked tremulously.

No, Rutter thought, but I may have found something that will help explain why he *went away*.

Nineteen

The Real McCoy Taverna was situated on the sea front in Larnaca. As the army Land Rover pulled up in front of it, Paniatowski noted that there were already a number of customers sitting at the tables outside the establishment, and that their main activity seemed to be gazing idly across the palm-lined promenade to the deep blue Mediterranean Sea which lay beyond it. They looked thoroughly contented with life, she thought – and why wouldn't they?

Inside, the taverna was darker and cooler. There were examples of local pottery on display in several niches in the walls, and photographs of visitors – apparently having an exceedingly good time – were stuck to the long mirror behind the counter. Heavy brass ceiling fans whirred overhead, and delicious smells of cooking wafted gently from the tiny kitchen which lay beyond the bar.

Ted McCoy himself was a large man, with broad shoulders and eyes as blue as the sea which was his neighbour. The eyes twinkled as he shook hands with Paniatowski, and beneath them a welcoming smile filled his broad face. It was hard to imagine that this man had once been a fearsome sergeant, the terror of new recruits.

'Are you here on business or pleasure, Sergeant?' McCoy asked from the other side of the bar, as he served Blaine and Paniatowski their drinks.

'Business,' Monika said. 'My mate Bill here thinks you might be able to help me with some information on men you might once have served with.'

McCoy's body was suddenly parade-ground stiff, and a steely look had entered his blue eyes.

He turned slightly, to face Bill Blaine. 'Is that right, Lance Corporal?' he asked in a voice which could have stopped a tank. 'You think I may be able to help with *information*? About men

I once *served* with?' The look on Blaine's face told its own story. The sudden dramatic change from Ted McCoy the genial host to Sergeant McCoy had left him completely pole-axed.

'Is that right?' McCoy repeated.

'I . . . well, you know . . .' Blaine mumbled.

McCoy turned his attention back on Monika Paniatowski. 'And suppose I did give you some information,' he said. 'Would I be getting any of the lads I mentioned into trouble?'

'Far from it, Mr McCoy,' Paniatowski promised, and though she hadn't flinched as Blaine had, she'd certainly wanted to.

McCoy opened the fridge behind him, and took out a bottle of Fix beer. There was a bottle opener lying to hand, but instead of using it he forced the metal cap off the bottle using only his thumb. It was a neat trick which was designed to impress – and it did.

'You're sure I wouldn't be causing them any grief?' he asked Paniatowski, before raising the bottle to his lips.

'Quite sure,' Paniatowski confirmed. 'In fact, by giving me information on them, you might just be saving their lives.'

Ted McCoy almost choked on the beer. 'You're joking, aren't you?' he asked, when the liquid had finally found the right channel and drained away.

'I wish I was,' Paniatowski told him.

'So how is anything I can tell you likely to prevent some poor bugger from getting the chop?' McCoy wondered.

'I'm afraid that at this stage of the investigation, I'm not at liberty to say,' Paniatowski replied.

'Suppose I was to say that unless you briefed me on what this was all about, I'd tell you nothing?'

'Then I'd be very disappointed.'

'But you still wouldn't tell me?'

'No, I wouldn't.'

McCoy was silent – and deep in thought – for at least a full minute.

Finally, he said, 'One of the things about being a sergeant for as long as I was one is that you learn to trust your own judgement about people. And it seems to me that even if you *won't* tell me what's going on, you're what the Yanks would call a pretty straight arrow.' He paused to take another swig of his Fix. 'So what do you want to know?'

*   *   *

Woodend looked down at the letter which officers from the forensic unit had rescued from the rubbish heap in Tom Bygraves' garden, and which was now sitting, safely and snugly, in the see-through plastic envelope. The right-hand side of the letter had been lost to the flames. The left side had been soaked by the water Rosemary Bygraves had poured on the heap in the interest of good-neighbourliness. Even so, the boffins had done a fine job, he thought. If he'd tried to do the same thing himself – with *his* ham-like hands - the bloody thing would probably have disintegrated.

He scanned the letter for the fifth or sixth time, then laid it on the desk, so that Rutter and Beresford, who had examined it a good few times themselves, could see it too.

> **READ THIS LETTER CARE...**
> **SEVEN YEARS AGO, YOU...**
> **RESPONSIBLE FOR A TERR...**
> **BEAR THE FULL CONS...**
> **BECAUSE OF WHAT YOU...**
> **HAS COME TO TAKE YOUR...**
> **WHITEBRIDGE POLICE HEAD...**
> **DO NOT DO SO, THERE AR...**
> **WILL BE USED.**
> **WHILE YOU STILL CAN.**

'Let's take it line by line, shall we?' Woodend suggested. 'The first one's easy enough, isn't it?'

Rutter and Beresford nodded.

'Read this letter carefully,' Colin Beresford said, putting both their thoughts into words.

'The second line talks about 'seven years ago',' Woodend said, 'an' I'd be willin' to bet my pension that what lay beyond the charred edge was: *you were in Cyprus*. Third line?' He grinned, despite himself. 'It could say: *you were responsible for a terrapin*, but I don't think so.'

'Could it be: *You were responsible for a terrible accident*'?' Bob Rutter suggested.

'Certainly a terrible *somethin'*,' Woodend agreed. 'And whatever it was, the writer's askin' Bygraves to take *the full consequences*.'

'And if he doesn't do it voluntarily, there are ways to make him do it?' Rutter wondered.

'In the light of what's happened to Pugh an' Lewis, I think it's more likely he was sayin' there are other ways to make him *pay*,' Woodend said.

'Do you think he threatened to hang them?' Rutter asked.

'He may possibly have mentioned the prospect of hangin',' Woodend said, 'but I don't really think there's enough space on the line for that kind of threat. Anyway, how would that fit in with the last few words that precede it? *There are ways of makin' you – hang*'?''

'You're right,' Rutter agreed. 'It isn't likely at all.'

'But there's no question about the last two lines,' Colin Beresford said. 'They have to be warning Bygraves that he should surrender himself to the police while he still can.'

'There's no *have to* about it,' Woodend cautioned. 'Given that half the letter's missin' we could have completely misinterpreted the whole thing.'

'Misinterpreted it?' Beresford repeated.

'Aye. For all we know, the complete letter could have said somethin' like, "Read this letter carefully. Seven years ago, your company sold me a sofa. I have not misused it, so you are responsible for the terrible condition it is in now, and must bear the consequences, because of what you promised . . ." He trailed off. 'You get the general idea, don't you?'

'But we don't believe that *is* what it said, do we?' Rutter asked.

'No, we don't,' Woodend agreed. 'We believe that this is a letter from a cold-blooded killer to a man who might well have become his latest victim by now. But does it help us at all? Does it get us any further on in our investigation than we were before it came into our possession?'

'Not really,' Rutter said gloomily.

'Do you remember a man called Terry Pugh?' Paniatowski asked Ted McCoy, as they faced each other across the counter of his bar.

'Terry Pugh? Came from Lancashire, like you sound as if you do yourself,' McCoy said immediately. 'Good with his hands. Was engaged to a girl from his home town, I think.'

'I'm very impressed,' Paniatowski said.

'Oh, it's not that difficult to recall the details, especially with a man like Private Pugh,' McCoy said modestly.

'From what I know of him, I wouldn't have thought he was really that memorable,' Paniatowski said.

'No, not for himself,' McCoy agreed. 'But, you see, he was a member of Matthews' Marauders.'

'What's that?' Paniatowski wondered. 'Some kind of special unit?'

McCoy laughed. 'Oh, it was special all right, but not *officially*, if you see what I mean.'

'No, I'm afraid I don't,' Paniatowski admitted.

'What made it stand out from the others was Jack Matthews himself, who was the finest non-commissioned officer it's ever been my privilege to serve with.'

'Who else was in the unit?'

McCoy scratched his head. 'Let me see now. There was Terry Pugh, as I've already mentioned, Reg Lewis, Tom Bygraves, Martin Murray, and, of course, poor bloody Mark Hough.'

Mark Hough! Who'd never once mentioned Matthews' Marauders in their conversations with him, Paniatowski thought.

'In what *way* was the unit special?' she asked.

'In the only way a unit *can* really be special in the army – it got involved in some bloody awful engagements with the enemy, and it survived the experience.'

'But that must have been true of many other units as well.'

'You're right. But no other unit got into as *many* engagements. And no other unit came out of them as unscathed as Matthews' Marauders did.'

'Unscathed?' Paniatowski repeated. 'What do you mean by that? Without casualties?'

'Partly that,' McCoy agreed. 'But there are other ways of being wounded, apart from being hit by a bullet.' He paused to take another swig of his beer. 'You can't really imagine what it's like to be caught in an ambush, unless you've experienced it yourself. You feel shattered when it's over. You know for a fact that your nerve's gone, and you don't think you'll ever get it back again. You usually do get it back, of course, but that takes time. Which is why I'd never even think of sending a unit out on patrol again for at least a week after an ambush – unless that unit happened to be Matthews' Marauders.'

'They were *that* impressive?' Paniatowski said.

'They were the best. But they also had what Napoleon thought was the most important quality in his generals.'

'And what quality was that?'

'Luck! But even their luck didn't last for ever. They blundered into an ambush one day, and Jack Matthews was killed. And then, the very same evening, Mark Hough fell out of the back of the Land Rover, and almost under the wheels of a lorry. The army investigators said he was lucky – there's that word again – not to have been killed, but I don't know whether he considered it lucky, because it must have been hard for a man who'd been as active as he'd been to be told that he'd never walk again.'

'How did the accident happen?'

'He was drunk as a skunk. They all were. They'd been out holding a wake for their fallen comrade. Can't blame them for getting drunk, though the Red Caps *could have* blamed them for stealing the Land Rover that Private Hough fell out of, if they'd had a mind to.'

'They *stole* a Land Rover?'

'Well, that's maybe a bit harsh. It was more like borrowing it without first getting permission – but even that's still a fairly serious offence under Standing Orders.'

'Were they punished for it?'

McCoy shook his head. 'No, for once the army chose to look the other way – to temper justice with mercy, as you might say. Everybody knew they'd taken Corporal Matthews's death hard, and what with Mark Hough getting crippled as well, it would have been almost inhuman to lock the rest of them up in the glasshouse. So what the authorities did instead was to ship them out immediately. All except for poor bloody Private Hough, of course. It was months before they dared move him – and even when they did, they had to fly a special ambulance plane in from England.'

'Have you got a phone?' Paniatowski asked.

'Over there on the wall.' He smiled. 'What's the matter? Missing your boyfriend all ready?'

Paniatowski smiled back. 'How did you guess?' she asked.

And then she went over to the phone and rang Whitebridge CID.

*   *   *

A cloud of gloom hung over Woodend's office, and for about five minutes nobody had said a word.

Finally, it was Beresford who spoke.

'If we could find the typewriter that the letter was written on, we could prove it was a match,' he said.

'True enough,' Rutter said, 'but to find it, we'd first have to know where to look.'

'Are we all in agreement that the letter Terry Pugh received – the one he kept readin' at work – is probably an exact copy of this one?' Woodend asked.

'Yes,' Rutter said.

'Almost bound to be,' Beresford added.

'So chances are that Reg Lewis got one as well. And so did the rest of the people on the list – if there *is* anybody else on the bloody list!'

The phone on his desk rang, and Woodend picked it up. 'Yes? . . . Good work! . . . No, I don't need to write that down . . . Have you come any closer to finding out exactly what ? . . . No? . . . Well, keep looking.'

He replaced the phone on its cradle. 'That was Monika,' he said.

'Has she . . . ?' Rutter began.

'She still doesn't know what this terrible "accident" or terrible "thing" that happened in Cyprus actually was,' Woodend told him, 'but at least she's been able to add a couple of names to our list.'

Twenty

There are six of them in the Land Rover, as it bumps its way along a dusty road at the base of the mountains.

Often, on such an expedition, they will be following up a lead provided by one of the legion of informers who operate on the island. But not this time. This foray is mainly to maintain 'visibility'.

'We have to show the Cyps that we're still around and have no intention of going away,' the briefing officer told them before they set out. 'We have to show them that we're still in charge.'

'And we have to hope that they don't notice that when night falls, we retreat behind our razor wire fences,' the men think – though they say nothing.

So the expedition's aim is not to engage with the enemy. It is simply to be visible. But if the unit does just happen to blunder across a group of EOKA terrorists, then it will be expected to do what it has been trained to do.

In the front of the Land Rover are Corporal Matthews and Private Bygraves. Matthews is unquestionably their leader, and not only because of the stripes he wears on his sleeve. The other men respect his calm and steadiness, and know the main reason the unit coheres so well is because of his influence. Bygraves, on the other hand, is much more a follower than a leader – competent enough to obey orders conscientiously, but unlikely to ever initiate any of his own.

The four men in the back of the Land Rover are playing a favourite game of theirs, which is called, 'What if?'

In many ways, it is a childish game, or at best an adolescent one. They know this, but are also silently aware that its very nature is perhaps its greatest strength. Because it enables them to face their fears without admitting that they are real fears at all – because it allows them to discuss these gut-churning concerns as if they were of no more importance than youthful pimples or squeaky voices.

'What if?' Murray begins. 'What if one of us was killed by an orthodox priest?'

'That's a difficult one,' Pugh says.

'No, it isn't,' Lewis says scornfully. 'If he kills one of us, he's the enemy – and if he's the enemy, he deserves to die himself. But him being a priest would make a difference to how I killed him.'

'How would it make a difference?' Murray asks.

'I'd make sure he died really slowly,' Lewis says with some relish.

'Why?'

'Because I used to be a choir boy, and that taught me to hate all priests.'

The others are slightly uncomfortable with the last comment, but then they often uncomfortable with the things that Lewis says. They do not think about their future beyond the army very often, but when they do, none of them really sees Lewis as being a part of it.

'Say the priest didn't actually do the killing,' Mark Hough suggests. 'Say he just facilitated it.'

'Facilitated it?' Lewis repeats. 'What the bloody hell does that mean?'

'Say he didn't do it himself, but still allowed it to happen.'

'You mean, say he led us into a trap?' Pugh asks.

'Either that, or while he didn't have anything to do with setting it up, he didn't warn us that there was a trap.'

'He's still guilty,' Lewis says. 'He still has to die.'

'I'm not so sure of that,' says Murray, who tends to take a wider view of most things than any of his comrades do – who sometimes seems capable of looking down from a great height at the situation they all find themselves in.

'Not sure!' Lewis repeats, contemptuously

'This is his country, after all.' Murray argues. 'He didn't invite us here, and I don't see why he's under any obligation to protect us.'

'We're British soldiers,' says Lewis, who has no time for the finer points of debate. 'And you're either for us, or you're against us.'

A girl, who looks no more than fifteen years old, suddenly appears at the side of the road and waves frantically at them to stop.

'Men are here!' she says, when the Land Rover slows to a halt and draws level with her.

'Men?' Corporal Matthews repeats. 'What men?'

'In village.' She points to a cluster of red-tiled houses about half a mile away. 'With guns,' she adds urgently.

'Are these men locals?' Matthews asks.

'Not understand.'

'Do you know them? Are they from the village?'

The girl shakes her head. 'No, not from village. Strangers. They come to rob our food.'

'They must be running very short of supplies in the mountains if they're prepared to take a chance like this,' Matthews tells his men. He turns back to the girl. 'Are they still in the village? Or have they gone?'

'Still in village,' the girl tells him. 'Go to taverna. Have many drinks.'

'How many of them are there?' Matthews asks.

The girl holds up her hand, and shows him three fingers. 'That many.'

'So there's three of them, and they're probably half-pissed by now,' Matthews says thoughtfully. 'What does your village look like?' he asks the girl. 'Can you draw us a map?'

The girl nods. She picks up a twig, and begins scratching in the dirt.

'Street,' she says, pointing to two parallel lines she has made.

'Understood,' Matthews said.

She draws a rough rectangle half way along the lines. 'That is . . . I don't know words.'

'The village square?' Matthews suggests.

'Yes, square. Taverna is on square. Men in taverna.'

'This is what we'll do,' Matthews tells his men. 'If we drive any closer, they'll probably hear us, so we'll leave the vehicle here with Bygraves, and the rest of us will make our way into the village on foot. Pugh and me will approach it from the west, the rest of you from the east. We'll converge on the taverna in exactly twenty minutes. With any luck, we'll capture these bastards without a shot being fired. Have you all got that?'

The men nod.

'Once we've got the Cyps in custody, I'll fire a single shot in the air,' Matthews tells Bygraves. 'That's the signal for you to slam your clog down on the accelerator, and get to the village as fast as you can. Drive straight to the square. We'll load up the prisoners, and be out of there before anybody knows what's happening.'

'What if there's more than one shot?' Bygraves asks, worried that he might find himself in a situation where he alone might have to take a decision.

'If there's more than one shot, it probably means that something's gone seriously wrong, my old son,' Matthews tells him calmly. 'In which case, we'll want you there even faster.'

The sound of the shot comes much earlier than it should have done, and it is rapidly followed by several more.

'Oh my God!' Bygraves moans, as he puts the Land Rover into gear, and presses down hard on the accelerator, exactly as the corporal has told him to.

It is hard to be sure of exactly what it is he is hearing over the roar of the engine, but as he gets closer to the village, Bygraves becomes convinced that it is more shooting.

'Please let it be all right!' he prays. 'Please! Let it be all right!

He has reached the edge of the village. The street is empty. There are no old women sitting in their doorways on short-legged chairs, no children playing in the street. No donkeys. No dogs. There is not even a chicken – and there is never a time when there is not even a chicken.

Everybody knew this was going to happen long before it actually did, Bygraves thinks.

Everybody but us.

He enters the square, and sees his unit immediately. They are crouched down, using the tables outside the taverna for cover, and firing across the square. But one of them is not firing at all. One of them is lying on the ground, not moving. And Bygraves' stomach lurches, as he realizes that that man is Corporal Matthews.

He slams on the brakes, and stops next to the taverna. Hough and Lewis continue to fire at the unseen enemy, but Pugh and Murray pick up Corporal Matthews and carry him to the vehicle. Once they have laid Matthews in the back, Pugh and Murray start firing again, and under the cover that provides, Hough and Lewis rush back to the Land Rover, and scramble in.

'Go, go, go!' Hough screams.

Bygraves slams the Land Rover into reverse, and as the tyres scream their protest, backs down the street as fast as the engine will allow. Only once they are clear of the village does he change gear, performing the tightest three-point turn he has ever managed, and speeding away.

The men in the back of the vehicle are huddled over Corporal Matthews. But they are not trying to help him - because he is beyond that.

Twenty-One

Priscilla Charlton looked up from the report she was studying on her desk, and smiled prettily at Woodend.

'How nice to see you again so soon, Chief Inspector Woodend,' she said. Then the smile faded, and she added, 'Even if the reason for your visit isn't exactly a pleasant one.'

He could understand Mark Hough's infatuation with the girl, Woodend thought. Truth to tell, he wasn't really all *that* far from being infatuated with her himself.

'Is your boss in?' he asked.

'He's nearly *always* in,' Priscilla said, a little severely. 'If he's not in the office, he's in his apartment, which is just above it. He works *far* too hard. I'm always telling him that. But why should he listen to me? *I'm* only his secretary.' A look of regret came to her face. 'I'm sorry, I should never have said that.'

'No?'

'No! He's not doing it just for himself – he believes it's his responsibility to keep his workers in a job, and sometimes I think he finds that responsibility very heavy indeed.'

Ah, to be young and idealistic, Woodend thought. To imagine that people always do things for the best of possible motives. But maybe he was being unfair. Maybe Hough was one of those men who *did* take his responsibilities seriously.

'And then there's all those cultural organizations that rely on him for support,' Priscilla continued. 'He once told me that if he couldn't be like the Borgias, he could at least be like the Medicis.' She frowned prettily. 'Do you know what that means?'

'Aye, surprisingly enough, I do,' Woodend said. 'I think I must've read it on the back of a Corn Flakes packet or somethin'.'

'Then I wish you'd explain it to me,' Priscilla Charlton said.

'The Borgias an' the Medicis were powerful families in Italy, a long time ago. The Borgias were great fighters – even though one of them was the Pope – but the Medicis put most of their efforts into encouragin' the arts.'

'How sad,' Priscilla Charlton said.

'Sad?'

'That Mr Hough would so much like to be one thing, but has no choice but to be the other.'

'At least he's doin' *somethin'*,' Woodend pointed out. 'At least he's doing what he *can*.'

Priscilla Charlton smiled gratefully at him. 'Thank you,' she said.

It was all suddenly getting a little too heavy, Woodend thought. He cleared his throat and said, 'So, if he's in, can I see him?'

'I'll just buzz through and inquire,' Priscilla told him. 'But there shouldn't be any problem, because I'm sure he wants Terry Pugh's murderer caught as soon as possible.' She smiled yet again, and the corners of her mouth dimpled. 'Besides,' she added, 'he *likes* you.'

An' I like him, an' all, Woodend realized.

Woodend's suspicions about the purpose of the two metal pillars connected by the steel bar, which he had noticed the last time he was there, were confirmed the moment he entered Mark Hough's office. Hough had parked the wheelchair under the bar, and, using only the power of his arms, was raising himself out of his seat and then lowering himself back into it.

'It's a terrible nuisance, doing this,' he said, puffing a little from the exertion. 'It gets in the way of serious work *far* too much. But my doctor says it has to be done, and I'd be a fool to pay him so much money and then not listen to his advice, wouldn't I?'

He lowered himself into the wheelchair again, and released his grip on the bar.

'Don't stop for me,' Woodend said.

'Glad for an excuse to give it up,' Hough told him. 'It's harder work than it looks.' He paused for a second, then continued, 'What can I do for you this time, Chief Inspector?'

'Terry Pugh, Reg Lewis, Tom Bygraves, Jack Matthews,

Martin Murray, an' you!' Woodend said, slowly and precisely. 'What's the first thought that comes into your head when you hear those names?'

'That three of them were murdered,' Mark Hough said, without any hesitation.

'That's funny,' Woodend told him.

'Is it? Why?'

'Because as I was drivin' over here, I was thinkin' about what your first thought would be, an' the answer that I came up with was Matthews' Marauders.'

Hough smiled. 'Well, you have been doing your homework, haven't you, Chief Inspector?'

'Aye, I have,' Woodend agreed. 'You formed your own little army within the larger army, didn't you?'

'Yes, I suppose we did. In fact, though I may not have used those exact words to you the last time you visited me, I certainly described us in somewhat similar terms.'

'That's true, you did,' Woodend agreed. 'Did you know that Tom Bygraves had gone missin'?'

'No, I didn't.'

'But you don't sound at all surprised that he has.'

Hough smiled again, perhaps a little sadly this time. 'Don't I?'

'What happened in Cyprus, seven years ago?'

'A lot of things happened, Chief Inspector, including my losing the use of my legs.'

'You got one of the letters yourself, didn't you?' Woodend asked.

'No,' Hough said.

'Wrong answer!' Woodend told him.

'Then what's the right one?'

'The right answer is, "What letters are you talking about, Chief Inspector Woodend?"'

Hough sighed. 'All right, if that will make you happy,' he said. 'What letters are you talking about, Chief Inspector Woodend?'

'The letters which reminded you of what you'd done in Cyprus, and advised you to give yourselves up to the police.'

'You've lost me,' Hough said.

'No, I haven't,' Woodend contradicted him. 'Have you thought through the implications of what's in those letters,

Mr Hough? Terry Pugh and Reg Lewis are already dead, Tom Bygraves might be, an' you – a man in a wheelchair – could well be the next man on the list.'

'That *is* a disturbing thought,' Hough said.

'Then why don't you *sound* disturbed?'

'Possibly because I am better able to take care of myself than you seem to think.'

'Indeed?' Woodend asked.

'Indeed!' Hough agreed.

'Would you mind tellin' me how?'

'One of the few sports still left open for me to compete in is competitive pistol shooting. And I'm really rather good at it.'

'What you're tellin' me, in a roundabout way, is that you have a gun?' Woodend asked.

'Exactly. A fully-licensed, perfectly legal, gun.'

'An' that you're more than willin' to use it to protect yourself?'

'As I understand it – and I'm sure you'll correct me if I'm wrong – the only justification for killing someone, under English law, is that your own life is threatened and flight is not an option.'

'Yes, that's more or less it,' Woodend agreed.

'Well, flight *isn't* an option for me, is it? I can move quite quickly in this chariot of mine, but nowhere near as quickly as most men can run.'

'Do you know what I think?' Woodend asked.

'How could I?'

'I think you don't *want* us to catch the man who murdered two – or possibly three – of your old comrades.'

'Then if that's true, I must be a very heartless creature, mustn't I, Chief Inspector?'

'An' the *reason* you don't want us to catch him is that you'd like him to come after you, so that you can shoot him.'

'There's a bill going through the Houses of Parliament at this very moment to abolish the death penalty for capital crimes,' Hough said. 'It is almost certain to become law by the end of the year. There will be no more hangings in England – at least, not judicial ones.'

'An' your point is that whoever killed your mates *deserves* to be executed,' Woodend said.

'An eye for an eye, and a tooth for a tooth,' Hough said.

'I've never had a great interest in the Bible, but it does seem to me that that particular statement makes a great deal of sense.'

'You can't simply ignore the law, an' go huntin' down killers yourself,' Woodend pointed out.

'Indeed I can't,' Hough agreed. 'I'd need legs to do that, wouldn't I? So the killer is in absolutely no danger from me – unless he seeks to make me his next victim.'

'What *did* happen in Cyprus?' Woodend asked.

Hough smiled again. 'Why are you so interested?' he wondered.

'Partly because you seem so reluctant to tell me about it,' Woodend countered.

'I assume that since you've come up with the names of what it pleases you to call "an army within an army", you have someone already in Cyprus making inquiries,' Hough said.

'That's right, I have.'

'Who?'

'Sergeant Paniatowski.'

Hough nodded. 'A good choice. She's a bright girl, and I'm sure she'll find out all you need to know.'

'You don't seem particularly bothered by *that*, either,' Woodend said.

'I'm not.'

'May I ask why?'

'Because by the *time* she finds out, I'll most probably have done what I need to do.'

Twenty-Two

There was an air-conditioning unit in Captain Howerd's office – Monika Paniatowski could see it, clearly projecting out of the wall – but instead of the happy humming and a cooling chill it should have been producing, there was only silence and stickiness in the room.

Maybe Howerd left it switched off because he liked to see the people who were sitting at the other side of his desk begin to sweat, she thought. Maybe he did it to show that a 'real' man like him could stand any amount of heat and discomfort. Maybe, even, it was not working simply because it had broken down. Whatever the reason, there was no escaping the fact that the office was an extremely unpleasant place to be.

Captain Howerd did not look exactly pleasant, either. Paniatowski searched her brain for the best word to describe the expression of his face, and finally settled on 'glowering'.

'You have only been on the island for a few hours, yet you are already putting in a request for access to our confidential files,' the captain said.

Paniatowski tried to ignore the beads of sweat which were already running down her brow.

'You're quite right, I am putting in a request,' she agreed. Then, after a pause in which Howerd had said nothing, she added, 'And am *I* right that you are refusing to grant that request, Captain?'

'No, you are not,' Howerd countered. 'At least, I'm not refusing *yet*. It is still conceivable that you can persuade me you have good reasons for wishing to see the files.'

'Still conceivable, is it?' Paniatowski asked, deadpan.

'But my problem with processing it, Sergeant Paniatowski, is that, try as hard as I might, I still fail to understand how you could possibly have amassed enough information, in such a short space of time, to merit such a request.'

He was using convolution and verbiage as a barricade, Paniatowski thought – which was just what men who found themselves in difficult situations often did. But he still did not *look* concerned.

'So that's your problem, is it?' she asked.

'That is correct.'

'Well, *my* problem is that, try as hard as *I* might, I fail to understand what would have prompted the army to ship four men out of here at extremely short notice, just a few hours after they had taken a vehicle without permission, and been involved in an accident in which the fifth member of their little group was seriously – and permanently – injured.'

Howerd frowned, but there was no sign of moisture in the furrows that created on his brow, and Paniatowski found herself speculating that perhaps, instead of blood, he had ice water running through his veins.

'Shipped out at short notice?' Howerd repeated musingly. 'I'm afraid I have absolutely no idea what you're talking about.'

'Of course you haven't,' Paniatowski said, as a drop of sweat fell from her face and landed with a plop on the desk. 'I wouldn't expect you to. You weren't here at the time that I'm referring to, Captain. Probably nobody who's currently serving in this camp . . .'

'In this Sovereign Base Area,' Howerd interrupted disapprovingly.

'. . . nobody who's currently serving in this Sovereign Base Area,' Paniatowski corrected herself, 'was here back then. But there will be records, compiled by people who *were* here then, won't there? The army prides itself on its records.'

Howerd sighed. 'Which particular records do you wish to see?'

'The service records of five private soldiers - Privates Pugh, Murray, Hough, Bygraves and Lewis.'

'Those records may no longer be lodged in the Sovereign Base Area,' Howerd said.

'Possibly not. But you won't know until you've looked for them, will you, Captain?'

'Anything else you'd like to get your eager little hands on, Sergeant Paniatowski?' Howerd asked, cranking up his already obvious contempt a notch further.

'Yes,' Paniatowski said, ignoring his tone. 'I'd like to see the report filed by the MPs who arrested the men I've just mentioned.'

'Do you know for certain that they *were* arrested?'

'No.'

'Well, then . . .

'But it would be strange if they *weren't* arrested, after stealing army property, wouldn't it?'

'I have only your word for it that any army vehicle was actually stolen,' Howerd said.

'And my *source's* word.'

'Who exactly is this "source" of yours?'

'An English soldier, who was here – in this *Sovereign Base Area* – at the time I'm referring to.'

'He may be playing you for the fool, Sergeant – having a joke at your expense. Or perhaps he's doing no more than trying to find a way to get into your knickers. Yes, that may be it. Perhaps all he wants is to "give you one". Or perhaps he's already "given you one", as a reward for the spurious information he's supplied you with.'

Now it was crudity, rather than verbosity, from which he was erecting his barricade, Paniatowski thought. And now he *was* starting to sweat.

'Strangely enough, the subject of "giving me one" never came up,' she said, almost sweetly – almost virginally. 'Or perhaps it's not so strange at all, since he's far too responsible a man to lie about such a serious matter, even if that would have given him the opportunity to bury the sausage.'

Howerd grimaced. 'I would not have expected such language from a so-called lady,' he said.

'And I would not have expected a so-called gentleman to set me off on that path in the first place,' Paniatowski countered.

Howerd searched around for another line of attack. 'You described this source of yours as responsible. Does that mean that he's an officer?'

'Are officers the *only* soldiers who can act responsibly?'

'Yes, based on my considerable experience in the army, I would have to say that they are.'

'All right, if you insist on backing me into a corner, I'll admit he *was* an officer,' Paniatowski lied.

'In that case, he was probably a very junior officer – one

who was not able to see the whole picture, as his superiors undoubtedly would have done.'

'What whole picture?'

'We were fighting a guerrilla war at the time, Sergeant Paniatowski. The men were under a great deal of pressure. So if a few of them *did* choose to bend the rules a little, it may have been decided by their superiors to take into account the stress they were under, and not to punish them too severely.'

'I see,' Paniatowski said.

Howerd smirked. 'I thought you might – in the end.'

'But sending them home can hardly have been regarded as a punishment *at all*,' Paniatowski said. 'Besides, I always thought that the tougher the situation, the more it became important to maintain strict army discipline.'

'You're a civilian,' Captain Howerd said impatiently. 'How could you possibly understand what it's like to be shot at, day after day? And when, on top of that, you lose a comrade like Corporal Matthews . . .'

He clamped his mouth so tightly shut that Paniatowski almost fancied she could hear his teeth crack.

'What was that?' she asked.

'What was what?' Howerd responded.

'You mentioned Corporal Matthews.'

'I was talking about what it's like to lose men in the field, Sergeant Paniatowski,' Howerd said, in a harshly rebuking tone. 'And if I happened to mention one of those brave men by name, it was probably because I saw his name on the list of the Fallen.'

'It's a long list, isn't it?' Paniatowski asked.

'Long enough. And every man who died did so in order that people like you could keep their freedom. So please don't insult those men's memory now by abusing that freedom.'

'It's a long list, but the name you remembered was Matthews's,' Paniatowski mused.

'That kind of thing happens. One name happens to stick in your mind, for some reason. You wouldn't understand the process, because you've never been under fire.'

'And did that list also tell you that the men who Matthews was with at the time he died also happen to be the ones I'm interested in?'

Captain Howerd was swollen with rage. 'I will process your

request for files, because that is what the War Office has ordered me to do,' he said. 'But until I receive instructions to the contrary, I can see no reason to tolerate having you in my office – so get out, and don't come back!'

Paniatowski rose to her feet. 'Thank you for that little talk, Captain Howerd,' she said. 'It's been most *illuminating*.'

When Woodend opened the door of the model shop and stepped inside, the old-fashioned brass bell rang loudly to announce his presence, but Martin Murray, who was bent over his huge model railway, retouching the scenery with a small and delicate paint brush, did not even look up.

'We're closed,' the shop owner said.

'Not to me, you're not,' Woodend told him.

With infinite care, Murray laid the paintbrush down and finally raised his head.

'You must be the police,' he said.

'Aye, I am,' Woodend agreed. 'But not the wet-behind-the-ears, butter-wouldn't-melt-your-mouth variety that you've had callin' on you before. I'm not a nice young lad like DC Beresford, I'm DCI Woodend – an' I'm a bit rough around the edges.'

Murray gave him a watery smile. 'Do you think you can frighten me?' he asked.

'Not as much as that mad Greek bugger who's out there somewhere can frighten you, no,' Woodend admitted. 'But I'm doin' my very best, given the limited amount of menace that I have at my disposal.' He paused. 'Why didn't you tell my lad what this was all about, when he came round this mornin'?'

'For the same reason I won't tell you,' Murray replied. 'Because it has nothing at all to do with you.'

'You're wrong there,' Woodend told him. 'When people get killed on my patch, it reflects badly on me.'

'I can't be bothered about that,' Murray said. 'My only concern must be my model.'

And he was just itching to get back to it, Woodend thought.

'Tell me about the model,' he said.

'Why should you be interested?'

'Because I'm interested in all *kinds* of things.'

Murray looked at him closely for the first time, as if trying to assess whether he was telling the truth or not.

'Very well,' he said finally, and a dreamy look came into his eyes. 'When I first started work on it, I thought it would take me six months or a year.' He laughed. 'How little I knew.'

'How long *did* it take you to finish it?'

'It's *never* been finished. There's always something more to do – some new way of improving it. I paint in a small lake, because I think it will look pretty, then realize it will make the land around it marshy, so I have to re-route the rail tracks. I read in a magazine about a better way of making model trees, and all the trees I've made so far have to go.'

'Doesn't it seem like rather a lot of effort?' Woodend asked.

'To strive to create a world that I can feel comfortable in? It seems like almost no effort at all.'

'You must really regret what happened in Cyprus,' Woodend said.

'I do regret it. I often wish it had been me, not Corporal Matthews, who caught the bullet.'

'I'm not talkin' about the ambush,' Woodend said.

'I know you're not,' Murray countered. 'But I *still* wish I'd been the one to get shot.'

'Still, when you're workin' on your model, everythin's all right, isn't it, Mr Murray?'

Murray shook his head. 'No. But at least it's *bearable*. And now, if you'll excuse me, I must get on and finish my work.'

'Finish it?' Woodend repeated. 'I thought you said it would never be finished.'

'No, I said it never *had been*,' Murray corrected him. 'But now it must be. However imperfect, an end has to be reached.'

'Because you fully expect to be murdered?'

'Perhaps.'

'An' yet you're not prepared to do anythin' at all that might prevent your death?'

'There's not a great deal I *can* do. I have put myself on the track, and the train will come, whether I will it or not.'

'You make me sick!' Woodend said.

'I make myself sick, too, most of the time,' Murray said mildly. 'But perhaps I won't make myself sick for very much longer.'

'For God's sake, be a man!' Woodend said exasperatedly. 'Don't just take what's being thrown at you! Fight back!'

'Perhaps I don't want to fight back.'

'I can't approve of what your friend Mark Hough's tryin' to do, but I can't stop myself admirin' him for tryin' to do it, either,' Woodend said.

'And just what is Mark trying to do?'

'Hasn't he told you?'

'No.'

'You mean to say that the two of you – who are probably the only two men from your unit still left alive – haven't been in touch?'

'Why should we have been?'

'I'd have thought that was obvious.'

'We have nothing to say to each other that has not already been said more than once.'

'I'll tell you what your pal Mark's doin', whether or not,' Woodend said. 'He's got a pistol, an' he's keepin' it by his side at all times. He *wants* the Greek to come for him, and when he does, he intends to kill him.'

Murray laughed, and continued to laugh until the tears ran down his bulbous cheeks.

'I wasn't aware that I'd said anythin' funny,' Woodend told him.

Murray made a concerted effort to rein in his laughter.

'I'm sorry,' he said, when he had it completely under control. 'That was very rude of me.'

'Well, now you've calmed down, maybe you can explain the joke,' Woodend suggested.

'Do you really believe what you've just said?' Murray asked. 'That Mark *wants* the Greek to come after him?'

'Yes, I do,' Woodend said seriously. 'From his perspective, it would seem to make perfect sense.'

Murray shook his head slowly from side to side. 'I wouldn't have believed it possible,' he said. 'You really don't know *anything* of what's been going on, do you?'

Twenty-Three

In accordance with the privileges reluctantly conceded to her by Captain Howerd, Paniatowski had a perfect right to drink in the Sergeants' Mess, if that was what she wished. But she didn't wish it. Instead, she chose to go to the NAFFI canteen with Lance Corporal Blaine, and, once there, she ignored the vodka which was smiling at her from the shelf, and asked for a nice cold glass of beer.

'Our Captain Howerd gave you the sweat treatment, did he?' Blaine asked, as he watched Paniatowski gulp the beer down.

'That's his standard trick, is it?' Paniatowski asked.

'One of many,' Blaine replied. 'The man knows more tricks than the most experienced whore in a Port Said brothel.' He blushed the moment the words were out of his mouth. 'Sorry, Monika. I forgot myself there.'

'Don't worry, I've heard worse,' Paniatowski assured him. She took another sip of her beer – a smaller one, this time. 'I've got a real problem on my hands, Bill,' she continued.

'And what problem might that be?'

'I don't think Captain Howerd's going to show me any of the records that I want to see.'

'Doesn't he *have to* show them to you? I thought you had friends who had friends in high places.'

'So I do. And Captain Howerd has to go through the motions of obeying their instructions. But he knows that he only has to stall long enough, and the information will reach me too late to do me any bloody good.'

'What records are you interested in?'

'I'd like to know what happened the night that those soldiers who Ted McCoy told us about stole that Land Rover. Which means I'd like to see the MPs' arrest report. But Howerd's not about to give that up without a very long and very bloody struggle.'

'Maybe you could approach the problem from another angle,' Bill Blaine suggested tentatively.

'What other angle?'

'Well, you can't find out what happened to the men, but maybe the vehicle's got its own story to tell.'

'Its own story?'

'There'll be a service log, won't there? And if anything happened to the vehicle in question that night, it will have been duly noted down.' Blaine suddenly began to look rather unsure of himself. 'I mean, I know that might seem like a bit of a long shot,' he continued, 'and after all, you're the one who's the detective, not me, but . . .'

'That's brilliant!' Paniatowski said.

'Is it?' Blaine asked. 'Are you sure?'

'*Absolutely* brilliant,' Paniatowski confirmed. 'Provided, of course, you've worked out a way to get your hands on the service log for of the particular Land Rover I'm interested in. Have you?'

'It might be a bit tricky,' Blaine admitted, 'but if we play it carefully, I think we should be able to manage it.'

Woodend, Rutter and Beresford were sitting at their usual table in the Drum and Monkey, though it did not quite *look* like the usual table, without a vodka glass in evidence.

They had been silent for some time, each one wrapped up in his own thoughts – though it was only in Woodend's case that the thoughts had been focused exclusively on the investigation.

'The thing is,' the Chief Inspector said, breaking the silence, 'both Hough an' Murray seem perfectly willin' to set themselves up as targets for our murderer – though, of course, for very different reasons. Well, I'm simply not goin' to let that happen. I will not allow Martin Murray to *be* killed, whatever his own personal inclination, an' I will not allow Mark Hough *to kill* the Greek, however much he might like to.'

'I thought you said that Martin Murray *didn't* think Hough wanted the Greek to come to him,' Rutter commented. 'I thought you said he thought it was very funny that that was what you *did* think.'

'Aye, well, when you've two conflictin' statements, you have to choose which one to believe, don't you?' Woodend said. 'An' which one would *you* believe? Are you prepared to take the word of a man who's built up his own thrivin' business *from a wheelchair*, and who – according to the inquiries I've made – is indeed a crack shot with a pistol? Or would you prefer to accept the ideas put forward by a pasty-faced bugger who spends his whole life playin' with model trains?'

'When you put it like that, there doesn't seem to be much of a contest,' Beresford said.

'No, there isn't,' Woodend agreed.

And yet, even though he sounded assured, he had to admit to himself that Murray's words had unnerved him – that even if the man was a complete nutter, his amusement had been genuine, and his belief that Woodend had got it all wrong seemed to be firmly held.

'Anyway, this is how it's goin' to be,' he told Rutter and Beresford. 'I've arranged for six officers – six *highly reliable* officers – to be posted outside Murray's shop, an' another six outside Hough's factory, which is also his home. Even if the Greek's got an accomplice – an' I don't believe he has – the two potential victims should be as safe as houses.'

'We don't yet know what's happened to Tom Bygraves,' Rutter reminded him.

'No, we don't,' Woodend agreed. 'But there are two possibilities, aren't there? The first is that he's escaped, an' is lyin' low somewhere. The second is that the Greek's got hold of him, an' is keepin' him prisoner.'

'Isn't there a third possibility?' Beresford asked.

'An' what might that be?'

'That the Greek's already killed him.'

'No, that isn't a possibility at all, lad,' Woodend said.

'Why not?'

'Because if the Greek *had* killed him, we'd have heard all about it by now. This isn't a killer who likes to hide his victims away – he wants to put them right out there on display, where as many people as possible can see them.'

In peacetime, the military motor pool kept almost as regular hours as any civilian business, and for the previous fifty minutes it had been winding down, so the only person still there when Blaine and Paniatowski arrived was the corporal responsible for locking up.

When he saw them approaching, a grin spread across the corporal's face. 'Well, look who's here, ' he called out. 'Strike me dead if it isn't the best centre forward what it's ever been my privilege to play alongside. How many goals was it you scored in that last match against the Cyps, Blainey?'

Bill Blaine looked suitably modest. 'You already know how many goals it was,' he said.

'I still like to hear it said out loud – from the bloke who actually slammed them in.'

'It was four.'

'Four! A hat trick plus one.' The corporal nodded his head in admiration. 'So how have you been, me old mate?'

'Not half bad,' Bill Blaine replied. 'Don't mind me dropping in on you like this, just as you're closin', do you?'

'Not at all,' the corporal said, 'especially when you've got a gorgeous lady in tow. Who is she anyway, this vision of loveliness?'

'Detective Sergeant Monika Paniatowski, of the Central Lancs Police,' Blaine said.

'Ooh, the law!' the corporal said, with mock concern.

Paniatowski gave him one of her widest – and sexiest – smiles. 'Just call me Monika,' she invited.

'I'll do that,' the corporal replied. 'And I'm Phil Campion, but everybody around here calls me Campo.'

'The thing is, Monika would like to get a quick shufty at some of your service logs,' Bill Blaine said.

Campo's face clouded over, ever so slightly. 'Have you got authorization?' he asked.

Blaine laughed.

'Authorization?' he repeated, as if the idea that it would be required had never even occurred to him. 'Why would we need authorization to have a gander at details of tyre pressure checks and oil changes?'

The cloud was still floating lightly across Campo's face. 'Well, regulations is regulations,' he said dubiously.

'Where our difficulty stems from, you see, is that Monika's had a bit of a run-in with "Frankie" Howerd,' Blaine explained, 'and now he's doing everything within his power to prevent her from doing her job properly.'

Campo nodded. 'She's not the first that's happened to,' he said. 'Howerd's a real swine.'

'And though she *could* go over his head – because she's got friends in the War Office – she's only here on the island for a short while, so there's not really enough time for that. That's why I was wondering if you'd let us have a quick peek now.'

'Just the service logs?' Campo asked, still sounding doubtful. 'No more than that?'

'No more than that,' Monika agreed. 'And I don't even want to look at *recent* ones, Campo. The ones that I'm interested in are from seven years ago.' She paused for a moment. 'You will still have them, won't you?'

'Oh, we'll have them, right enough,' Campo assured her. 'The army never throws *anything* away.'

'We shouldn't need more than ten minutes all told,' Bill Blaine said, sensing a weakening on his footballing friend's part.

'The service logs are all on that shelf over there,' the corporal said, pointed with his thumb. 'But, having said that, I'm afraid I can't possibly allow you to examine them.'

'Not even if . . .' Blaine began.

But Campo held up his hand to silence his friend. 'Look, I'm a reasonable man, and I want to explain to you, right down to the tiniest detail, why I can't let you see them,' Campo said. 'But before I can give you that explanation, I've simply got to pay a visit to the latrines.' He winked. 'My stomach's been upset all day, you see, so I imagine I'll be gone for ten or fifteen minutes.'

And without saying another word, he left the room.

It did not take Blaine and Paniatowski long to find the service logs for the right date, nor to establish which vehicle Tom Bygraves and his comrades had used.

'This is the only one that went out that night,' Bill Blaine said, 'and, strangely enough,' he grinned, 'nobody seems to have signed for it.'

No, they wouldn't have, Paniatowski thought. You don't sign for a vehicle you're stealing.

'It did forty miles on that particular expedition,' Blaine said, then he whistled softly.

'What's the matter?' Paniatowski asked.

'It'd already had a full service the previous day, but they

did a real number on in when it came back. There was a full mechanical check, two of the tyres were changed, it was given a complete wash-down, and the back end of the chassis was given a whole new paint job.'

'And that's unusual, is it?' Paniatowski asked.

'The paint job?'

'Yes.'

'Not *too* unusual. The Army likes to keep its vehicles looking smart, you have to understand, even when it's involved in combat situations. It thinks that gives it a psychological advantage over the bedraggled enemy.'

'Well, then . . .'

'But they're not normally that keen on appearances that they'll go to the trouble of re-spraying a vehicle overnight.'

Twenty-Four

The barriers had been delivered to the ruined abbey by lorry, earlier in the day. They were made of tubular steel, were each ten feet long and were painted bright yellow. Once they'd been unloaded, they were immediately set up around the perimeter of the abbey.

Though they were known as *crowd-control* barriers, the title was not strictly accurate, since they came only to waist height and could be toppled over by someone who was even *slightly* determined. Their true function was as 'indicators' of the line between the area set aside for the audience and that reserved exclusively for the performers, and though they would have been of little use at a violent political demonstration or an over-emotional football match, the organizers of this particular event were confident they would serve their purpose well enough.

The large man with unruly grey hair was standing on the *performance* side of the barriers, but was watching the crowd on the other side, which had been building up since darkness began to fall. He was not alone. Beside him stood a blonde woman who was both much younger and much smaller than he was. She was an 'off-comer', a term which in Dunethorpe could well have meant she'd been born a dozen miles away, though, in her case, it was closer to a couple of hundred.

The woman, who had been christened Josephine but was always called Jo, pinched the man lightly – and affectionately – on the arm, and said, 'Well, I'll say this much for you, you seem to have got us the best seats in the house.'

The man, Chief Inspector Baxter, chuckled. 'Best *seats*?' he repeated. 'In case you haven't noticed, we're standing.'

'The best *view* in the house, then,' Jo corrected herself.

'Well, there have to be some perks to being a bobby,' Baxter replied. 'And I am sort of on duty.'

'But we are still "sort of" on a date?'

'Oh yes. There's absolutely no doubt about that.'

She was a lovely woman, Baxter thought, and he enjoyed her company. And if, as sometimes happened, he found himself comparing her to Monika Paniatowski, he immediately pushed those thoughts back into the darkest recesses of his mind.

'There's quite a crowd,' said Jo, looking across at the barriers.

'Yes, there is,' Baxter agreed. 'There are those who say that the only time Dunethorpe looks as if it has any kind of future is when it's celebrating its glorious past.'

Jo crinkled her nose. 'That sounds a bit cynical.'

'You're right,' Baxter conceded. 'But there's a grain of truth in it, for all that. Historically, you see, while Dunethorpe never came close to matching York in power or influence, wool did make it rich, and for a couple of hundred years or so it was *something*. And what is it now, Jo?'

'I don't know,' the woman said. 'I'm just an off-comer, after all. What do you – a man born and brought up here – think it is?'

'I think it's a sleepy little market town that only comes alive once every five years, when it stages the Mystery Cycle as part of the Dunethorpe Festival.'

'You were going to tell me all about how the Cycle started,' Jo reminded him.

'Oh yes, so I was,' Baxter agreed. 'It began way back in the Middle Ages. What it was intended to be was a cunning combination of religious expression and education.'

'Education?'

'That's right. Everybody was supposed to know their Bible, but very few people could read it for themselves, so the Mysteries were a way of teaching them biblical stories. Each guild was made responsible for staging one particular story, you see, and . . .'

'What's a guild?'

Monika Paniatowski would probably have been able to work that out for herself – or have made a stab at guessing what it was, Baxter thought. But then Monika would never have grown to love him – and he thought that Jo just might.

Baxter lit up his pipe, and took a few puffs. The air around him was filled with light blue smoke.

'A guild was a professional body which controlled one particular trade,' he explained. 'The Cordwainers' Guild, for example, supervised everybody working in the leather industry. It set the length of apprenticeships, the quality of work that was expected, and even the price. Functions that are nowadays supervised by any number of government bodies – or do I mean *busy*bodies? – were all under the control of the guild.'

'So if you wanted to stage something as elaborate as a mystery cycle, it was the guilds you went to?' Josephine asked.

'Exactly,' Baxter agreed, pleased that she'd grasped the point. 'So, as I was saying, each guild was given its own story to tell. Originally they performed their little pageants in wagons on the streets. The wagons moved around, so that instead of you coming to the play, the play came to you. But when the whole thing was revived, after the war, it was decided to stage it in the ruins of the abbey.'

'And is it still the guilds who run it?' Josephine asked.

'Yes, although they've had to be revived, too, because some of them haven't existed for at least a couple of hundred years.'

'And each guild still does it's own thing?'

'Correct. The Builders' Guild will give us the story of Creation, just as they always did, the Mariners' Guild will present the tale of Noah's Ark, and, of course, the Butchers' Guild have been put in charge of the Crucifixion.'

'You're making that last bit up,' Josephine said accusingly.

Baxter laughed. 'I promise you, I'm not,' he said.

And he wasn't.

When the abbey had been closed, under orders from King Henry VIII, its lands had been seized and its roof removed, but it had otherwise been left intact. Now, after five hundred years of relentless Yorkshire wind and rain, only two walls remained standing, but they were more than enough to give an idea of how impressive and imposing the edifice had once been.

Of the two walls, the one facing the crowd was in the better state of repair. Its base rose thirty feet into the air, and was capped by a row of stone arches – once holding huge stained-glass windows – which added another forty feet to its height. Behind the wall – and out of sight of the audience – was a complex and recently-erected system of scaffolding, and standing on this scaffolding was a man dressed entirely in white and wearing a long beard which was starting to itch. He was God for the night, but once the performance was over he would revert to be being plain Albert Doddsworth, bricklayer.

The lights which had been illuminating the whole of the abbey grounds were suddenly extinguished, and were replaced by a single spotlight in the arch just above Doddsworth's head.

The bricklayer climbed the scaffolding, stopping when he was framed in the archway. Ahead of him, he could see only darkness, though he knew that there were thousands of people watching his every move.

He cleared his throat. 'I am the Lord God!' he said, and was startled by how loudly his words seemed to boom back at him when picked up by the hidden microphones. 'I have created the heaven and the earth, and onto the earth I have created, I have put Man.'

A second spotlight illuminated the base of the wall, revealing a man in a skin-tight flesh-coloured leotard, who was looking up at his God.

'I am Adam,' he said, though he was really a plasterer called Billy Higgins. 'Thou hast created me, and I do worship Thee.'

Albert Doddsworth nodded, in what he hoped was a God-like way, and wished his false beard didn't itch quite so much.

Tom Bygraves was lying in the back of the black van. His wrists and ankles were bound tightly, and every time the van turned a corner sharply, he rolled from one side of it to the other. At that moment he was thinking only of the pain which made his muscles burn and his limbs ache. But he knew, subconsciously, that that would not last – knew that soon another wave of fear would engulf him, and he would begin screaming for mercy again.

The van slowed, then came to a halt. He heard the driver's door open, then the sound of footsteps as the driver walked around it. Next the back doors opened, and the Cypriot climbed in.

'Where are we?' Bygraves croaked.

'Why should you care?' his captor asked, kneeling down beside him.

'Please, I'd like to know.'

'Well, since you seem so interested, I will tell you. We are parked in a lay-by outside Dunethorpe.'

'And why . . . why have we stopped?'

'Ah, that is a much more intelligent question,' the other man said, rolling his prisoner over, until he was pressing against the side of the van. 'We have stopped because I need to give you an injection.'

Bygraves felt his bowels turn to water. 'You're . . . you're going to kill me,' he moaned.

'You have known that for a long time,' the Cypriot told him. 'But if you think the injection will be lethal, you are wrong. That would be too easy a death – too merciful a punishment.'

'Then what . . .'

'The injection will cause temporary paralysis,' the Cypriot said, wedging Bygraves against the side of the van with his knees, and using his freed hands to unbutton his prisoner's left shirt sleeve. 'You will not be able to move, but you will be conscious. You will be able to understand exactly what is going on, and when death comes, you will feel it just as much as your poor victim did.'

'Please . . . !' Bygraves gasped.

'Let us play your game again,' the other man suggested. '*What if* you knew you were about to hang, but could do nothing about it? Would you feel regret for what you had done – or only regret that you had been caught.'

'I do regret it!' Bygraves said. 'I regretted it the moment it was over, and I've never stopped regretting it since.'

'Then you should have taken the opportunity to surrender yourself to the police, as you were instructed to,' his capture said harshly.

'If . . . if you let me go, I promise I'll do just that.'

'Too late,' said the other man, picking up the syringe and looking for a suitable vein.

Noah had survived the Flood. Moses had delivered his people from Egypt and into the Land of Milk and Honey.

The Cycle moved on to the New Testament – the birth of Jesus, the miracles, the arrest.

'What comes next?' Jo asked Baxter. 'The crucifixion?'

'You'd think that would be the next logical step, wouldn't you?' Baxter agreed. 'And in all the other cycles I've heard about – the York Cycle and so forth – that's exactly what *does* come next. But we're awkward buggers in Dunethorpe, and we do things differently from everybody else on principle. Besides, we like things to be clear cut, and we hate to see any loose ends left dangling.'

'Loose ends? What loose ends?'

'Well, we've seen the villain of the piece – Judas – being villainous, haven't we?'

'Yes?'

'And now, being the plain-speaking, plain-living people we are in Dunethorpe, we want to see him punished for it.'

'I beg your pardon?'

'We want to see Judas top himself,' Baxter said.

Judas Iscariot – better known as a plumber called Ted Osslethwaite – appeared in the window archway with a rope around his neck.

'I have betrayed my master for thirty pieces of silver,' he said.

He had another line still to deliver, and in the first few rehearsals, he had said it almost immediately, much to the director's frustration.

'We need a dramatic pause,' the director had told him.

'A dramatic pause?' repeated Osslethwaite, who knew a great deal about U bends and ball-cocks, but very little about acting. 'What's a dramatic pause?'

The director had looked up to the sky, as if badly in need of some divine guidance. 'Count to ten before you speak again,' he said, spacing out his words as if talking to a simpleton. 'And count *slowly* . . . one elephant, two elephants, three elephants . . .'

Now the rehearsals were over. This was the real thing, and Osslethwaite – determined to get it right – began his counting now: 'One elephant . . . two elephants . . . three elephants . . .'

Though he'd never intended to – though the director would later be furious that he had – he found himself glancing back over his shoulder, at the scaffolding a couple of feet below him, where he had placed the dummy which was due to take his place.

'Four elephants . . . five elephants . . . six elephants . . .'

Once he'd delivered his second line, the lights would all go out for ten seconds.

'And *only* ten seconds,' the director had said emphatically, 'because if it's any more, some of the audience will start to think it's funny. Then we'll get catcalls and giggles, and the whole atmosphere will be destroyed.'

Ten seconds then – in which time Osslethwaite was expected to climb onto the scaffolding himself, pick up the dummy and throw it through the archway, so that when the lights came on again, what the audience would see Judas hanging from the wall.

It shouldn't be a difficult thing to do, even in the dark, because he'd practised it enough.

'Seven elephants . . . eight elephants . . .'

Osslethwaite was beginning to feel mildly troubled. When he'd glanced back, he'd seen the dummy just where it should be, right enough, but he'd also got the impression that there were a couple of people lurking in the shadows.

And they shouldn't have been there, because the director had made it quite plain that when you weren't on stage – or *about* to be on stage – you should keep well away from the set.

'Nine elephants . . . ten elephants!'

'I am no longer worthy to live on the green and beautiful earth that the Lord my God has provided for me!' Osslethwaite-Judas said. 'I will kill myself.'

The lights went out, and Billy Osslethwaite was on the point of turning round when he felt a sharp blow to his head, and *his* lights went out as well.

The first time Baxter had been alone in the dark with a girl, he had been sixteen, and they had been at the cinema. Then, he had taken the opportunity to steal a hurried, furtive kiss. Now, he felt the return of that urge, but instantly recognized the absurdity of following it through, since the girl in question this time was actually a woman, and in a couple of hours or so they would be in bed together.

Or maybe it wasn't so absurd after all, he told himself. Maybe he *should* treat Jo as if she were his first girlfriend, and he was totally infatuated with her.

But then the lights came on again, and the decision was taken out of his hands.

He looked up at the arch, expecting to see the Judas-dummy hanging from it.

But he didn't see that at all!

What he *did* see was that there were two men standing in the archway, although one of the men seemed only to be standing by virtue of the fact that the other was holding him up. And the man who needed assistance had a noose around his neck – a noose which was connected to the buttress by a length of rope.

The man who could stand unaided looked around him, and then threw the second man off the ledge. For just a moment, the second man was in free-fall, then he ran out of rope, and came to a jerky halt.

The audience, who had not been expecting anything as spectacular as this, gasped in amazement. And then slowly, they began to realize that this wasn't part of the show at all – that this was a real hanging, and the man who was now swinging slowly from side to side – like a malfunctioning pendulum – was probably dead.

'Oh, my God, how terrible!' Jo gasped. 'Hold me! Please hold me!'

But she was talking to empty air, because Baxter was already sprinting towards the wall.

Twenty-Five

B axter was running at a speed which would have surprised him if he'd stopped to think about it. But he didn't stop – and his mind had other things to ponder on.

In all his years on the Force, he'd never actually *seen* a murder being committed, but less than a minute earlier, all that had changed. The nutter from Whitebridge had struck again, and this time the bastard had had the gall to do it on *his* patch.

The wet grass squelched under his feet, but he did not worry about slipping and falling. He had never felt more sure-footed. He had never felt fitter. He would catch this killer if it was the last thing he did.

He reached the abbey wall, and sprinted round to the other side – the back-stage area, where the murderer had used the scaffolding to carry his victim up to the point of execution. Cast and crew were milling around. Some of them seemed well-aware that *something* had gone wrong, but still had no idea what it was. Others were only *too* aware of it, and at least three of this latter group looked as if they were about to be sick.

'Did anybody see where he went?' Baxter bellowed, without even bothering to explain who the 'he' was.

A man in a black beret – who was probably the director – took a couple of steps forward.

'It's . . . he was . . .' he stuttered.

'Just point, you bloody fool!' Baxter barked.

The man in the black beret raised his hand, and pointed with a trembling finger into the darkness which lay between the ruins and the boundary wall.

Baxter looked up at the scaffolding. 'Can the fellers working the spotlights hear me?' he shouted.

The men called back that they could.

'Then swing the bloody things round so I can see where the bastard's gone,' Baxter told them.

The lights were swung, and the strip of land between the abbey and the boundary wall was suddenly as bright as day. And there was the killer – running as fast as he could towards the wall, but in an awkward lop-sided way, as if he'd injured himself climbing down from the scaffolding.

Baxter dashed after him. The best he could hope for – given the lead the other man had – was to catch him half-way over the wall, grab his leg, and drag him back down again. But even that hope quickly faded. The killer had already straddled the wall, and while Baxter was still at least twenty feet from it, he dropped over the other side.

The wall was around twelve feet high, and the chief inspector took a flying leap at it. He felt his hands make contact with the top of the wall at the same moment as his sternum slammed into the brickwork. He was winded, but his hands maintained their grip and, gasping for breath, he heaved himself up.

From the top of the wall, he heard an engine roaring to life, and saw a black van pulling away. He dropped to the ground, and immediately stepped out into the middle of road.

Several cars were approaching the spot, but a souped-up Cortina – travelling at well above the speed limit – was much closer than the rest. The driver of the Cortina saw Baxter standing there and waving his arms, and pulled hard on the steering wheel to slue the car to the right. His intention was clearly to get past this maniac as quickly as possible, but when the maniac moved in the same direction himself, the driver realized that was not going to happen, and slammed on his brakes.

The Cortina came to a skidding halt just three feet from where Baxter was standing.

The driver, trembling with a mixture of fear and anger, stuck his head out of the window and screamed, 'What do you think you're doing, you bloody moron? I could have bloody killed you!'

Baxter advanced a couple of feet, holding his warrant card in front of him. 'Police!' he said.

It was a magic word which instantly drained away the driver's anger – though not his fear. He pulled his head back into the car, and said, 'I swear to you, officer, I'm perfec'ly sober.'

'I'm commandeering this vehicle,' Baxter told him.

'Commandeering? What does that mean?'

'It means I need it – and I'm taking it.'

'Are you allowed to do that?' the Cortina driver wondered.

Baxter opened the door. 'Out!' he ordered. 'Or I might just see if you really *can* walk in a straight line.'

The man climbed out the car, and Baxter quickly slid into the driver's seat. He gunned the engine, and, with a screech of protest from the tyres, the Cortina shot forward. As it disappeared into the distance, the owner found himself praying that he would get it back in one piece.

Baxter no longer had visual contact with the van, so he was going to have to guess where the killer would be heading. If he was in the man's shoes himself, he thought, he would want to get away from Dunethorpe before the police had time to react and started setting up road blocks. That meant he would probably be heading for the by-pass – and chances were that he didn't know all the short cuts that a local man did.

A route – almost as straight as the crow flies – was already taking shape in Baxter's mind. He took a sharp turn to the right, and plunged into an estate of Victorian terraced cottages.

He drove down the narrow streets with his lights flashing and his hand almost permanently on the horn. He took corners on two wheels, praying as he did so that no one had parked illegally close to those corners – because if they had, he would go right up their arses.

He saw that his recklessness had been rewarded as he reached the mile-long, sloping slip-road which led down to the dual carriageway. There was the black van, just ahead of him. The driver was getting as much out of the engine as he possibly could, but it was no match for the souped-up Cortina.

The road was wide enough for the Cortina to overtake the van – but only just. If the van chose to swing out as he was passing it, there was a fair chance that, with its superior weight, it could knock him off the road, and send him hurtling down the embankment to the fields below. Clearly then, his brain told him, the safest thing to do – the only *sensible* thing to do – would be to simply keep following the van until they reached a safer place to overtake. But even as these thoughts were going through his mind, his foot was already pressing the accelerator right down to the floorboards.

The van had been picking up speed as it went downhill, and now it was moving almost as fast as the Cortina. When Baxter drew level with it, he could see the van driver looking down at him, and read in the man's eyes that at any moment he intended to swing the van out.

He needed a diversion, Baxter thought. *Any* diversion!

He pulled his pipe out of his pocket, the bowl in his hand, and pointed the stem towards the van driver. It didn't look much like a gun, but at that speed – and in those conditions – it was close enough to fool the killer for a second. The Cypriot ducked his head, and Baxter was past him.

The Cortina had soon pulled a couple of hundred yards away from the van. It was now or never, Baxter decided. He hit the brakes, and pulled hard on the wheel. His vehicle slewed across the road, its tyres screeching, its gearbox almost swallowing itself. The Cortina came to a rocking halt, with its wheels no more than a few inches from the edge of the embankment.

Baxter flung open the door, and dived free of the Cortina. He went into a roll, and only stopped when seven or eight feet clear of the vehicle. As he scrambled to his feet, he could see that the black van was still heading towards him.

The driver still had time to slam on the brakes and put the van into reverse gear, if that was what he wanted to do. But he showed no signs of any such inclination. Instead he seemed to be concentrating on coaxing every available ounce of energy out of his engine.

'He's decided that if he turns back now, he's finished,' Baxter thought.

And the van driver was right in that assumption. The only chance he had escaping now was ramming the Cortina out of his way.

The van hit the car with a sickening thud. The Cortina rocked, and even moved a little.

But not enough!

Nowhere near enough!

The van's engine bellowed like a dying animal, and then – but for a hiss of stream and the creaking of twisted metal – it fell silent.

Baxter ran around the car to the van. As he wrenched open the van door, he was expecting resistance. But there was none.

The driver was slumped over the steering wheel – and it didn't take a doctor to see that he was dead.

Mr Forsyth sat in his room at the Foreign Office, looking at the secure-telex machine which had been spewing out ribbons of information for quite some time.

'So the Cypriot's dead,' said Barrington, who was reading the same information over his shoulder.

'Yes, he is,' Forsyth agreed.

'Then all your troubles are over, aren't they?'

Forsyth swung his chair around, so that he was facing the man who he had come to regard as his protégé. 'You disappoint me,' he said.

'Do I? Why?'

'Because a few gothic murders, in a part of the country that none of us would ever visit through choice, have never really been of much concern to us. Our primary interest has always been in covering up what went on in Cyprus seven years ago.'

Barrington flushed, like a cocky schoolboy who had suddenly and unexpectedly had the full extent of his ignorance revealed.

'I appreciate that,' he said, 'but I would have thought that now the killer is dead, the murder investigation would no longer have the impetus to . . .'

'Monika Paniatowski is still in Cyprus,' Forsyth interrupted him. 'Furthermore, she seems to have been making unexpectedly good progress in her inquiries, so that while she's not yet discovered the awful truth, she's getting rather close to it.'

'Then she should be pulled out immediately,' Barrington said.

'Indeed, she should,' Forsyth agreed. 'And how, exactly, do you think we should go about doing that?'

'We should contact someone in the military with the authority to rescind her privileges.'

'General Doyle, for example?'

'Yes, he would be a good choice.'

Forsyth sighed. 'General Doyle is spending the night with his mistress. She is a woman of rather bizarre sexual tastes, and she seems to suit him perfectly. He thinks I don't know about her, and I want him to *continue* thinking that until the

Service is in real trouble, and we desperately need his backing. Which means that for tonight at least, we cannot contact him.'

'General Parkinson?' Barrington suggested.

'General Parkinson is currently in the operating theatre, having something unspeakable done to his haemorrhoids.'

'General Hatton?'

'General Hatton is the one who secured the privileges for Sergeant Paniatowski in the first place. He did it to oblige a pal of his in the RAF, and he will not take kindly to any suggestion from us that he should let that pal down.'

'So what *can* we do?'

'Tomorrow morning, General Doyle will appear at his desk in the War Office – no doubt limping slightly – and I will immediately ask him to do what is necessary.'

'But if this Paniatowski woman's as good as you say . . .'

'She's very good,' Forsyth said. 'But even someone as talented as Monika couldn't possibly blow the whole thing open in just a few short hours.'

Twenty-Six

The Chief Constable had all the morning papers spread out on the desk in front of him. The headlines told their own story:

'Whitebridge Hangman' Dead
High Speed Car Chase Sees End of Northern Killer
Lancashire Monster Dies

Marlowe picked up one of the papers, scanned the story, then threw it back on the desk in obvious disgust.

'Well, you haven't exactly covered yourself in glory with this case, have you, Chief Inspector?' he asked.

'At least the killer's been caught before he could do any *more* harm,' Woodend pointed out mildly.

'By the *Yorkshire* Police,' Marlowe countered. 'He committed two of his murders in Lancashire, and got away with them, but the moment he tries the same thing across the border, he's caught.'

Woodend could have pointed out that the killer had taken far more chances with his third murder than he had with the previous two – that there was a big difference between killing his victim near a lonely canal bank and killing him in front of several thousand people – but he knew he would only be wasting his breath.

'I'll be nothing but a laughing stock at the next meeting of the Association of Chief Police Officers,' Marlowe complained. He sighed heavily. 'Still, I suppose I must do what I can to save you from the vultures waiting out there for their press briefing.'

'Thank you, sir,' Woodend replied. 'It's very kind of you. An' despite what anybody else might say, *I* know you're not only doin' it because you can't save yourself without savin' me first.'

'That remark is bordering on the insolent, Mr Woodend,' Marlowe said angrily.

'Is it, sir?' Woodend asked innocently. 'And there was me thinkin' I was only bein' nice.'

Henry Marlowe tried to think of a suitably cutting comeback, and failed completely.

'How much longer do you intend to allow Sergeant Paniatowski to swan about in the sun, at the taxpayers' expense?' he demanded, shifting his ground for a fresh attack.

'I'll tell her to come straight home as soon as I get the chance to speak to her.'

'And why haven't you spoken to her *already*, pray tell?'

'Because I don't know exactly where she is. I rang Akrotiri, an' they told me she'd left the base.'

'It's typical of you to lose track of your own people,' Marlowe said contemptuously. 'Shall we get this press briefing over with?'

Woodend shrugged. 'I suppose we might as well.'

The press room was crowded with reporters, but Marlowe kept his eyes on Williams, who he had now firmly identified as Enemy Number One.

The Chief Constable cleared his throat. 'Previous to the dramatic events of last evening, our own investigation here in Whitebridge had already uncovered much of the information that I am now about to give you,' he said unconvincingly. 'The killer's name was George Niko . . . Niko . . .

'Nikopolidis,' Woodend supplied.

'Thank you, Chief Inspector,' Marlowe said, flashing him a quick and venomous glare. 'The man was a Greek Cypriot, and is believed to have been heavily involved in the EOKA terrorist campaign which was waged on that unhappy island some years ago. We have learned that he lived quite openly on Cyprus since its independence, and only came to England a few days ago. We consider it highly probable that these three recent murders were only the latest in a long line of killings, and you can all thank your lucky stars that the Lancashire Police were more on the ball when it came to apprehending him than those investigating his previous crimes seem to have been.'

'But you *didn't* apprehend him, did you?' Williams interrupted. 'He crashed his van and killed himself.'

'That is undoubtedly true,' the Chief Constable agreed, 'but had he not been involved in that fatal accident, we would certainly have arrested him within the next few hours.'

'And Tom Bygraves would still have been dead,' Williams pointed out. 'Isn't this simply a case of, "The operation was successful, but the patient died"?'

'It is always so very easy for you gentlemen of the press to take a negative view of the way things develop, but we working bobbies prefer to be more constructive,' Marlowe said, a little shakily.

'And another thing,' Williams pressed on. 'Why did this Nikopolidis *want* to kill these three sons of Whitebridge?'

Marlowe sighed. 'I thought I had already explained to you that the man was a natural killer, and that he once worked for EOKA. His three victims had all served Her Majesty's Government proudly – and no doubt bravely – in Cyprus, and it was probably the case that, in his sick mind, he thought he was exacting his revenge on the whole British Army.'

'I can see that,' Williams conceded.

'Good. I am pleased you finally seem to have caught up with the rest of us,' Marlowe told him.

'But what I *don't* see is why he chose these three particular men. Of the thousands of soldiers who served in Cyprus, what was it about them that made them so *special* to him?'

Marlowe looked to Woodend for help.

'We don't know,' the Chief Inspector admitted.

'What Mr Woodend means is that *no one* can *ever* know,' the Chief Constable said hastily. 'Niko . . . this Greek . . . was clearly a madman. There is no logic to his choice of victims, except perhaps a twisted logic in his own diseased brain.'

'He had no trouble at all in finding these victims of his, though, did he?' Williams asked.

'I beg your pardon?'

'If I was a Greek Cypriot, living on an island in the middle of the Mediterranean Sea, I don't think I'd have any idea of how to locate three soldiers who hadn't been on the island themselves for over seven years.'

'But then you do not think *at all* as he did, because you are not a homicidal maniac,' Marlowe said. He permitted himself a small smile. 'At least, Mr Williams, I sincerely *hope* you're not.'

* * *

The Cypriot Chief Inspector's name was Andreas Karamanlis. He looked a little like Anthony Quinn had, when playing the Greek patriot in *The Guns of Navarone*, and Paniatowski wondered if he'd seen the film – and if he had, whether that was the moment when he had decided it would be a good idea to grow a thick moustache and smoke a curved pipe.

Karamanlis' office had the same cluttered appearance as her own boss's, though, living in Lancashire as he did, Woodend would have had no use for the ancient but powerful fan which was clattering away noisily in the corner of the room.

'I must tell you, Sergeant, it is a real pleasure to speak to a British copper again,' Karamanlis said.

'In Lancashire, sir, we prefer to call ourselves bobbies,' Paniatowski told him, with a smile.

Karamanlis returned the smile. 'Of course you do,' he agreed. 'I should have known that, because the UKPU was drawn from forces all over your country, and there were both coppers *and* bobbies.'

'What's the UKPU?'

'It is, or rather, it *was*, the United Kingdom Police Unit. I take it you have never heard of it.'

'The initials didn't mean anything to me,' Paniatowski admitted. 'but now you've given me its full name, it does ring a bell – if only a very vague one.'

'Then perhaps I should fill you in on a few details,' Karamanlis said. 'Is that the correct term – *fill you in on a few details*?'

'It's perfect.'

Karamanlis lit up his pipe, and puffed away for a few seconds.

'Until 1955, the Cyprus Police was run on British lines – we were a colony of yours, after all – though it was made up entirely of Cypriots,' he said. 'But when conditions here started to deteriorate, the Governor decided the CP was simply not equipped to deal with the situation. Policemen were identified with the colonial power, you see, and so were not always popular with the civilian population. Besides, it was claimed that the police had been infiltrated by EOKA.'

'And had it?'

Karamanlis shrugged. 'I suppose there was a certain

justification, in some cases, for the belief. At any rate, a decision was made to bring in British policemen to supplement
the work of the local force. They were all volunteers who
came out here to serve for twenty-one months, and they were
all promoted by one rank, so that constables became sergeants,
and sergeants became inspectors.'

'How many of them were there?'

'There were a hundred and fifty of them initially, though
their number eventually rose to over two hundred and fifty.'
Karamanlis chuckled. 'At first, I think, some of them saw it
as no more than a very long holiday.'

'But it wasn't?'

'Not at all. They were, in fact, putting themselves into a
very dangerous situation. They carried weapons for their own
protection, which they would not have done in your own
country, and, in addition, they were escorted everywhere by
armed soldiers. But even so, in the three years they were here,
seven of them were murdered, and eleven seriously wounded.'
The Chief Inspector puffed on his pipe again. 'But you are
not here to listen to me talk about what is now no more than
ancient history, are you, Sergeant Paniatowski?'

'In a way, I am,' Monika Paniatowski countered. 'I'd be
very interested to learn about any serious crimes which might
have been committed on the ninth of June, 1958.'

'You are being very specific,' Karamanlis said.

'Yes,' Paniatowski agreed. 'I am.'

The Chief Inspector swung his chair round, opened his
filing cabinet, and pulled out a battered cardboard file. He
flicked through the pages until he came to the right one,
consulted it for a moment, then said, '*Any* serious crime?'

'*Any* serious crime,' Paniatowski agreed.

Karamanlis frowned. 'There were two on that date – though
since one of them involved the British Army and EOKA, it
might be more accurately called an "act of war" from one
side of the fence, and an "act of terror" from the other.'

'And what would you call it?' Paniatowski wondered.

'That would depend on whether I was thinking as a
policeman or as a patriot,' Karamanlis replied enigmatically.
'At any rate, the act of war/act of terror occurred in the afternoon of that day. A British Army patrol was ambushed, and
the corporal leading it was killed.'

'That would be Corporal Matthews,' Paniatowski said.

'Yes, but how would you . . . ?'

'What about the second crime?'

'That same night, a young girl disappeared from the village in which the ambush had taken place. She has not been seen since, so she is presumed dead.'

'Could you give me any more details about that incident?'

'She was a very lively young woman, by all accounts. She was very interested in astronomy – which is unusual for Cypriot girls – and that night she had gone out to look at the stars. She never returned home.'

'You gave me all that information without looking down at your file once,' Paniatowski said.

Karamanlis smiled wistfully.

'You suspect that I have a personal involvement in the case, and you are right,' he said. 'I was, indeed, part of the team which investigated the poor girl's disappearance. My boss at the time, Chief Inspector Harding, was very angry about the case – almost unprofessionally so. But we understood the reasons for his anger – we knew that he had two young daughters of his own and we were very much in sympathy with him.'

'So he pulled out all the stops, did he?'

'He most certainly did. He told us that even in troubled times like those were, the disappearance of a child was simply not to be tolerated. He cancelled all leave, and put every available man on the investigation.'

'But you still didn't find anything that might have helped explain what had happened to the girl?'

'No,' Karamanlis agreed. 'But in our own defence, I must point out that we were only working on the investigation for a short time before we were pulled off it again.'

'But I thought you said that your Chief Inspector Harding was keen as mustard to solve it.'

'So he was. But the situation changed after he had spoken to your Special Branch and Military Intelligence.'

'And what did *they* have to say, that cooled his enthusiasm?'

'That a roving band of Turkish Cypriot vagrants – men of the worst possible class and kind – had been spotted near the village that very night, and that it was probably they who had taken – or murdered – the girl.'

'And you accepted that?'

'Why would we not have? The Turkish Cypriots and Greek Cypriots were as much at each other's throats then as they are now. Perhaps even more so. There had already been several inter-communal murders that very year. It seemed highly probable, given that the Turkish scum had been spotted in the area, that they were responsible.'

'And no attempt was ever made to track this band of Turkish Cypriots down?'

'None,' Karamanlis admitted, looking a little ashamed. 'But that was not our choice – it was a *political* decision that we drop the case.'

'How did the disappearance of a young girl ever manage to become political?' Paniatowski wondered.

'It was not the disappearance that was political, it was the nature of the probable perpetrators.'

'I still don't understand.'

'It was felt that once the men had returned to the Turkish area of the island, it would have been very difficult to identify them, and that even if we *could* identify them – and establish conclusively that they had been near the village – we would still find it impossible to prove that they had murdered the girl.'

'Still, there would have been no harm in trying, would there?' Paniatowski said.

'That is where you are wrong,' Karamanlis told her. 'It was also felt – and I happen to agree with this – that by even *attempting* to make an unmakeable case, we would be running the risk of further inflaming the violence between the communities, and that, as a result, even more innocent people would die. And so the girl – the poor *child* – became simply another casualty of war.'

'You've been very helpful, and I mustn't take up much more of your time,' Paniatowski said. 'But before I go, I do have just one more question.'

'Yes?'

'About how far is it from the Akrotiri base to the village where the girl disappeared?'

Karamanlis thought about it. 'Eighteen or nineteen miles, I would guess,' he said.

And there had been forty miles on the clock of the stolen Land Rover, Paniatowski thought.

She shook hands with the Chief Inspector, and took her leave. When she stepped out onto the street, the bright sunlight almost blinded her for a few seconds. Then her eyes adjusted, and she looked around for Lance Corporal Bill Blaine and his Land Rover.

There was no sign of either the lance corporal or the vehicle, but two severe-looking military policemen were very much in evidence, and the moment they saw her, they began to walk towards her in a most determined manner.

Twenty-Seven

Considering the amount of alcohol they have consumed, they should have reached some kind of philosophical plateau by now, and be saying things like, 'Well, if a bullet's got your name on it, there's nothing you can do about it.'

Failing that, they should at least have reached the stage at which it was possible to re-write the past, in order to turn events which had either been mundane or unpleasant into amusing anecdotes – 'Remember that time Jack Matthews pretended he was going to shoot those three Cyps if they didn't tell him what he wanted to know. I don't know if they believed him, but I certainly bloody did, and I was near shitting myself.'

Neither of these states has been achieved. They have been drinking, but they are not drunk. They are speaking – occasionally – but they are not really saying anything. It is as if their nerves and feelings are coated in a layer of ice, and will remain coated until one of the unit has the nerve to start a fire.

It is Reg Lewis who strikes the tinder. 'What if?' he says. 'What if your corporal was killed by a bunch of cowardly bastards in the hills? What would you do then?'

If they were still playing the game **as** *a game, someone would come back with an immediate answer, but this is real, and there is a long pause before Tom Bygraves says, 'What can we do?'*

'We can go back to the village,' Mark Hough says, with a determination which takes all them – including himself – by surprise.

'And do what?' Terry Pugh asks.

'We won't know till we get there,' Martin Murray says, grasping the existential moment.

And suddenly they are all agreed. They have no plan. They have no real expectations. But it seems the right thing to do.

* * *

The guards on the gate are only too well aware that these five men do not have permission to take the Land Rover out at this time of night. But they also know what the men have been through in the previous twelve hours, and so, instead of raising a hand or lowering the barrier, they choose to look the other way.

The Land Rover leaves the camp, and heads towards the hills. Bygraves' driving is erratic, because now he really is drunk. Now that they are finally taking action, they are all drunk.

They park close to the village, on almost the same spot where they had parked earlier in the day. They climb down from the Land Rover and look around them, waiting for Corporal Matthews to tell them what to do next – for though they know he is dead, they have still not quite realized it.

As if Matthews's spirit has taken control of him, Hough begins to walk towards the village, and the others follow. They still do not have a plan, but they are hoping that something will happen to give them a sense of direction.

And something does! What happens is the girl!

This is the second time they have seen her in a single day – and after the first there were bloody consequences.

They do not know what she is doing outside the village at that time of night. They will never know. But there – bathed prettily in the pale moonlight – she undoubtedly is.

She sees them, and turns to run back to safety. She never has a chance. She is little more than a child, while they are fit adult males, and before she has gone more than a few yards, Reg Lewis has brought her down in a rugby tackle.

Lewis clamps his hand over the girl's mouth, but not quickly enough – and not completely enough – to prevent her from biting it.

'Little bitch!' he moans.

Then he lifts her skirt and pulls it up over her face, pressing down on the part of it which is covering her mouth, so that she is effectively muffled.

Events have been moving so quickly that none of them has really had time to think, but now, looking down at the girl – her thin bare legs kicking helplessly in the air – they know that some kind of decision has to be made.

'What are we going to do with her?' Bygraves asks in a

panic. *'We can't let her go, because if we do that, she'll run straight back to the village.'*

Lewis is still holding the girl's skirt tight around her head, but his eyes are on her legs.

'I've no intention of letting the little bitch go,' he says. *'She's the spoils of war.'*

'You're . . . you're going to rape her?' Murray asks, troubled.

'I'm certainly going to stick one to her,' Lewis says. *'Whether it's rape or not is another matter. Her father and her brothers have probably all had her already. Why shouldn't I?'*

'I'm not sure it's right,' Murray said.

'She got our corporal killed,' Lewis says angrily. *'What are we going to do about it? Give her a prize for it?'*

'No, but . . .'

'Pugh, you take her arms,' Lewis says. *'Bygraves, you take her legs – and make sure you keep them well spread.'*

The two men hesitate, then a cloud drifts over the moon, and it seems almost as if it is a signal – a permission – for them to go ahead. Terry Pugh grabs the girl by the wrists, Tom Bygraves by the ankles, and Reg Lewis stands up in order to properly unbutton his flies.

Lewis takes her roughly and quickly, and when he has finished, he says, *'So who's next?'*

Nobody speaks.

'We're all in this together,' Lewis says. *'We're Matthews' Marauders, and whatever one of us does, the rest of us have to do as well.'*

It makes sense. If they are to punish the girl, they should all punish the girl. And if they are to bear the consequences of their actions later, they should all have taken part in those actions.

Pugh follows Lewis, Bygraves follows Pugh, Hough follows Bygraves, and finally – though it is clear that he doesn't want to do it – Murray follows Hough.

For the first few minutes, the girl was struggling, but by the time Murray enters her, she is perfectly still.

Murray finishes quickly, and gets to his feet. He looks as if he wishes he was dead.

'What happens next?' Bygraves asks. *'Do we let her go?'*

'How can we let her go?' Lewis asks contemptuously. *'She's*

seen us, hasn't she? We know we haven't done anything wrong – anything she hasn't asked for – but we could still all get twenty years for this.'

'Then we . . . ?' Bygraves begins.

He says no more, but he doesn't need to. Ever since Lewis penetrated her, they have known they have gone beyond the point of no return. Ever since then they have all understood – though they may not have acknowledged it – that they were going to have to kill her.

Lewis picks up a large stone from the ground.

'We all have to do it,' he says. 'We all have to strike a blow so we don't know which of us killed her – so we all share the responsibility.'

The other men – even Murray – nod sombrely.

The girl's head is still covered by her skirt. Lewis smashes his rock down on it, and there is the sickening sound of bone splintering. The others follow suit, though none of them with the force that Lewis has employed.

'What now?' Bygraves asked.

It is at this point that Mark Hough takes charge. 'We have to get rid of the body,' he says.

'Why can't we just leave her here?' Pugh asks.

'Because if they can't find the body, they can't prove she's dead,' Hough explains. 'If they can't find prove she's dead, then they can't charge us with her murder.'

The others shiver at that last word. They know they have killed the girl, but they have not been thinking of themselves as murderers. Now they see that that is exactly what they are.

'What do we do with her?' Bygraves asks.

'We throw her into the sea,' Hough says. 'It's the safest way.'

They load the girl's body into the back of the Land Rover – it does not take up nearly as much space as Corporal Matthews's body had – and drive to the cliff tops. The sea is deep at this point, and there are strong currents. With any luck, the body will never be found.

The moon comes out as they are lifting her from the Land Rover, shining on her thin young legs which are sticky with dried sperm and stained with blood.

Blood! A virgin's blood!

'Cover her legs,' Hough says.

'What's the point of that, when we're about to throw her over the cliff?' Lewis asks.

'It's the decent thing to do,' Hough tells him.

'Decent?' Lewis says, incredulously.

'Cover her legs!' Mark Hough repeats, in a tone which suggests that if they do not do exactly as he says – and immediately – then more blood will be spilled that night.

Lewis shrugs, and pulls back the skirt from over her face. And then they see it.

'Oh, my God!' Bygraves moans.

'It's the wrong girl!' Murray gasps.

It's the wrong girl. She looks similar to the one who led them into the ambush – she may even be her sister – but she is the wrong girl!

'Let's get her over the cliff quickly,' Pugh says.

As if that will make a difference. As if, as she plunges towards the sea, she will miraculously become the right girl.

There is a bottle of whisky crammed down between the seats in the Land Rover. The unit did not touch it on their way out to the village, but now, on the journey back to camp, it is opened and passed around.

They are very drunk now. Drunker than they can ever remember being before. But for some of them, at least, the image of the dead girl – the wrong dead girl – will not go away.

As they are approaching the camp, Mark Hough notices the dark stain on the floor of the Land Rover. More blood! From her head! From the injuries that they inflicted.

He struggles to his feet.

'What the bloody hell are you doing?' Bygraves asks.

'Want to be sick,' Hough groans.

He grasps hold of the cover frame, leans out over the back of the vehicle, and throws up all over the road.

In the front of the vehicle, Tom Bygraves has just been handed the whisky bottle. He raises it to his lips and glugs it down. As the fiery liquid burns his throat, he finds himself wishing that Jack Matthews was there, to tell them what to do next. But if Jack Matthews had been there, he would never have allowed them to get into this fix in the first place.

Bygraves is still drinking when he swings the Land Rover

around a bend on the wrong side of the road. It is then that he sees the lorry heading straight towards them. He drops the bottle, and wrenches desperately at the wheel.

The Land Rover swerves, its tyres screeching their protest, the air suddenly filled with the smell of burning rubber. He misses the lorry by inches, but now the Land Rover is in danger of coming off the road completely. He pulls hard on the wheel again, and the vehicle is more or less pointing in the right direction. He applies the brakes – none too gently – and the Land Rover comes to a juddering halt.

'You almost killed us,' Reg Lewis screams.

'No harm done,' Bygraves replies weakly.

The truck has stopped, too, and the driver and his mate are running back down the road.

'Tell them we had some sort of mechanical failure,' Terry Pugh says. 'Tell them the steering slipped.'

But the two running soldiers never reach the Land Rover. Instead, they come to a halt besides something lying in the road.

'Where's Hough?' Martin Murray asks worriedly. 'He was here a second ago.'

But that is not quite accurate. He was there ten or fifteen seconds earlier. Then, as the Land Rover swerved, he had gone flying through the air. His body had struck one of the lorry's big wheels. He had bounced off it immediately, but the damage had already been done.

Part of his spine is crushed, and he will never walk again.

Twenty-Eight

The two MPs marched Monika Paniatowski into Captain Howerd's office, stamped their feet in the approved manner, then wheeled round, and left.

'Your privileges have been revoked,' Howerd said, his voice thick with fury. 'You are no longer welcome on either the island of Cyprus or within the Sovereign Base Area. The next military flight leaves for Britain in a little under an hour, and you, Sergeant Paniatowski, will be on it.'

'What about my friend's friend in the War Office?' Paniatowski wondered. 'How's he going to take this?'

Howerd gave her a savage smile. 'It would appear, from a communication I have recently received, that he has been overruled by people with even more power and influence than he has himself,' he said.

'I need to ring my boss,' Paniatowski said.

'You mean, you'd *like* to ring your boss,' Howerd said.

'No, I mean I *need* to. His instructions to me were that I should call him every few hours, and we haven't been in contact since last night.'

'Well now, isn't that too bad,' Howerd said. 'But unfortunately for you, making phone calls over British Government lines is one of those privileges which has been revoked.'

'And when was this decision to revoke my privileges made?' Paniatowski asked.

'That is of no interest to me, and no business of yours, Sergeant. It is enough for both of us to know that they *have* been revoked.'

'If I had to guess, I'd say the decision had been made within the last hour and a half,' Paniatowski mused. 'To be even more specific, Captain Howerd, I'd say that it was made some time between me walking into Police Headquarters and me walking out again.'

'You had no right to take it on yourself to speak to the local police!' Howerd said. 'No right at all.'

'You told me that I could talk to anyone I wanted to,' Paniatowski reminded him.

'I meant anyone *within reason*, as well you know,' Captain Howerd countered.

'Corporal Matthews was killed in an ambush, and the same night, his mates stole the Land Rover and went back to the village where he'd died. And when they returned to the base, whoever was the base commander at the time flew into a complete panic, didn't he?' Paniatowski asked.

'You're babbling!' Captain Howerd said.

'There were two courses of action the man in charge *could* have taken,' Paniatowski continued. 'The right one – the *decent* one – would have been to have all five of them arrested. The wrong – but *practical* – one would have been to keep them in isolation for a couple of weeks, then slip them quietly away when no one was looking. But he didn't do *either* of those things, did he? *Because* he was in such a panic, he shipped the four who could be moved out the very next morning. And that left a trail which it hasn't been too difficult to follow.'

'I don't know what you're talking about,' Howerd said.

'I've lost count of the number of times you've told me that,' Paniatowski replied. 'But however many times it's been, it's never been even remotely true, has it? You had nothing to do with the incidents I keep referring to. You weren't even here at the time. But the army was here, and since you *are* the army – and the army is *you* – to all intents and purposes, it's just the same as if you *had* been here.'

'I neither know, nor care, what that deranged Cyp chief inspector of police told you,' Howerd said, 'but for your own sake, I would strongly advise you not to repeat anything that he may have communicated to you. In fact, if you wish to salvage what little may possibly be left of your own career, you would be wise to forget that you have ever visited Cyprus at all.'

'When your people pulled the police off their investigation into that young girl's disappearance, they claimed it was because they didn't want to inflame the Greek Cypriot community against the Turkish,' Paniatowski said. 'But that wasn't true, either, was it? What they were really worried about – what they were scared shitless over – was the possibility that once the truth got out, the Greek community would turn on the *army*.'

'There was no link between the girl's disappearance and the army,' Howerd said stubbornly. 'But if there *had* been – and if the police had uncovered it – can you even begin to appreciate how many more British lives would have been lost? And I don't just mean soldiers. I'm talking about soldiers' *wives* as well. And soldiers' *children*.'

'So the men involved with whatever happened to the girl were allowed to get away with it – until now,' Paniatowski mused. 'Do you know, there's a part of me that hopes we'll never find the chap who's killing them off.'

'I'm sure there is,' Captain Howerd said. A cruelly amused smile came to his lips. 'You want to ignore the law, and decide for yourself how justice will be served. But doesn't that make you just as bad as you seem to think we are?'

The constables had been on guard outside the model shop all night, but once the news of Nikopolidis' death had been announced, there seemed no point in keeping them there any longer, and the order had come through for them to withdraw.

Martin Murray had watched them leave without either concern or regret. What had to happen, had to happen – and the only question was whether it would be sooner or later.

He was putting the finishing touches to his model railway – his own private world – when he heard the doorbell ring, and the sound of rubber on tiles which followed it.

'Nikopolidis, the Cyp who killed Pugh, Lewis and Bygraves, is dead,' his visitor said.

'I know he is. I heard it on the radio.'

'So now there's a problem.'

'Is there?'

'Oh yes. Since he's dead, he cannot complete his work. But it must *be* completed.'

Murray had still not looked up from his model railway. 'I need five more minutes to finish off what I'm doing,' he said. 'Will you allow me that?'

'You're not going to put up any sort of fight?' his visitor asked, surprised.

'Did you expect me to?'

'I thought it might be a possibility.'

'*What if?*' Murray asked. 'What if I decided to resist you?'

'Then I'd have to find some way to overcome that resistance.'

'It wouldn't be easy.'

'No, it wouldn't.'

'And though it might result in my death, I would not die in the manner you would wish me to.'

'That's true. But I can only do what I can – what I am *able* to.'

'I won't resist you,' Murray promised. 'What would be the point of it? I should have been hanged seven years ago. We both know that. It would have been a merciful release for me if I had been. But now the time has finally come, and I will not struggle against the inevitable.'

'This isn't some kind of trick, is it?' his visitor asked suspiciously. 'You're not simply stalling me until the police arrive?'

Murray laughed. 'I haven't even looked at you yet – I have more important things to do – but from the moment you entered this shop, you have not taken your eyes off me for a single second. Isn't that true?'

'Well, yes,' the visitor agreed.

'You should have looked around the shop,' Murray told him. 'If you had done, you'd no longer have any doubts about the seriousness of my intention.'

The visitor did now look around, and when he saw what was in a corner of the room not visible from the window, he said, 'I am sorry I ever doubted you.'

'So you will now allow me the five minutes I requested?' Murray asked.

'Of course,' his visitor agreed.

Twenty-Nine

The two young military policemen, who'd been charged with the responsibility of ensuring that Paniatowski did exactly what she'd been ordered to do, were nowhere near as stern and forbidding as the ones who had taken her into custody outside the police station. On the contrary, they seemed to be enjoying what they considered to be a really rather pleasant assignment.

'It's a pity you can't stay a few more days,' one of them – who said his name was Brian – told her. 'We've got a dance on Saturday, and there's always a shortage of ladies.'

'You see, it's all very well dancing with your best mate's missus,' said the other – Chris – 'but somehow it's not the same as having a girl of your own on your arm, is it?'

'No,' agreed Paniatowski, who knew something about loneliness. 'It probably isn't.'

They were standing in a shaded area at the edge of the tarmac, watching a Blackburn Beverly, surrounded by a heat haze, being unloaded. Once the cargo had been removed, the plane would be made ready for take-off, and then the no-longer-welcome guest herself would be escorted on board.

Paniatowski was feeling vaguely dissatisfied, but that dissatisfaction had very little to do with the obvious pleasure she knew it would give Captain Howerd to see her leave the island.

The simple truth was that while she had done the job that had been asked of her, she still did not feel that she had actually contributed much to the investigation which was being conducted back in Whitebridge.

True, she had found out what had really gone on that night in June 1958, but that was another crime in another time, for which the surviving miscreants might still be punished – though she doubted they would.

True, too, she had, thanks to Sergeant McCoy, identified

the men on the killer's list, but no doubt Woodend would have
got those names from another source easily enough.

She wished she could talk to Woodend at that moment,
partly so that he could reassure her that her own efforts had
been of value to the team, partly because she was bursting
to know what developments there'd been back home. But
that was not to be, because Brian and Chris – despite their
obvious friendliness towards her, would never disobey
Captain Howerd's orders and allow her to use the phone.
And she knew that for a fact – because she'd already asked
them.

So, all in all, she thought, her little jaunt to Cyprus had
turned out to be an almost complete waste of time.

One of the lorries pulled away from the plane. It passed
within a few feet of where they were standing, and Paniatowski
noticed that several of the packing cases bore the name of a
company she recognized.

'Do you buy a lot of stuff from Hough Engineering?' she
asked Chris and Brian.

'We wouldn't know about that,' Chris said. 'We don't get
involved in the technical side of things.'

'Still, I suppose the desk wallahs must buy a fair amount
from the company, or it wouldn't have been worthwhile
Mr Hough coming out here himself, would it?'' Brian added.

'Hough? Coming out here himself?' Paniatowski repeated,
almost stunned by this new information.

'That's right,' Brian agreed.

'You're sure about that?'

'Definitely. The reason we remember it particularly is
because he paid us to drive him into Nicosia on our day off.
Bought us a bloody marvellous slap-up meal, too, though we
never asked him to.'

'It *was* bloody marvellous,' Chris agreed. 'And he didn't
even get a taste of it himself, because while we were stuffing
our faces, he was off on his own, doing a bit of business.'

'What kind of business?' Paniatowski wondered.

'Don't know. He didn't say – and we didn't ask.'

Hough in Cyprus! Hough doing 'business' in Nicosia!

The idea that was forming in Paniatowski's mind seemed
so incredible that it simply couldn't be right.

'And you're sure it was Hough himself,' she asked

desperately. 'It couldn't have been one of his sales' representatives, could it?'

'Told *us* his name was Hough,' Chris said. 'And I know this isn't going to sound very logical, but when a man in a wheelchair tells you something, your natural inclination is to believe him.'

'We've had it all wrong from the start!' Paniatowski thought.

But that wasn't strictly true, she thought. They'd had it all right – *and* all wrong.

'I have to make a phone call,' she said.

'Now we've already told you that isn't possible,' Chris said, slightly reprovingly.

'Yes, I know – but the last time I asked, I didn't realize it was a matter of life or death,' Paniatowski told him.

'It can't be that serious,' Brian said.

'It *is* that serious,' Paniatowski said urgently. 'I promise you it is.'

The two MPs exchanged questioning glances, then Chris shook his head and said, 'Sorry.'

'Then could you make a call?' Paniatowski asked desperately.

'I suppose there's no harm in that,' Chris conceded.

'Ring Whitebridge Police headquarters. Ask for Chief Inspector Woodend, and tell him that Matthews Marauders killed a girl – and that Mark Hough's made a recent visit to Cyprus.'

'Is that it?'

'That's it.'

'But will it mean anything to him?'

'Oh yes,' Paniatowski said heavily. 'It will mean a *great deal* to him.'

There were three of them in the car which screeched to a halt in front of the model shop. Woodend – the driver – was the first to get out of it, but Rutter and Dr Shastri were not far behind him.

Woodend tried the main door to the shop, and when he found it was locked – as he had fully expected it to be – he kicked it open without a second's hesitation.

He saw Martin Murray immediately. It would have been hard to miss him. The model shop owner was hanging from a rafter in the corner of the room which was not visible from the window, his head lolling to one side, his tongue protruding from his mouth.

'See what you can do for him, Doc,' the chief inspector said, without even an ounce of expectation in his voice.

Dr Shastri looked first at Murray's face, and then at the pool of liquid which had collected on the floor.

'He's dead,' she said. 'He has been for some time. There is an envelope pinned to his chest, and no doubt there is a letter inside it.'

'Unpin it, please,' Woodend said, almost lethargically.

'You are sure?' Dr Shastri asked. 'Might I not be contaminating important evidence in the process?'

'No.'

Dr Shastri shrugged. 'Very well, it is your business,' she said, and unpinned the envelope. 'Good heavens, it is addressed to you, my dear Chief Inspector,' she continued.

'Aye, I thought it might be,' Woodend said.

'How strange that you would ever have had such thoughts,' Dr Shastri said. 'In all my experience of dealing with suicides, I don't think I have ever come across one in which the suicide note was actually addressed to a policeman.'

'I don't think it *is* a suicide note,' Woodend said.

'What else could it be?'

'I suspect that it's much more in the nature of Martin Murray's last will an' testament.'

'Curiouser and curiouser,' Dr Shastri said.

'Open it, please, an' let's see what it has to say.'

Dr Shastri split the envelope open with her fingernail, and extracted a single sheet of paper.

'Dear Chief Inspector Woodend,' she read, 'I believe you understand what my model railway means to me, and I would ask you to do all that you can to find it a home where it will be truly appreciated.' She paused. 'That's all he says.'

Woodend nodded. 'Got any really pressin' engagements this afternoon, Doc?' he said.

'I will have to perform the autopsy on our little friend here, but I can always put him on ice, if needs be,' the doctor said. 'Why do you ask?'

'Because I think it's more than likely that we'll be needin' your services *again*,' Woodend told her.

*　　*　　*

Priscilla Charlton was at her desk, and – as usual – greeted Woodend with a cheery smile.

But that smile soon disappeared when she noticed the grim expression on his face.

'Has . . . has something happened?' she asked.

And by that, she meant, 'something *bad*'.

'Where's your boss?' Woodend asked.

'On the top floor. In his apartment. It's most unusual for him to go up there at this time of day, but that's what he's done – and he left strict instructions that he wasn't to be disturbed.'

'I bet he did,' Woodend agreed. 'Have you got a key to the place, Miss Charlton?'

'Yes, I have. But I'm not sure that Mr Hough would want me to . . .'

'Then give it to me, for Christ's sake!' Woodend snapped. 'Don't you understand, woman? I'm tryin' to save his life!'

Mark Hough's apartment had once been the warehouse for the cotton mill which had functioned below it, and Hough had retained many of the original features. Thus, with the exception of the walled-off bathroom, it was a single open space. Thus, it had rafters rather than a ceiling.

And thus, there was still a door in the middle of the wall, through which cotton bales had been hauled in the old days, with a gibbet on the outside which had done the hauling.

That door was open, and Hough was sitting in his wheelchair very close to the edge. There was a noose around his neck, formed from part of the rope which had been tied around the gibbet.

'It's not as easy as it looks for a man in a wheelchair to get a rope over that gibbet,' he said conversationally, when he saw Woodend standing in the doorway that led from the lift. 'But then, there are many things that are not all that easy to do when you're in a wheelchair.'

'I'm sure that's true,' Woodend said, taking a couple of cautious steps towards him.

'Stop!' Hough ordered him. 'If you wish to talk, then we will talk. But if you come any closer than you are now, I will propel my chair forward immediately, and within moments, my neck will be broken.'

'So it will,' Woodend agreed. 'As long as you've got your calculations right. But if you haven't, of course, you'll either strangle to death or else decapitate yourself.'

'I have my calculations right,' Hough assured him. 'I'm no bungler like that fool Nikopolidis.'

'You recruited Mr Nikopolidis on your trip to Cyprus, I take it,' Woodend said.

'That's right.'

'An' how did you persuade him to help you? Was it through money? Or was it through the promise of revenge?'

'Both. I paid him a considerable amount of money. And why not? I knew I would have no further use for it. Revenge certainly came into it, too. The girl who we killed . . .' He paused. 'You do know about her, don't you, Chief Inspector?'

Woodend nodded. 'I don't have details yet – I won't get them until I can talk to Monika – but I think I've got the general idea.'

'The girl we killed – after we'd brutally *raped* her – was some sort of vague cousin of Nikopolidis's. But then, on that island, all the Greeks are related to each other, if you look back far enough. So, overall, I don't think it was either money or thoughts of revenge which finally brought him to Britain to do the job for me. I think it was the excitement.'

'You think he found what he did *excitin'*?'

'Oh, very much so. He was an EOKA terrorist – or freedom fighter, as I'm sure he would have called it – for over four years, and his life was in danger every day of that time. Then the peace came, and he almost died of boredom. I gave him the chance to live again – to take on an enemy much more powerful than he was, against whom he knew he was almost certain to lose. I wouldn't be at all surprised if he crashed that van deliberately.'

'Why?'

'So he could die on a high note.'

'Was it your idea to make the hangings so exotic?' Woodend asked.

'No. I wanted those men hanged, but I didn't care how few – or how many – people saw the result. Nikopolidis, on the other hand, wanted his work to be admired in all its gory detail.'

'But it was you who suggested the idea of the Dunethorpe Festival to him, wasn't it?'

'What makes you think that?'

'Are you denyin' it?'

'No, I'm just curious about your reasoning.'

'He'd never have heard of it, comin' from Cyprus as he did. But you knew all about what went on during the Mystery Cycle. After all, you were one of the sponsors.'

'Very well worked out!' Hough said approvingly. 'And you're quite right, of course – Dunethorpe was my idea.'

'So you wanted him to get caught?'

'No, not at all. The only reason I proposed Dunethorpe was as a way of protecting him.'

'Are you serious?'

'Completely. As risky as I knew the festival would be, it seemed a lot safer than the crazy ideas that Nikopolidis was coming up with himself. I wanted him to stay alive, you see. I wanted him to finish the job I had recruited him to do.'

'He'd have killed you, too, in the end, you know.'

'Of course he would. I fully expected him to. But he needed me as a way of getting at the others – he needed me to provide the logistics for him – and so I would have been the last man to die.'

'Why?' Woodend asked.

'Why would I have been the last man to die? I thought I'd just explained that.'

'You know what I meant. Why did any of this have to happen?'

'We committed a crime for which we should rightly have been hung. What more do I need to say?'

'Why wait seven years?'

'Perhaps it took seven years for the deep remorse to truly eat its way into my soul.'

Woodend shook his head. 'That may have been true in Martin Murray's case. In fact, I'm sure it was. That's why it was so easy for you to persuade him to hang himself.'

'Yes, you're right about that,' Hough agreed. 'When I went to his pathetic little shop, he showed me the rope he'd already prepared.'

'But what's true for Martin Murray isn't true for you.'

'Then what *is* true for me?'

'The way I see it,' Woodend said, 'you thought for quite a while that you'd already been given your fair share of punishment for killing the girl. You were crippled, an' that was enough. As for the others, you were perfectly content to let them live with their own consciences, an' if they could just shrug off what they'd done, then that was their own affair.'

Hough smiled. 'So what suddenly turned me into the Mad Hangman of Whitebridge?' he asked.

'Love,' Woodend said.

'Love?'

'You fell in love with Priscilla Charlton. You dreamed of marryin' her, an' havin' her bear your children. But, of course, that was never goin' to happen. Still, you thought you could reconcile yourself to that. Then you met Terry Pugh – purely by accident – in Whitebridge town centre . . .'

'You're doing nothing but blowing hot air,' Hough said.

'What's the matter?' Woodend challenged. 'Are you afraid you can't handle the truth?'

Hough considered the question for a moment, then shook his head and said, 'No, I can handle it. You carry on.'

'You met Terry Pugh in town, an' he told you that his wife was expectin' a baby. Suddenly, the balance you'd established in your life just disintegrated. It didn't seem fair, did it? The two of you had both had a hand in killin' the girl, yet he was goin' to have kids, an' you weren't. *That's* when you decided that justice had to be done. At least, justice is what you decided to called it.'

'It *was* justice,' Hough said angrily.

'Yes, I'm sure that's what you told yourself. I'm sure you argued that it *had to be* justice, because you were goin' to die, too.'

'That's exactly it.'

'But you'd reached the point at which you considered that your own life wasn't worth livin' anyway, so what did it *matter* if you did die?' Woodend shook his head slowly, from side to side. 'It wasn't the search for justice that was drivin' you, Mr Hough. It was *anger*. It was *envy*.'

A tear began to trickle down Hough's cheek. 'Do you have to try and rob me of my last illusion, Chief Inspector?' he asked.

'Yes, I think I do,' Woodend told him seriously.

'In God's name, why?'

'Because it's my duty to do all that I can to stop you from

killing yourself. And the more you see it as some grand noble act, the more you're likely to do it. But it isn't noble at all, Mr Hough. It's petty an' it's peevish.'

'So what's the alternative to killing myself?' Hough asked. 'A lifetime in prison? Because they're never going to let me out, you know.'

'Probably not,' Woodend agreed. 'But you're a very talented man, an' you could do a lot of good for the world, even from prison. An' when you do eventually die, you'll have the opportunity to die like a man, instead of like a snivelling wretch – which is just what you'll be if you kill yourself now.'

'You make a strong case, Chief Inspector,' Hough told him. 'But unfortunately, not strong *enough*.'

His hands grasped the wheels of his chair, and he propelled himself forward. The chair flew through the air, then plummeted to the ground. Hough remained, swinging at the end of a rope, a few feet below the level of the floor.

He had been right about one thing, Woodend thought – he *had* calculated the necessary length of the rope perfectly.

Thirty

'What have you got to say about the bloody mess you've got us into, Chief Inspector Woodend?' Henry Marlowe demanded, in a voice that was almost a roar.

'The mess *I've* got us into?' Woodend replied.

'That's what I said. Not only have we had three murders in the last few days, but we've had two suicides in the last few *hours*. And let's just take a closer look at those two suicides, shall we?'

'If you like.'

'The first one had such an element of coercion to it that it was *virtually* a murder. And as for the second, that was dramatic enough to ensure it will be on the front page news tomorrow morning – and probably for days after that.' Marlowe paused for a second, but only to draw breath. 'Have I missed anything out, Mr Woodend?' he continued. 'Is there some further disaster I've not even heard about yet?'

'You're wrong about Martin Murray's suicide being coerced,' Woodend said. 'Mark Hough's intervention might have speeded the process up a little, but he would almost certainly have killed himself eventually.'

'What are you talking about!' Marlowe demanded. 'Don't you realize that I don't give a toss about Murray's state of mind. All I care about is how bad this makes us look.'

'I don't see how we could have handled it any differently,' Woodend told him. 'We're simply not trained or equipped to deal with professional assassins, which is what Nikopolidis more or less was. An' how likely did it seem that Hough was behind the whole thing – that he was intendin' to die himself?'

'You should have spotted it sooner,' Marlowe said.

'Aye, you're right,' Woodend agreed. 'Not that it would have made much difference to the outcome, even if I had.'

'It would have made a difference to this *police force*,'

Marlowe said. 'It would have made a difference to your future *prospects*.'

'I beg your pardon, sir?'

'I have to inform you, Chief Inspector Woodend, that as from this moment you are suspended on full pay.'

'Until when?'

'Until a board of inquiry can be convened to investigate your mis-handling of this case.'

'You mean to determine whether or not I *did* mis-handle it,' Woodend suggested.

'No, I meant exactly what I said,' Marlowe told him.

Woodend nodded slowly. 'So the board's report is already written, is it? At least in your head?'

'Yes, it is,' Marlowe said, with unusual candour. 'I intend to break you, Chief Inspector. I shall take no personal pleasure from it, but that is what I intend to do.'

'I don't think you're bein' *quite* honest about that last point, sir,' Woodend said. 'The truth is that if you *can* break me, you'll be chuffed as little apples.'

'Perhaps you're right – in the long term,' Marlowe conceded. 'Perhaps, at some time in the future, I will be able to truly savour the process I am about to initiate. But at the moment, I am simply doing whatever I can to ensure my own survival.'

'An' there's no room in the lifeboat for two,' Woodend said.

'Just so,' Marlowe agreed. He held out his hand, palm upwards. 'If you don't mind, I'll take your warrant card now, Chief Inspector.'

An air of gloom hovered over the team's usual table at the Drum and Monkey that night.

'Have you spoken to Monika, sir?' Rutter asked, more to fill in the silence than because he wanted to hear the answer.

'Aye, I have spoken to her,' Woodend replied. 'Her plane was diverted to somewhere down south, so she'll not be back till the mornin'. She's not exactly pleased about it, but at least it means she's been spared havin' to attend this mournful bloody gatherin'.' He took a slug of his pint. 'An' while we're on the subject of my wake, I'm not entirely sure you two lads should be here, either. Now I've been given the black spot, you might be well advised to pretend that any past association you've had with me was certainly not a matter of choice on your part.'

'It doesn't work like that, sir,' Beresford said, and his tone was very gentle, as if he were talking to an injured bird. 'We're on your team, and we'll continue to be on it until there's no team to be on.'

'Too bloody true,' Rutter agreed. 'Anyway, I'm confident you'll beat this thing, sir.'

'I'm not so sure you're right about that,' Woodend said. 'The press will be screamin' for *somebody's* blood, an' I have to admit, I'm likeliest-looking donor. Anyway, why *should* I fight it? I'm only a few years away from retirement, an' while the pension won't be exactly wonderful, I'll be able to live off it, as long as I watch the pennies carefully. Who knows, I might just move to Spain, an' set up a private detective agency with my mate Paco.'

'It doesn't sound like you,' Rutter said dubiously.

'Doesn't it?' Woodend asked. 'Listen, for the past twenty years I've been puttin' more hours into the job than Soft Mick. I've worked till my back ached an' my head was spinnin'. I've seen things that would probably turn most men's stomachs – an' which have certainly turned mine. An' on top of that, I've had to serve under a long line of dickheads, culminatin' in the Dickhead-in-Chief, Henry-bloody-Marlowe. Who needs it?'

Rutter grinned. '*You* do,' he said.

'Aye, you're right,' Woodend agreed with a sigh. '*I* do.'

'Phone call for Mr Rutter,' the landlord called across the bar.

'Better take it,' Woodend said. 'It could be that they've already assigned you a new boss, an' he's wonderin' what you're doin' still dancin' the hornpipe on a sinkin' ship.'

Elizabeth Driver was lying in a deep luxurious bath, in a hotel where her bill – when it was finally presented – would just about equal the national debt of a small country. She was not alone in the bath, but she had given the muscular young man who was sharing it with her strict instructions that he should keep quiet while she made her phone call – and since she had delivered the instructions in words of one syllable, she was fairly confident that he had understood her.

'Rutter,' said a voice at the other end of the line.

'Oh, hello, darling!' Elizabeth Driver said – then wondered

immediately if 'darling' was not pushing things a little too far, a little too fast.

'Is that you, Elizabeth?' Rutter asked.

No 'darling' from him in return, then, so perhaps she'd better cool things off a little.

'I heard on the news that you've solved the case of the headless man,' she said.

'In a way – and at a cost,' Rutter told her.

'At a cost?'

'Cloggin'-it Charlie's been suspended. He doesn't think he'll survive the board of inquiry.'

'But that's terrible!' Elizabeth Driver gasped.

'Don't pretend to be upset about it, Liz,' Rutter said. 'You never did like the man.'

There was an element of rebuke to his tone, she thought, but at least he was calling her Liz, which was a definite improvement.

'You're right that Mr Woodend and I haven't always got on,' she agreed, 'but I've always respected him for the good bobby he is, and I had been hoping that, as we got to know each other better, we'd learn to like each other more – if only for your sake.'

'You never cease to surprise me,' Rutter said. 'There I was, thinking you'd be over the moon that he was about to lose his job, and instead you really sound quite distressed.'

'I *am* distressed,' Elizabeth Driver said.

And so she was. Charlie Woodend was going to be one of the cornerstones of her book. She didn't want him crucified now – she wanted him crucified when she was in a position from which she could hammer in the nails personally.

'I've got another piece of news,' Rutter said. 'And it's good news, this time. Louisa is coming to Whitebridge next week.'

'Who?'

'Louisa. My daughter!'

'Oh, Louisa,' Elizabeth Driver said. 'Must be a bad line, because I could have sworn you said something else. Yes, that *is* good news.'

She was simply going to have to cosy up to the snotty little brat if she was to get really close to Rutter, she told herself. It would be a strain, but it would still be a relatively small price to pay for having a best-selling exposé handed to her on a platter.

'I'm really looking forward to meeting the little poppet,' she continued. 'Listen, darling, I simply have to go now, because I'm working to a very tight deadline on my latest story, and my editor will go absolutely bananas if I don't manage to meet it.'

'If you're that busy, then it was very nice of you to find the time to ring me,' Rutter said.

'It wasn't nice at all,' Elizabeth Driver told him. 'I rang you because I *miss* you.'

It was a rather good closing line, and so she hung up immediately.

The man at the other end of the bath smiled amiably at her, reminding her of a none-too-bright puppy who only wants to please.

'Finished?' he asked.

'The phone call's finished, but I'm certainly not,' Elizabeth Driver told him. 'You remember that thing you were doing to me earlier?'

'Yes?'

'Do it to me again.'

Most of the customers in the public bar of the Drum and Monkey noticed the new arrival almost the moment he came through the door. Perhaps it was his expensive herringbone suit which immediately attracted their attention, or perhaps it was the aura of self-confidence which seemed to encase him. Whatever the cause, the man himself did not seem aware of the minor sensation he was causing, and having located Woodend, he made a bee-line for his table.

'Good evening, Chief Inspector,' he said.

'Good evening to you, an' all,' Woodend replied. He turned to Beresford. 'This is Mr Forsyth. He's a spy.'

Forsyth laughed lightly. 'Mr Woodend will have his little joke,' he told Beresford. 'In point of fact, I'm no more than a very minor official in the Foreign Office.'

'A spy,' Woodend repeated.

'Have it your own way, Mr Woodend,' Forsyth said easily. 'Would you excuse us for a few minutes, Constable Beresford?'

'How do you know my name?' Beresford asked.

'You've not been listenin', lad,' Woodend told him. 'He's a *spy*.'

Beresford stood up. 'Well, I'll . . . if you'll . . . call me when you need me, sir,' he said awkwardly.

'Don't worry, I will,' Woodend replied.

Forsyth sat down in the seat that Beresford had vacated. He was holding something in his hand, and now he laid it flat on the table. It was Woodend's warrant card, and at even the sight of it, the chief inspector's hands began to itch.

'I've just had a most interesting chat with your chief constable,' Forsyth said. 'Apparently, he now thinks that he acted rather hastily earlier. He's completely given up the idea of convening a board of inquiry, and is hoping that you'll be willing to report for duty tomorrow morning as if the whole unpleasant scene in his office had never happened.'

'How the hell did you manage that?' Woodend wondered.

'Oh, it was easy enough,' Forsyth said lightly. 'Everyone has secrets they'd rather not have made public – and we know what most of them are.'

Woodend looked down at his precious warrant card, but, as hard it was to restrain himself, he still made no move to pick it up.

'Go ahead,' Forsyth said encouragingly. 'It's yours. Take it!'

'Before I do that, let's talk about just what it's goin' to cost me,' Woodend replied.

'I'd be more than happy to, Chief Inspector,' Forsyth agreed, 'but first I'd like to order a drink.'

He signalled to the waiter. It was a minimalist gesture, but the man noticed immediately, and came straight over to the table.

'I'll have a double of the best malt whisky you have on offer,' Forsyth said. 'And a pint for you, Chief Inspector?'

Woodend looked down at his glass, which was almost empty. 'Thanks, but I'm all right for the moment,' he said.

The waiter – well aware of the chief inspector's drinking habits – did his best to hide his look of astonishment. 'Are you sure about that, Mr Woodend?' he asked.

'I'm sure,' Woodend told him. 'You'd better go an' get that expensive malt whisky, before there's a run on it.'

The waiter nodded, and returned to the bar like a man in a trance.

Once he'd gone, Forsyth said, 'It's my job to keep the lid on things, but I'm rather afraid you're the kind of chap who likes to show everybody what's still bubbling up in the pot.'

'Go on,' Woodend said, non-committally.

'All five men who were involved in that rather unpleasant incident in Cyprus seven years ago are now dead. And that being the case, we would rather like you to consider the matter closed.'

'An' what about the other buggers?' Woodend asked.

'Which "other buggers" are you referring to?'

'You know that as well as I do. I'm talkin' about the army officers who were in charge at the time – the ones who knew what had gone on, an' decided to cover it up.'

'I'm sure they acted from the best possible motives.'

'Best possible motives?' Woodend repeated. 'In law, we call what they did bein' "an accessory after the fact".'

'In diplomacy, we call it choosing the option likely to cause the least damage within the context of the bigger picture.'

'So that's the price, is it?' Woodend asked. 'I keep my job as long as I'm prepared to let the guilty parties get away with it?'

'Essentially.'

Woodend took a swig of what was left of his pint. 'I won't do it,' he said firmly.

'I could make sure that any inquiry that was held went heavily against you,' Forsyth pointed out. 'You might not only lose your job – you might lose your pension, as well.'

'I still won't do it.'

Forsyth looked pained. 'Oh dear, you're going to force me to be unpleasant, and I was so hoping to avoid that,' he said.

'Be as unpleasant as you like,' Woodend invited.

'Very well. How is Sergeant Paniatowski coming to terms with being a killer?'

'You what?'

'We both know that Sergeant Paniatowski did something at Haverton Camp which resulted in the death of a very prominent person.'

'It was his own actions which killed him.'

'True. But she was the one who made those actions possible, and – as I think I may have said at the time – we could make out a case for charging her with manslaughter if we chose to.'

'You also said *at the time* that it would cause your masters considerable political embarrassment if she ever actually went to trial – an', as far as I can see, that's not changed.'

The waiter returned with the malt whisky. Forsyth gave him a pound note, and waved away the change.

'You're quite right about that, of course, Chief Inspector,' he said. 'But it would also cause my masters considerable embarrassment if this Cyprus business ever became public knowledge.'

'An' you don't want to have to deal with two embarrassments at the same time, do you? So even if I do go public with this Cyprus business, you'll still leave Monika alone.'

'You've certainly made a good logical case for that, but it ignores the *realpolitik* of the wider picture,' Forsyth said smoothly.

'Does it?'

'Indeed it does. If we let you get away with this, it gives those who find themselves in a similar position in the future the licence to believe they can do the same as you have done. You are the first crack in the dam, and if we don't staunch it now, the deluge will follow.'

'Which, in the interest of justice an' open government, might not be a bad thing,' Woodend pointed out.

'We simply can't allow that to happen,' Forsyth continued, ignoring him. 'And if, in order to avoid such a situation arising, we have to deal with two embarrassing situations tomorrow morning, then we will grit our teeth and do just that. In other words, if you raise the issue of Cyprus again, we *will* prosecute Sergeant Paniatowski. And furthermore, we will win – because nobody, not even you, believes that the judicial system can remain impartial when it feels the whole weight of government pressing down on it.'

Woodend picked up his warrant card, slipped it into his pocket, and stood up.

'I suddenly feel the need for a breath of fresh air,' he said.

'I'm sure you do,' Forsyth agreed. 'But please do remember, Chief Inspector, that it is because of organizations like mine that there is still fresh air for you *to* breathe.'

'An' *you* should remember that you can sometimes pay such a price to keep the air fresh that eventually you can't hide the stink *whatever* you do,' Woodend countered, heading for the door.

Author's Note

Several of DCI Woodend's earlier cases are mentioned during the course of this book, and for any readers interested in following them up, I have listed below where they can be found.

The Helen Dunn kidnapping occurs in *The Red Herring*. Paco Ruiz, the Spanish detective, helps Woodend make his case in *The Butcher Beyond*. Maria Rutter is murdered in *Dying in the Dark*, and Bradley Pine is disembowelled in *Sins of the Fathers*. And finally, the Haverton Camp murder is central to *A Long Time Dead*.